"Maybe ... ut going back ... er

AUTHOR NOTE

When I wrote SALVATION IN THE RANCHER'S ARMS it was intended as a stand-alone book. I had no plans to return to the thriving little town of Salvation Falls. I was merely passing through. But in the process of telling Caleb and Rachel's story I couldn't help but wonder about the future of the handsome (and quite single) Sheriff Hunter Donovan. Needless to say my curiosity won out and back to Salvation Falls I went.

As it turns out, the town has some secrets yet to tell about past loves and old betrayals. Both of which come back to haunt Hunter when an old love, Meredith Connolly, returns to town with justice on her mind.

SALVATION IN THE SHERIFF'S KISS allows me to explore the extremes people go to when trying to protect those they love and to discover how the results alter and change the lives of those involved.

It was a delight to return to Salvation Falls once again, and I hope you enjoy reading Hunter and Meredith's story.

SALVATION IN THE SHERIFF'S KISS

Kelly Boyce

A life-long Nova Scotian, **Kelly Boyce** lives near the Atlantic Ocean with her husband (who is likely wondering what he got himself into by marrying a writer) and a golden retriever who is convinced he is king of the castle. A long-time history buff, Kelly loves writing in a variety of time periods, creating damaged characters and giving them a second chance at life and love.

Books by Kelly Boyce
in Mills & Boon® Historical Romance:

SALVATION IN THE RANCHER'S ARMS
SALVATION IN THE SHERIFF'S KISS

Visit Kelly Boyce's profile page
at www.millsandboon.co.uk

In memory of my grandmother, Eileen Boyce,
for always believing I could do it. It meant the world.

Chapter One

Colorado Territory, November 1876

"Hoo-wee! That was a tough one!"

"That's one word for it," Sheriff Hunter Donovan muttered, bending over to swipe his hat off the saloon floor. He brushed it against his leg then jammed it back onto his head, giving his deputy an exasperated glance. The way the kid was grinning from ear to ear, you'd think he'd lassoed a wayward bronco, not helped take down three brawling idiots too stupid to know when to quit.

It was hard to believe only five years separated their ages. Had he ever been that young and foolhardy? If so, he'd be sure and stop by old Sheriff McLaren's grave and issue a most heartfelt apology.

"Aw, hell, Sheriff. It ain't so bad. Beats sittin' around all day staring at the walls."

Hunter scowled. "Being a sheriff isn't about having fun, Jenkins. It's about keeping the peace, stopping these kinds of things before they happen. You need to be vigilant, because if not, people get hurt." He'd learned that one the hard way. Unfortunately, it was Sheriff McLaren who had paid the price.

"I know, I know," Jenkins said, his affable smile still in place. "I jus' hate it when there's nothin' exciting to do is all."

Hunter refrained from telling him there was always plenty to do—people to check in on, disputes to mediate, help to offer. He could stand a little idle time to try and bring Jenkins up to speed on what it meant to be a sheriff. It wasn't all shoot-outs and saloon fights. Wearing the badge also meant the town's safety and well-being would become his responsibility. That people would rely on him. It was a bit like a family in a way, not that Hunter's own family, broken as it was, provided the best example in that regard.

And now, more than ever, it was important to be vigilant. Ever since the train station had been put in on the outskirts of town it seemed every piece of riffraff had found their way to Salvation Falls to try and pick up work at the lucrative ranches in the area. Although, in his estimation, they spent as much time drinking whiskey and beer in the three saloons dotting Main Street as they did actually working.

One of said riffraff rolled over onto his back and groaned. "We was jus' havin' a conversation about Yucton bein' guilty or not. Didn't mean no harm."

Hunter gazed down at Roddy Lewis. He was a regular hand from Hunter's father's ranch, the Diamond D. "Perhaps you should try agreeing to disagree the next time. It's up to the courts to decide Yucton's fate. Not you."

Bill Yucton had become another thorn in his side. Everyone in town had an opinion on his guilt or innocence and no one seemed shy about spouting off about it. Or about the events of seven years ago he was being tried for.

He glared over at Kincaid, the bounty hunter who had brought the outlaw to town. He'd said little about where he'd found Yucton, or why it was the man had arrived with his hands unbound, more than willing to ride into town despite knowing it could spell his doom. There was something fishy about the whole thing.

"You could have helped," he said, addressing the bounty hunter. The man had turned in his stool at the bar and watched the fight without so much as lifting a hand.

He did so now, however, holding up his shot glass filled to the brim with watered-down whiskey. "Didn't want to spill my drink."

"You keep drinking at this rate and you'll burn through the bounty you collected before the trial even starts."

If it started. The circuit judge was taking his sweet ole time getting here. A wire had arrived this morning. The appointed judge had met with an unfortunate accident. It would be another week at least before a replacement could be found and sent their way.

"Can't see how my drinkin' is any of your business, Sheriff. Thought you'd be a bit more appreciative. I did bring in a wanted man, after all. Made the world a safer place, putting one more outlaw behind bars."

"Right. Because Bill Yucton was such a huge threat."

Fact was, Kincaid was right. Yucton was a wanted man, but the law around here hadn't been looking for him. He'd been part of an outfit that had rustled some cattle from the Diamond D and got caught, but Yucton had managed to somehow slip out of the jail and disappear into the night. Sheriff McLaren hadn't bothered gathering a posse to set out after him and eventually, after the trial in which the two remaining rustlers had been dealt with, folks around Salvation Falls seemed happy to put the whole sordid matter to sleep. Hunter counted himself among them and he sure didn't appreciate it being resurrected now.

He pointed at the bounty hunter. "You and I need to have a conversation about Bill Yucton real soon."

Kincaid eyed him for a brief second, downed his drink then motioned for another one. "Can't say I have much to say."

But Hunter did. It had been bugging him for the past several days. There was no reason in the world for Bill Yucton to come back here. Yet here he was, taking up space in one of the three jail cells in Hunter's office. To top it off, the bounty on Yucton wasn't paid out by the U.S. Marshalls Service. It was a private bounty offered to anyone who brought him into Salvation Falls to stand trial for a crime committed over seven years ago.

"You plan on sticking around these parts?"

Kincaid grinned. Weathered lines creased the corners of his eyes, beaten in by the elements and adding an incongruent nature to the man's age, though Hunter suspected he wasn't much older than his own thirty years.

"Might. Never know when you're going to need help with the rowdies."

"Because you've been so helpful thus far." Sarcasm saturated his words.

Kincaid shrugged and turned his attention back to the drink Franklyn set in front of him, putting an end to their conversation.

Hunter returned to Jenkins who had hauled the current band of rowdies to their feet. Hunter would worry about Kincaid later. So long as he was sticking around, there would be time to question him further about the mysterious return of the wayward Bill Yucton. He knew there was more to the story than he was hearing. Instinct kept telling him something wasn't right. Instinct and Sheriff McLaren's dying words. Words that had haunted him since Abbott Connolly had stood trial for rustling cattle from the Diamond D Ranch seven years ago.

Dig deeper.

He'd heeded the sheriff's words, but it had come to naught. There was nothing new to find. The evidence was what it was, and it had sent Abbott Connolly to prison.

Hunter and Jenkins herded the stumbling men down to the opposite end of the street and shoved them all into one small cell. Bill Yucton lay prone on his bed, his legs crossed at the ankle and his hat covering his face. He lifted the brim far enough to slide a gaze at his new neighbors, then dropped it back in place.

The fire in the woodstove had dwindled during their absence and the cold air from outside had made the interior a bit nippy. Hunter crossed the room to the woodstove and stoked the embers, putting another log on. He'd put on a pot of coffee just before getting called down to The Seahorse to break up the fight. By now it had likely thickened to a warm sludge. He poured a cup anyway. He'd long ago given up on drinking a decent cup of coffee.

"Get these three settled in," he said, and headed back out the door.

Once outside, he leaned against the exterior wall of his office. Things were starting to quiet down. The twilight hour. His favorite time of the day. It was the one brief respite where the town took a deep breath, held it for a moment, then slowly exhaled. The sun had started its descent, leaving the tips of the mountains burnished in bronze and the sky streaked with orange and purple. The colorful display never failed to take his breath away. He'd lived his whole life under the shadow of those mountains and the effect had never lessened.

It was the one thing about ranching he'd taken a shine to, the amount of time he spent out of doors, riding the range. But all that would change when he took over the business from his father. He'd spend more time dealing with the management and money and less time actually doing the day to day. The thought saddened him. He had no true interest in the job. He liked what he did now.

He'd taken on the role of deputy nearly ten years ago after an argument with his father. He'd been barely twenty, brash and determined to create his own identity apart from the Donovan name. And he had. More importantly, he'd discovered he loved doing it.

And soon it would be Jenkins's job, if he could bring the kid up to snuff.

He leaned a shoulder against the post next to the steps that led into the street and stared up at the vista, breathing in the evening. It gave him a sense of peace, of belonging. He knew it would only last as long as the sunset, though. Come nightfall, the loneliness would sink in. He'd eventually retire to the room he kept above the jailhouse and the emptiness would mock him. The memories would seep through the cracks in the walls and remind him of everything he'd lost.

Maybe when he moved back to his father's house and took over the business, the memories would stay put and not follow him there. He doubted it, but it was the only bright spot he could find about giving up his badge and returning to the Diamond D Ranch.

He scowled at the fading sunset. The idea of turning in his badge stuck in his craw in the worst way. He hated to do it, to give up the only thing that gave him a reason to get out of bed in the morning. But as his father constantly reminded him, he had a duty to his family.

What was left of it. It had been just him and his father since Ma had hightailed it out of town when he was fourteen. He tried not to blame her. Get right down to it, his father was a first-rate bastard. He'd spent his whole married life and longer mooning over another man's wife instead of his own, turning bitter when he couldn't have her. Hunter hadn't heard from Ma since she'd left. Sometimes on nights like this he wondered where she'd got to. Was she happy? Was she even still alive? Why hadn't she thought to take him with her? He didn't let the thoughts linger for long, though. Turned out Ma was as interested in being a mother to him as Vernon was in being a father. He guessed that there wasn't enough about him to love. At least that's what he believed for the longest time until someone else had shown him different.

Someone who had made him dream of a future full of possibilities he'd never considered. Of having a home. Of coming through the door once the sun had sunk into its nest behind the mountains and the stars took over the heavens, and being met by a passel of smiling children and a loving wife with pale blond hair and dazzling blue eyes who'd welcome him with open arms.

He'd come so close to having that once, but… well, he'd come close but not close enough.

Now, here he was pushing thirty and all he had to show for himself at the end of the day was the tin badge pinned on his chest.

"The men should sober up soon enough," Jenkins said, coming up behind him. Hunter welcomed the interruption. He didn't like wallowing in maudlin thoughts for too long. They had a way of making a man see all the things he'd done wrong in life. It could be a long list. "I can spring them once the sun goes down, send 'em on home if you want."

"Let them sweat it out for a bit," Hunter said. "Maybe it will give them pause if they think they might be bunking down here for the night."

"Yucton wouldn't like that. Says he don't cotton to neighbors much. 'Specially smelly drunks who don't have the sense to know when to keep their mouths shut."

Hunter scowled. "You tell Yucton we're running a jail, not a damn hotel. If he wanted to choose his neighbors he should have chosen not to break the law."

That's the way it worked in Hunter's mind. You broke the law, you paid the price. It was as simple as that. At least it should be. But justice could be a mercurial mistress.

"Hey, ain't that…?" Jenkins took a step forward and squinted through the early-evening light. Hunter followed his gaze.

His heart stuttered and his breath along with it.

Jenkins made his way to the edge of the planked sidewalk and leaned against the railing, a smile breaking across his young face. "Well, I'll be hog-tied and roasted on a spit. Will you look at that?"

Hunter couldn't look at anything else. Every muscle in his body went still as rigor. Had someone hog-tied him and roasted him on a spit, he wasn't sure he would even notice. He knew what he was seeing. He just couldn't believe it. Or didn't want to.

"Meredith."

He hadn't spoken her name aloud in seven

years, but it slipped off his tongue now as if it had been yesterday, bringing with it all the emotions he'd kept neatly tucked away deep inside. They rushed out now, caring little for neatness or order as each one raged through him and left him standing in front of his office wrecked and broken as if no time had passed at all and she was riding out of town instead of back in.

He'd known this day might someday come, but he had prayed it wouldn't almost as fervently as he'd hoped it would.

And now it had.

Meredith Connolly sat in the wagon, her fingers grasped tightly around the handles of the small valise resting in her lap. The boned construction of her corset helped keep her back ramrod straight but her shoulders ached from the strain of holding them back while keeping her chin high.

She'd had no intentions of riding into town the way she had ridden out of it seven years earlier with a crushed spirit, broken dreams and empty bank account. Granted, the riding into town was mostly for show. Her aunt had squirrelled away some money from her business as a seamstress, a business Meredith had learned backward and forward, but it wasn't substantial. She'd inherited enough to arrive back in Salvation Falls in style and start over. After that, it would be up to her. A fact that suited her just fine. She didn't put much stock into relying on others. Not anymore.

Pride held her posture in check when her muscles began to ache from the effort. The plumed ostrich feather in her hat bobbed in her peripheral vision, blotting out the image of Hunter Donovan every time the wagon's wheels hit a new rut in the road. Even from halfway down Main Street she had recognized his likeness, the relaxed posture as he leaned against the post outside the sheriff's office, every bone in his body a study in ease. He was too far away to see the details of his face, but she didn't need to. She'd memorized every line, every contour long ago.

She recognized the moment he realized who she was. Though his stance did not alter, the coffee mug in his hand went slack, its contents dribbling out and hitting the toe of his boot. She wouldn't blame him for not recognizing her straightaway. Coifed and dressed to the nines as she was, it was a far different picture she presented than the one he was familiar with.

She refused to look his way, to give the strange tingling in her belly any credence. It was only nerves, nothing more. She had put away the feelings she'd harbored for Hunter Donovan a long time ago and she had no intentions of hauling them back out now.

Once upon a time, he'd told her she wasn't good enough to take the Donovan name. Well, she would show him. She would show everyone who'd thought it impossible a Connolly would ever amount to much.

Meredith turned her gaze to the craggy mountains off in the distance. Their panoramic landscape refused to be ignored. It had been too many years since she'd seen the view. Its potency had not lessened since then. If anything, the sun-brightened tips of the mountains looked even more golden against the twilight-streaked sky than she remembered. The wildness of it called to her, penetrating the polish and sophistication Boston had adorned her with.

The wagon jostled to a stop and the driver, a man she didn't know, hopped down.

"Meredith!"

Bertram Trent's robust voice cut through the melee of people milling about at the end of the day. He bustled toward her and shooed the driver off, helping her down on his own. He had always struck her as a tangible version of Old St. Nick, and in the seven years she'd been gone time had only solidified the image. Thick white hair with a matching beard framed a round face and apple cheeks. Even his blue eyes sparkled with a merry twinkle that never seemed to dim. She set aside her valise and let him assist her down. Her feet no sooner touched the ground than he enveloped her in a warm embrace.

"Bertram! It is so wonderful to see you."

"And you, my dear girl." He pulled away and held her at arms' length, giving his head a small shake. "As I live and breathe you are a sight for these old eyes. Every bit the vision of loveliness your mama was."

"Oh, pish." Meredith smiled at the compliment but shook her head. Vivienne Connolly had been a raven-haired beauty with the warm olive skin of her Irish ancestors. Even illness hadn't been able to rob her of it. Meredith, on the other hand, was fair-skinned and prone to burning whenever the sun found its way beneath her bonnet. "We both know I favor my father in that regard."

"I don't remember your pa being quite so pretty, or dressed in such finery."

Meredith glanced down at her traveling dress. It had wrinkled somewhat from the trip but had fared better than she expected. Aunt had allowed her a new dress each season once Meredith convinced her it was the best way to advertise their services. Business had picked up afterward, and soon Meredith began designing her own patterns, of which this was one.

"I suppose it's a far cry from what I wore when I left."

When she'd left, she'd barely had more than the worn-out clothes on her back, a suitcase full of bad memories and a broken heart. Now she returned a woman of some means, with the knowledge of how to run her own business and succeed in doing so. Never again would she have to rely on the charity of others or worry where her next meal was coming from.

"Indeed. Now how was your trip? Never did cotton to riding the rail. Seems a dangerous way to go if you ask me. Thing moves faster than a body ought to in my opinion."

Meredith smiled. "It didn't move fast enough in my estimation. But I'm happy to be home. Happier still to find a proper bed to sleep in."

"Come, come then," he said, reaching past her to retrieve her valise. "Your room is ready and waiting. Top floor. Nicest one The Klein has to offer, just as you requested."

"Thank you, Bertram. I do appreciate all the effort you've put in on my behalf."

"It's nothing. I'm glad to be of service. How are you doing?"

"I'm fine." The lie tripped easily off her

tongue but left behind a bitter residue. Her father had returned to Salvation Falls a month before in a casket. She hadn't seen him since she'd left town. She wouldn't see him now. The knowledge left her hollow and hurting.

"Good, good." Bertram held out his arm and she slipped her hand through it, noting the fine fabric of his coat. Business must be good. With the growth of the town, she had no doubt Bertram's client list had grown. She was happy to see the old lawyer still prosperous after all this time. Though he spoke occasionally of retirement, she doubted it would ever come to that. He enjoyed his work, enjoyed the people and the challenge of the law.

He'd been a godsend when she'd needed it most, even if the result hadn't been what they had both wanted.

"I was sorry to hear about your aunt."

She accepted his condolences with a nod of her head as they stepped inside the hotel and out of the cold bite of the November evening. "It was difficult, but she had been ill for quite some time. In some ways, it was almost a relief knowing she didn't suffer any longer." Though she and Aunt Erma hadn't seen eye to eye on many issues, Meredith had always appreciated the woman who had taken her in when she'd had nowhere else to go.

"Well, it's good to have you home. I only wish it was under happier circumstances." Bertram patted her hand in a grandfatherly gesture that warmed her heart. As much as she had come to appreciate Aunt Erma, her aunt had never been an outwardly warm woman. Meredith had missed the connection a thoughtful touch brought.

Bertram extricated himself for a moment and went to the front desk where a trio of finely dressed people stood chatting. She looked them over and recognized the rich fabric of the women's dresses. The younger lady in particular caught her eye. Her dove-gray dress was constructed of multiple pieces draped over each other and the bodice, cuffs and skirt were trimmed in royal blue velvet. Meredith knew from experience the amount of work that went into creating such a complicated garment and could only stare in appreciation.

The young lady must have felt her gaze and turned. Her ebony hair stood in stark contrast to her pale grey eyes and ivory complexion. A fairy-tale princess plucked from the pages of a book Meredith might have read as a child. Her cool gaze slid over Meredith with little expression before she turned away.

Bertram returned with the key to her room and noted the direction of Meredith's gaze. "Oh, heavens, let me introduce you to the Bancrofts. They're new in town. Looking to buy property and settle from what I hear."

She stopped Bertram when he took her arm. "Perhaps another day," she said. Seeing Hunter had left her rattled. She wanted to escape to the quiet of her room and regain her weakened composure. "I find I'm quite exhausted from my travels."

He patted her hand. "Of course, my dear. Silly of me." They turned away from the Bancrofts and Bertram escorted her up the stairs to her room, stopping outside the door and pressing the key into her hand. "The boys will bring up your trunks shortly."

"Thank you, again, Bertram. You've made my homecoming much easier."

The older man nodded and let go of her hands. "You've only to call on me if you need anything. My offices and apartments are still in the same spot. Don't hesitate."

"I won't." She leaned in and gave her old friend a peck on his bearded cheek. "Good evening, Bertram."

"Will you visit your father tomorrow?"

She took a deep breath. "Yes, I believe I will."

It wasn't the visit she had envisioned with Pa, not the one she had hoped for, but it was the only one she would get. Sadness seeped into her bones, and with it came a deep sense of regret.

And failure.

Bertram's voice softened. "Would you care for some company?"

She shook her head and fought back a sudden urge to cry. She had forgotten what it was like to have someone show true kindness and caring. She took a deep breath and swallowed against the lump in her throat. She didn't have time for tears.

"Thank you, Bertram, but I'll be fine. I plan on visiting Bill Yucton afterward."

"See if you can't convince the old rascal to avail himself of my services, would you? He's yet to hire himself proper counsel and time is running out."

"I will. Good night, Bertram."

She entered the room and listened as Bertram's heavy footfalls disappeared down the hallway. The room left her awestruck. In all her years living in Salvation Falls, she had never even set foot inside the Klein's lobby, though she'd peered inside the doors while running errands for her mother and one day dreamed of seeing the rooms upstairs.

She was not disappointed. Her suite was separated by an archway allowing for a sitting room in front and a bedroom in back. She could see the bed from where she stood. A colorful quilt in burgundy, white and green covered the thick feathered mattress, and Meredith longed to sink into it. A bell pull hung near the bed, and another one in the sitting room. She had only to give them a yank and one of the hotel staff would arrive to see to her requests.

What would the townspeople think to see Abbott Connolly's daughter living high on the hog in her luxurious hotel room wearing the height of Paris fashions? That she was someone to be noticed? Listened to? She hoped so. Because they certainly hadn't listened to poor little Meredith Connolly, the girl who wore charity cast-offs and whose family struggled to put food on the table. She'd learned the hard way if she was going to accomplish what she had come home to do then she needed to set herself up as someone of account, even if it meant using up the nest egg Aunt Erma had left her.

She crossed to the bedroom window and pulled back the heavy brocade curtain, letting in what little light remained in the evening. The sunlight was beginning to fade and the moon had yet to make an appearance, leaving the main thoroughfare ensconced in a shadowy haze. Outside, activity was minimal—that much hadn't changed. Salvation Falls, despite its growth, was still a family town, settled and well-lived. This was the time of day when people went home to their families. In another hour, those without such ties would begin to crop up to take the night air, visit the saloons, maybe find themselves some companionship paid for by hard-earned or ill-gotten coin. The town had two faces in that respect and once the night encroached, the town changed hands. She'd always liked that part of the day, watching the two sides ebb and flow. They rarely seemed to butt up against each other, and in the bright light of the sun they existed amiably enough.

Her traitorous gaze wandered to the jailhouse, but Hunter was no longer there.

Had he gone home? Did he have a family now? The thought cut into her, slicing through the well-constructed walls she'd built. How close she had come to that being her life. How quickly it had been torn away.

Part of her had hoped Hunter would have pulled up stakes and moved on, but she hadn't put much stock in it. He lived and breathed this town and its people. It ran in his blood, flowed through his veins and beat in his heart. He would never leave until they put him in the ground, just as they had the sheriff before him. Even then, he would likely still linger like a ghostly specter refusing to leave. The way he had haunted her.

The rebellious thought wound its way loose from her subconscious. She tried to tamp it down, but once free, it demanded attention. Her heart raced and her pulse jumped. Even in thought, her body's response to him belied the number of years since she'd last laid eyes on him.

She shook her head. It was strange to be back, to be a stranger in a town so familiar she could envision every inch of it by simply closing her eyes. It smelled and sounded the same, as if nothing had changed. And yet everything had.

She had.

Meredith let the curtain drop and turned away from the window, wishing she could shut out his memory with as much ease, but she knew from experience that would not happen. And sooner or later, she would have to deal with him in the flesh. There was no way around it if she wanted to see Bill.

She reached into the sewn-in pocket of her traveling dress and retrieved the wire Bertram had sent her the day before she left Boston.

BILL YUCTON IN CUSTODY. STOP.
WISHES TO SEE YOU UPON ARRIVAL.
STOP. BEST REGARDS. BT. STOP.

She refolded the message with her fingers and slipped it back into her pocket. She hadn't seen Bill in forever. Why did he want to meet with her now? And what in Heaven's name had possessed him to return to Salvation Falls?

A knock sounded at her door. Meredith left the bedroom and crossed through the sitting room, happy to finally have her trunks arrive. She wanted nothing more right now than to rest her weary head on the soft, feathered mattress.

She opened the door wide and swept her arm toward the far wall. "You can put the trunks right over here."

But it wasn't her trunks waiting for her on the other side.

It was her past come to call.

Chapter Two

Meredith was saying something as the door opened but the words died on her tongue. Not that it mattered. Hunter's brain had stopped working the moment he laid eyes on her up close. It simply fizzled out and rolled over like a possum playing dead.

She looked different. Poised and sophisticated in her fancy green dress that reminded him of spring leaves newly budded.

Lord. Was he really going to wax poetic about her dress? *Focus man!*

A feat much easier said than done.

Surprise brightened her eyes, which were far bluer than he remembered, but she schooled her features quickly, and in a blink of her eyes it disappeared until he wondered if he had seen it at all. His own recovery proved slower coming. His tongue remained tangled behind his teeth and all he could do was stand there and stare like a first-rate idiot. She was the one who finally broke the growing silence.

"Can I be of some service to you, Sheriff?"

He didn't miss the way she stressed the *sheriff* bit, cutting it off sharply at the end. He'd been newly appointed shortly before her departure. He remembered how it had filled her with hope, as if it would somehow change things, make them better. And he remembered how he'd taken that hope and crushed it. Guilt clawed at his insides.

"I saw you arrive. Figured you'd come to see your pa."

"Did you?"

It wasn't much as far as conversations went. She'd yet to fully open the door and the way she had one hand on the doorframe and the other one on the inside doorknob, it didn't appear she was interested in having an extended chat.

He tried again. "I thought I'd come over and pay my respects."

One blond eyebrow arched upward. The hat she'd worn earlier with the strange feather thing jutting out was gone, but the wild mane of wheat-blond hair that taunted his memories remained tamed and twisted into submission, save for one curl dangling just in front of her left ear, as if it refused to be constrained by the pins she'd inflicted on the rest of it.

"Your respect?" The frost from her words brushed against him like a bitter wind and pulled his attention away from her hair.

"Yes. That's right." He didn't like the tone in her voice. It set him on edge, as if whatever answer he gave would be the wrong one. Women had a funny way of doing that. He'd never quite figured out how they managed it but—

The frost turned to shards of ice. "Given that I never had your respect in the past, I see no reason for you to pay it now."

And there it was.

Hunter's face burned. He wanted to defend himself, but what ammunition did he have? She was right. He hadn't treated her with respect. He had meant to. His intentions were honorable in that regard, but it hadn't turned out that way. Instead, he had jilted her in the worst possible way and at the worst possible time. Still, the remark hurt and he shot back without thinking.

"Nice room. Quite a step up for you."

Anger and pride hardened her features. Stupid. He should have left well enough alone. Heck, he probably shouldn't have come over here in the first place. A fact he realized too late.

"I don't see how my accommodations are any of your business."

Her arms crossed just beneath her chest, pushing the soft mounds upward enough to draw his attention. He quickly looked away, but not quick enough to stop his body's reaction. She'd always done that to him. He'd been a fool to think seven years would lessen the effect, smother the need. It hadn't. If anything, it had only intensified. He just didn't realize it until she opened the door and everything she was, everything she had become, reached across the threshold and slammed into him with the ferocity of a runaway horse.

"Being Sheriff makes a whole host of things my business."

"Well if I intend to break the law, I'll be sure and let you know. Now if you'll excuse me." She moved to close the door. Without thinking—because, really, why start now?—he stuck his foot out and pressed his weight against it. She looked down at his foot, then met his gaze. A low fire kindled in her eyes, but not the kind he remembered.

"What do you think you're doing?"

Hell and damnation, he was making a total muck of this, but he'd stepped in it now and there didn't seem to be a graceful way to pull his boots out of it. He'd come here with one intention—

to find out how long she planned on staying in town—and the next thing he knew, he was jamming his foot in her door like he had some right.

"Are you planning on staying long?"

"That is none of your concern." She pushed at the door, but he kept his foot lodged in place receiving a deathly glare for his trouble.

"I'm going to keep my foot here until you tell me."

"Then I'll scream until—"

"Until what? Someone sends for the law?" He tapped a finger against the tin badge pinned to his chest and smiled. "At your service, ma'am."

Somebody ought to shoot him now. Given Meredith looked angry enough to spit, he guessed she'd be the first to volunteer. The thought sent his attention to her mouth. Bad idea. Full lips he'd once kissed with more passion than a body could contain were pulled into a tight line. It did nothing to diminish how badly he wanted to kiss them all over again, taste her sweetness, lose himself in her. Damn it!

"If I tell you why I'm here, will you go away?"

"Likely." But he didn't want to. As much of an idiot as he was making of himself just being this close to her again made him feel alive. He hadn't felt this good since…well, since before she'd left.

"Fine. I have moved back to Salvation Falls for good."

"For good?" He wasn't sure how he felt about that. He had a sinking feeling if she stayed put he'd spend the rest of his days reveling in his stupidity every time she came within sight.

"Yes. I plan on opening my own business."

"And what business might that be?" And when had she become Little Miss Entrepreneur? She had never expressed an interest in running her own business before. Before, she'd wanted to get married, have babies. His babies. And as stupid as it sounded even to his own ears, the idea that she no longer wanted that felt like a betrayal. He really was losing his grasp on his sanity.

"A dress shop." Her chin lifted and pride shone past the irritation in her eyes. "I design and sew my own creations, as well as patterns I have sourced from Paris. I owned a successful dress shop in Boston and now I plan on doing the same here."

Hunter tried to marry the idea of the sweet, loving girl he had known with the confident businesswoman who knew her own mind and was willing to give him a piece of it with little provocation. It created a strange dynamic, a potent infusion that made him want her even more for reasons he couldn't even determine.

"I see."

"So glad to hear it. Will you remove your foot from my door now please?"

"Is there a problem here?"

Hunter turned, the movement forcing him to remove his foot from where he'd propped it against Meredith's door. Coming up the hallway was the gentleman who'd arrived in town a little over a week ago. Bannerman...? Baxter...? Bancroft. That was it. Anson Bancroft.

"Mr. Bancroft." Hunter looked up at him. He had to. Even at six feet, the man had a good half foot on him. A person could get a crick in the neck holding a long conversation with this man. Not that he seemed prone to long conversations. The most Hunter had ever gotten out of him was a nod of the head in passing. Hunter did the same now to the two well-dressed ladies who flanked either side of him. "Mrs. Bancroft. Miss Bancroft."

"Oh, good evening, Sheriff Donovan. You remember Charlotte, of course." He didn't, given that they had never been introduced, but that little detail didn't seem to derail Mrs. Bancroft. "Say hello to the nice sheriff, Charlotte."

Charlotte tilted her head and gave him a half smile he recognized as forced. From the look of her, trussed up like a doll with not a hair out of place and an expression of bored superiority resting on her pretty features, Hunter guessed she didn't often deign to fraternize with someone as lowly as the town sheriff. Although he was certain if she knew he was set to inherit one of the largest ranches in the area she'd sing a different tune.

Given the way Mrs. Bancroft continued her jabbering, she already knew which way the wind blew on that account. "And how are you this evening, Sheriff? Such a lovely evening. We thought we might all take a stroll before supper. Perhaps you would like to join us?"

"Uh, thank you, but no." He gave his most charming smile to soften the refusal. "I'm afraid I'm on duty tonight, ma'am."

"Oh, of course, of course." She tapped his arm with her folded fan and tittered. "Such a horrible thing, this trial. Best to see the man pay for his crimes, I say, but I'll leave that to the men to decide, of course I will."

Bancroft ignored his wife's chatter, a habit Hunter suspected he used on a regular basis out of self-preservation, if nothing else. Instead, his gaze landed on Meredith. "Are you all right? Miss Connolly, is it?"

"Yes, I'm fine. Thank you for your concern.

Sheriff Donovan was, in fact, just leaving. Weren't you, Sheriff?"

It angered him how much he missed hearing her call him by his name. Sheriff Donovan made it sound like they were strangers, and they were far from that. He didn't care how many years had passed.

Burrowing past his anger, however, was the sudden realization that Bancroft had referred to her by name. Strange, given she had only just arrived.

"Do you know each other?"

Bancroft's gaze hit him full force and a strange chill reverberated up his spine. The man was an imposing figure, Hunter would give him that, but this was something else. This was instinct telling him to pay attention, but to what?

"I ran into Mr. Trent. He indicated Miss Connolly had recently returned to town."

The explanation was reasonable. He himself had watched Bertram Trent meet Meredith at the hotel and see her inside. And yet...

"If you do not require assistance I will bid you good evening, Miss Connolly." Bancroft touched the brim of his hat and strode down the hallway, his wife dithering after him, his daughter bringing up the rear, her pace much more sedate.

He turned back to Meredith. She had started

to close the door. He stopped the door with his hand this time, garnering another glare.

"What now?"

"I don't believe we were done with our conversation."

"I'm quite certain we were."

She was probably right. There wasn't much else to say. He'd asked his questions and she'd reluctantly answered. He was stalling, not ready to cut the fragile connection, one-sided as it was. "So you're staying. Opening your own business."

"Yes."

"That's it?"

"Oh, well, there is one more thing on my agenda."

The way she said it, the corners of her mouth curling upward, made the hair on the back of his neck stand at attention. It made other parts of his body take notice too, but he was trying to ignore them.

"And that is?"

"I plan on proving my father's innocence once and for all."

He wasn't sure what he'd been expecting exactly, but it hadn't been that. His hand fell away from the door and he took a step back. Meredith didn't hesitate. She took the opportunity to slam the solid oak door in his face, missing his nose by a mere inch.

* * *

Meredith slid down the door. The damask silk of her dress scraped against the smooth wood and bunched on the floor at her feet. Her fingers shook as she plucked at the buttons lining the front of her dress. When she'd freed enough of them she switched her attention to the hooks holding her corset together. She'd often bemoaned her slight frame, but for now she was thankful she didn't have to cinch her corset within an inch of her life to create the illusion of a small waist. It allowed her the ability to pop the hooks without too much struggle. Bit by bit the constriction released, but her breath did not come any easier.

Why had he insisted on coming over here? What had he hoped to accomplish? Hadn't he caused her enough grief upon her exit from Salvation Falls? Was it truly necessary for him to heap more upon her now that she had returned? She knew she had to face him sooner or later, there was no way around it, but could he not have allowed her to arrange the meeting on her terms, in her own time. When *she* was ready.

Would she ever have been ready?

She closed her eyes, but the images that riddled the back of her lids did nothing to ease her state of anxiety. Tangled bodies, hungry mouths, searching hands.

Her eyelids flew open and she popped a few more hooks for good measure. Her skin burned, scalded by his nearness, by the unexpected assault on her senses. It wasn't fair.

But perhaps expecting fairness from the likes of Sheriff Hunter Donovan had been overreaching. If fairness had been a part of his make-up, he would have married her proper. Instead, he'd turned his back on her and sent her to Boston, soiled and used, where no respectable gentleman would even think to offer for her. Not that she would have let them even if they had. Aunt Erma had it right. Better a woman learn to live under her own steam than to rely on something as silly and transitory as love.

Love.

She scoffed at the word now, but once upon a time she had believed in it with everything she had in her. Mama and Pa had set the example and she'd grown up in a house filled with love and affection. She'd had every intention of following in their footsteps, even thought she'd found the right man to do that with.

She'd been wrong.

Her parents had been the exception to the rule. The rule being that love was not something solid and strong. It was weak and fleeting and deserted you without hint or warning or reason. All it left in its wake were memories, and oh, how those could taunt. She drew up her knees and dropped her forehead to rest against them.

She had made the right decision to forsake such a fair-weather friend. Besides, she was a businesswoman now. Independent. She didn't have time for softer emotions or relying on others. It was better that way. Really.

Oh, but the audacity of Hunter Donovan to show up on her doorstep and demand to know what she was doing here, stirring up everything old and stored away. The bravado! He had no right. No right at all.

Anger sluiced through her veins and teased her jagged nerves. Seeing him had left her unbalanced. Throughout her trip back to Salvation Falls she had wondered if the years would have left him untouched. They hadn't. Instead they had honed the young man he'd been into a sharper image, chiseled in the fine details, added layers. The lankiness of youth had been replaced with lean muscle and an air of almighty confidence that told him he had the right to show up at her door and demand answers to his questions.

What had he seen when he looked at her? She dared glance at the full length mirror on the opposite wall. Her reflection was captured there, undone and pooled in wrinkled silk damask. Had she at least appeared poised when facing him? Or had he been able to see through the facade to how his sudden appearance had rattled her?

Her fingers tangled into her dress to keep them from shaking, but her insides did not comply. They roiled and twisted around the memories she had buried deep, coaxing them back to the surface. She tried to stuff them back down, but their residue lingered, sweet and intoxicating, bitter and hateful.

Tomorrow she would have to face him again. To do battle with her memories. Seeing him, standing close enough to touch him made every scar he'd laid across her unruly heart throb with pain and regret.

How much could a body withstand before it suffered too much? Before the floodgates opened and dropped her to her knees.

She had a sinking feeling she was on the verge of finding out.

Chapter Three

Going to see Meredith last night had been a colossal mistake. He'd blindsided her and as a result she'd gotten her back up. Then Bancroft and his brood had descended poking into their business. Hunter loved this town, but just once he'd like to do something without everyone in Salvation Falls dipping their toe into his life like they had some right to it.

He wondered if that was how Meredith had felt when he showed up at her door like a puffed-up buffoon and demanded to know what her intentions were. He groaned and dropped his forehead onto the smooth surface of his desk, banging his head lightly against the wood. He should have tried a softer approach but it had been so long since he'd tapped into anything remotely resembling a soft emotion he wasn't even sure he'd remember how. His job as sheriff demanded he be strong, steady, often tough and forceful. Softness didn't enter into it.

Given their parting seven years ago and the circumstances surrounding it, he had to expect he'd be the last person she'd want to see. If only he'd cooled his heels long enough yesterday to remember that before he went barreling over there to pound on her door.

Hindsight was a rather smug beast.

He lifted his head and leaned back in his chair, swinging his feet up onto the corner of his desk. Her return had set him on edge, no doubt about it. If he'd thought he had locked away their past and put it to rest, her arrival had proved him wrong. On first sight of her, everything had come rushing back in a tidal wave of memories. The good. The bad. The incredibly ugly.

To this day he still wasn't sure which one outweighed the other. He couldn't think of the good without the bad and ugly creeping in, and so he'd put them all away. Tucked them down deep where he didn't have to look at them or face what he had done. It had been hard enough to do when she wasn't here. He suspected it was going to be damned near impossible if she was front and center in his life day in and day out.

He needed to convince her to return to Boston. This time, however, it was for his safety, not hers.

It didn't help matters that he'd spent the better part of the night tossing and turning trying to figure out how he was going to accomplish such a feat when it was obvious she wasn't interested in one word that came out of his mouth. By the wee hours of the morning he was no closer to a solution. He'd dressed and come downstairs to his office to relieve Jenkins. With Bill Yucton's penchant for escape, he wasn't taking any chance of leaving the man unwatched.

He pushed himself out of his chair and crossed over to the woodstove, stoking the fire to ward off the cold creeping down from the mountains. He poured another cup of coffee. He had hoped the first cup would awaken enough of his faculties to force the image of Meredith from his mind, but he was three mugs in now and her image still lingered. A strange mesh of the girl from his memories and the woman she had become.

Time had left her skin smooth, untouched. The freckles he remembered were no longer in evidence. Her ivory skin did not appear to have met with the sun's rays in some time. Maybe it didn't shine much in Boston. And her eyes. Lord help him. The cornflower blue seemed even more brilliant against her flawless skin than he remembered. They'd stared at him in surprise when she first opened the door. He watched myriad emotions scuttle across them like fast-moving clouds when a storm was brewing.

Her words drifted back to him as they had over and over again through the night.

I plan on proving my father's innocence once and for all.

That could prove problematic.

He took a sip from his mug and winced. The sludge tasted like a disgusting mixture of burnt tree bark and dirt. He should have let Jenkins make a pot before he took Yucton to the bathhouse. He'd enlisted Kincaid's aid in transporting the prisoner. The bounty hunter had been none too pleased to be roused from his slumber, but since he'd taken to bunking in the empty cell to sleep off his latest bender, Hunter figured he wasn't in a position to argue.

Besides, he needed some time to think.

The return of Bill Yucton and Meredith Connolly at the same time was a bit too coincidental for him to swallow. He'd never put much faith in happenstance. Then again, he hadn't put much faith in anything of late.

He stared at the narrow file cabinet wedged under the small window next to his desk. He kept meticulous files, a trait McLaren had not shared and not one Jenkins seemed inclined to pick up.

He'd had to go into the bottom three drawers repeatedly to refile whatever he'd given to Jenkins. It was as if the boy had never been introduced to the alphabet.

But the top drawer he'd left alone. It had been two years since he'd opened it and pulled out the worn leather notebook. Years earlier, he'd gone over its contents six ways from Sunday, reread every word he'd put into it in the vain hope they would reveal whatever it was he was missing. They hadn't, and so he'd stuck it in the drawer and tried his best to wash his hands of it.

Dig deeper...the trial...syndicate...

The words had confused him at the time and haunted him ever since.

Sheriff McLaren had been like a father figure to him, more so than his own father ever had. In the wake of his death, Hunter had done his best to look at Abbott Connolly's trial from every direction. But in the end, it was what it was. A straightforward case of cattle rustling with one alleged accomplice saying he was there and another claiming he wasn't. If they hadn't found a few of the stolen cattle on Abbott's small piece of property perhaps the trial would have had a different outcome, but they had found the cattle, and in the end, it was all the jury needed to convict.

Hunter walked over to the cabinet and pulled

at the top drawer. It stuck, as if telling him what he already knew. He was wasting his time. No amount of digging on his part had revealed any great secret or explained what Sheriff McLaren had meant by *syndicate*. His dying declaration remained a mystery and Hunter had been forced to accept the fact it meant nothing. Likely the fatal wound he'd suffered had left him confused in his last moments of life and he'd simply been rambling. Doc Whyte said that could happen.

Still...

The memory of that day continued to trouble him. He'd come upon the scene too late. McLaren had been coming back from a routine checkup on old Mrs. Dunlop when he was gunned down by two men in cold blood. Hunter had heard the shots and come running. The shooters had taken off, no reason or explanation given for the attack, and McLaren lay dying in the street. He gripped Hunter's wrist when he reached him and his eyes, though filled with pain, were sharp and alert. The man knew he was dying. He'd gathered what was left of his strength and pushed out the words with the last beats of his heart.

It had to mean *something*! But what? And why? If Abbott knew, he wasn't talking. No one was.

He gave the drawer another yank, harder this

time. It opened with reticence, the leather note-book exactly where he'd left it two years ago. He reached in and fingered the twine wrapped around it. He didn't need to look inside. He'd long since memorized every note he'd written. It wasn't much.

Outside, the steady chink of chains and boots moving in tandem on the planked walkway her-alded the prisoner's return. Hunter slammed the drawer shut and turned toward the door as Yuc-ton crossed the threshold, Jenkins close on his heels. Kincaid was nowhere to be seen.

As if reading his mind, Jenkins hooked a thumb over his shoulder. "Kincaid stopped on the way back for a drink. But we got the stink washed off ole Bill here and he's clean as a whis-tle. Willie gave him a change of clothes jus' while his own are gettin' laundered."

Hunter ground his teeth together, his mood souring by the minute. He wanted to continue his conversation with Kincaid. The man knew more than he was saying. Hunter had sent Meredith away once before for her own safety. If there was any kind of a threat being resurrected by Yuc-ton's trial, he needed to know. He'd be damned if he let any harm come to her after what he'd given up to secure her safety in the first place.

"Much obliged for the bath," Yucton said,

reaching up with both hands to tip the brim of his hat, but the chains prevented him from reaching. He inclined his head instead, as if they'd done him a favor.

"Wasn't doing it for you, Yucton. Quite frankly, I was getting tired of smelling you."

A low rumble emanated from Yucton's chest as Jenkins opened the middle cell door and waited for him to walk inside before he reached through the bars to unlock the shackles. Despite his best efforts, Hunter had yet to get a rise out of his prisoner or to figure out why he'd willingly returned to Salvation Falls.

Jenkins walked over to the hook next to the woodstove and hung the shackles on it. "Heard you paid Meredith a visit yesterday."

Hunter scowled. News in this town moved with the swiftness of a wildfire caught in the wind.

"I did." He didn't bother mentioning it had been a disaster. He preferred to keep his private business just that—private.

Jenkins, on the other hand, had no such compunction. "Heard it didn't go so good?"

"And where did you hear that?"

"Mrs. Bancroft mentioned it to Eunice at the pie shop who told Saul over at the bakery and when I went past he told me. Said Mrs. Bancroft claimed she'd run into you in the hallway at the Klein and it looked like the two of you were exchanging words. Said you had your foot stuck in her doorway so she couldn't close it."

Fantastic. That's all he needed—people jawing about him and Meredith. It had created enough of a stir the first time around, given their family histories.

"This town needs to mind its own business. Now go find Kincaid and make sure he isn't so far into the whiskey he's passed out by noon." He barked the last order harsher than he needed to.

"Sure thing, boss," Jenkins said, his affable manner never showing any signs of the rebuke he'd just received. His deputy was so good-natured Hunter worried he'd never develop what it took to take over as Sheriff. Hunter was tough on him, maybe tougher than he needed to be, but he knew what this job required, what it could take out of you. Oftentimes, you had to make hard choices. Jenkins needed to be prepared for that.

He wished he had been.

"That Abbott Connolly's girl you're talkin' about?"

Hunter turned and stared into the middle cell. Yucton leaned forward, his arms resting against the crossbar. He'd pushed the hat back from his face revealing the plethora of lines beaten into it from a lifetime of hard living.

"It might be." He eyed Yucton with caution.

"Real shame about what happened to that family." His expression remained unchanged, but something in the prisoner's tone had changed. Hardened. "Ain't it, Sheriff?"

The small hairs on the back of Hunter's neck prickled. "You got something you want to say about it?"

"Believe I just did."

Hunter gave Yucton a fierce glare but the man didn't flinch. He was a cool customer. Hunter was both irritated and impressed.

"Given you're being tried for the same crime Connolly committed, I'd think you'd be a bit more concerned about yourself and not his kin. Especially given how things ended up for him."

"I'll worry about myself. You just worry about Abbott's girl."

The hairs on his neck now stood at full attention. "Why would I do that?"

"You ever hear tell of a group called the Syndicate?"

Hunter froze. "No. What does this Syndicate have to do with Meredith?"

Yucton stared at him for a long, silent moment. "You just make sure you keep her safe.

Believe you made promises in that regard. Am I right?"

Hunter's throat closed and his heart pounded deep inside his chest. "What do you know about it?"

"Maybe Abbott trusted you, but I haven't made up my mind about that. You're still a Donovan, after all."

Hunter took a step closer to the cell. "What's that supposed to mean?"

Yucton didn't answer him. He pushed away from the bars and returned to his bed. "You just keep her safe. That's all you need to know."

But it wasn't all he needed to know. Not now that another piece had been added to the puzzle of McLaren's last words. When Hunter had made his promise to protect Meredith years before, it had been made blindly to a father desperate to protect his daughter. At the time, Hunter had thought Abbott had been worried about leaving her alone in the world, her reputation damaged by the verdict delivered upon him. Now he wasn't so sure.

But if Yucton had the answers, he kept them to himself as he lay down and pulled his hat over his face, cutting off any further conversation. In the silence, the outlaw's words rang in Hunter's ears and slithered like poison through his veins.

You're still a Donovan after all.

He was nothing like his father. Everyone in town knew that. At least, he hoped they did. He'd spent most of his adult life trying to prove it, as if by doing good he could erase the horrible moment when he kept his promise to a convicted thief and broke the heart of the woman he loved.

Not that it mattered now, he supposed. Meredith was back and it was clear her animosity toward him still boiled beneath the surface. And all the good he'd tried to do as sheriff, the life he'd built, such as it was, was coming to an end. The truth of it chafed hard against his soul. His future opened up before him like a yawning abyss. But one thing was for certain—before he turned in his badge and accepted his fate, he was going to get to the bottom of whatever was going on.

Which meant another conversation with Meredith Connolly.

Meredith pulled the wool shawl tightly around her shoulders to ward off the chill of the late-autumn morning. She had almost forgotten the feel of Colorado in November. Not that it didn't get cold in Boston, but it was a different cold, coming off the water in the harbor and giving the air a sense of salty dampness. Here the cold had a brittle quality to it, as if you could reach out and snap it in half.

She took a deep breath and let its freshness fill her lungs in the hopes it would give her courage. Bertram had offered to escort her this morning, but she had declined. She wanted her first visit with her father to be on her own. She wasn't certain she could maintain her composure and she didn't want Bertram to see her break down. She couldn't afford weakness. She needed to remain strong.

Easier said than done. Her plan had already been put in jeopardy by Hunter's surprise visit. Seeing him had left her shaken, the memories rushing back and assaulting her from all sides. She tried to avoid them, skirt around them, but they showed her no mercy. Further proof love was to be avoided at all cost. Even when it was over it refused to leave you in peace.

She walked to the church and turned onto the narrow dirt road across the street from the white clapboard building, its spire cutting like a sword into the stark gray sky. Graves dotted the horizon, more than she remembered, each one punctuating the passage of time. Despite the added population and slight change to the landscape, Meredith needed no assistance in finding her way. She had walked the pathway a hundred times over in her memories.

The crisp morning breeze ruffled her hair and nipped at her skin. She paid it little heed as she trudged on, following the winding path toward the thick oak tree in the distance. Beneath it, her mother had rested these past seven years. Her father, for only one month.

She stopped at the top of the hill and walked to the outer edge of the tree's reach. Gathering her skirts, she knelt between the two markers, one made of stone faded and already weathered by time, the other a wooden cross bearing Pa's name and dates indicating the start of his life, and its end. She would have the stone mason carve a proper headstone to match Mama's, but not yet.

She wanted the words beneath his name to read *an innocent man*, and have everyone in town know the words as truth.

"Good morning, Mama." She touched the browning grass where it covered her mother's final resting place. Someone had been keeping the grave up. It was free of weeds and a small bouquet of hardy autumn flowers tied with string had been placed in front, weighted down by a rock on their stems. Bertram likely, though he hadn't mentioned it. Either way, she was touched by the gesture, by the idea that someone had watched over Mama when she had been unable to. She would make a point to thank him.

Meredith reached out and touched the flowers, wilted and brittle now, their colors faded. Much like her memories. She would never forget her mother—that was impossible. But sometimes, when she tried to capture the full picture in her mind, so many facets were muted. The sound of her laughter had become distant, the way light danced in her eyes, the sharp, delicate bones of her face. She could see one at a time, but never all at once. A deep sadness invaded her bones and seeped into her heart.

"I came home, Mama."

She knew that would please her mother. She'd always loved having her small family close. Thrived on it. She'd lost her own parents at an early age and had been forced to fend for herself. A dangerous proposition for a woman, but Mama had managed. She'd found work cleaning house for the Donovans. It put food in her belly and a roof over her head. For a while, her mama said, it had been enough. But then things changed. The elder Donovans passed away, and their son, Vernon, developed ideas she didn't agree with. At the same time, she met Meredith's father, and after that—she remembered her mother's smile when she told this part of the story—her whole life changed.

It had made Meredith believe in love, at least for a little while. But she'd long since shelved that belief. As much as love could lift you up it could just as easily throw you down. And the landing left you broken and battered beyond repair.

Meredith wondered if her mother had any inclination then how much her rejection of Vernon Donovan would change the course of their lives.

Meredith shifted her weight and faced her father's grave. The newly tilled ground formed a gentle mound. He'd rested here only a month and the grass had not had time to take hold before the cold weather swooped down in earnest and impeded its growth.

Her fingers ran over the dates burned into the wood. The last image she had of her father was sitting in the cell at the sheriff's office before he was transported to prison in Laramie. He'd refused to let her come with him. He'd been adamant about it and enlisted Hunter's help to keep her in Salvation Falls.

But Hunter had had other ideas.

The memories of that horrible time beat against her without remorse. A sob welled up in her throat. She tried to swallow it down as she always did but it refused to budge, demanded its freedom. Meredith fought it as best she could, but it was no use. Somewhere inside she had believed things would right themselves, but they never had

"Oh, Pa…"

The sob erupted from her, and behind it came all the others she had suppressed over the years. Tears obscured her view. She tried to fight them, but it was no use. Her strength gave out and she let her body fall across his grave. The need to hold Pa just one last time, to feel the safety of his arms, his gentle voice telling her everything would be fine, overwhelmed her. She cried unrestrained, all the pent-up emotion she'd held in for so long pouring out with her tears. She'd lost everyone she'd loved: Mama to illness, Pa to injustice, Hunter to betrayal.

She consoled herself with the fact she would never need to know loss again, but it was cold comfort and it only made the tears come harder.

Hunter hesitated, not wanting to disturb such a private moment, but the shaking of Meredith's shoulders and muffled sobs were enough to get his feet moving before his brain or common sense could catch up.

He slowed as he reached her, thrown across her pa's grave. She hadn't heard him approach and he wasn't sure how to let her know he was there. Given their last interaction, he doubted she would appreciate his intrusion. Still, he couldn't just walk away when she was in distress.

He crouched down. The hard ground and dry grass crunched beneath his weight.

"Meredith?"

Chapter Four

Hunter placed a hand on Meredith's back. The contact was exhilarating, which was almost as disconcerting as her tears. He wasn't sure what to do about either. Seeing her so distraught cut into him, finding every last crack in the walls around his heart and seeping through until their foundations began to crumble. God help him. He thought he was stronger than this.

Meredith whirled about, dislodging his hand. Her hair slipping free from its pins on one side creating a cascade of curls that bounced against her shoulder. A smudge of dirt bruised her cheekbone. The disarray reminded him of the girl he'd once known and a strong keening pierced his insides.

"What are you doing here?"

She wore another fancy dress today, this one a light copper with odd swirly designs on it in red and blue. The color somehow made her eyes even bluer. Or maybe that was the sheen of tears.

"Uh…" He'd tried not to glance down at the bouquet of flowers in his hand. They seemed a bit pathetic, small and inconsequential, but when he attempted to move the flowers out of her line of sight, she caught the motion. Her gaze flitted from the flowers in his hand to the withered batch on her mother's grave before returning it to him. She hiccupped then sniffed.

"You?" Disbelief filled her voice. She blinked, her lashes spiky from the tears.

He supposed it would be a bit ridiculous to deny it. He'd been caught red-handed, so to speak. Still, how did he explain it to her? He'd been doing it regularly since she'd left Salvation Falls and seven years later he still couldn't explain it to himself. Guilt could make a man do crazy things.

"Yeah, me." He looked away, embarrassed, but his gaze soon swung back, hungry for a glimpse of her, no matter the upheaval it caused the rest of him.

Her expression softened, a heady mix of uncertainty and something else that drew him in. Without thinking, he lifted a hand and gently brushed his thumb across the moist dirt clinging to her cheek. Her eyelids fluttered, thick lashes spiked with the remnants of tears creating crescent shadows across the tops of her cheekbones. Her skin was as soft as he remembered and he itched to touch her again, but she'd moved away from his reach and he didn't dare make a second attempt. She reminded him of a deer caught unaware in the woods, spooked by an unexpected noise.

He cleared his throat, needing to break the strange tension between them. She'd always had the power to do that. Entrance him until everything else but the two of them faded away. "I'm sorry about what happened to your pa."

He'd wanted to write. Composed the letter a dozen times over in his head. He knew Bertram would get it to her, but everything he came up with sounded trite and lacking. In the end, he'd left it alone, knowing she didn't want to hear from him either way.

"When they brought your father home I made sure they did right by him. Buried him next to your ma like he'd asked."

She nodded, the only hint she'd heard. She didn't look at him. Her small fist clenched and unclenched in the folds of her skirt. The wool shawl had slipped from her shoulders and pooled around her hips. She shivered.

"It's cold out here, Meredith. Why don't you

come back to the office? I'll put a pot of coffee on. It'll warm you up."

She sniffled and glanced up, her gaze hitting somewhere over his shoulder. When she spoke, her voice was thin and reedy, her throat stripped raw from crying. "I've tasted your coffee."

"My abilities have improved." One golden eyebrow arched upward. "Slightly," he amended.

Her gaze dropped to the flowers in his hand. "Why did you bring those?"

He lifted the small bundle and searched for the right words to make her understand, make her hate him a little less. "I knew you'd want to see her grave taken proper care of. And I figured if you were here, you'd put the flowers on yourself."

She reached up and tucked her hair back into place. He wished she hadn't. He loved seeing it down. His fingers itched to run through it. He swallowed. No, up was definitely better. Safer.

"So you're my proxy." The idea sat with discomfort on her furrowed brow.

"Guess so."

She was silent a moment, then her chin tilted upward. The formality returned to her voice and he could feel the distance between them grow. "Thank you for that."

"No need." He figured he owed her that much.

Given how he'd failed her on so many levels, this small gesture was almost laughable but he didn't want her gratitude. He didn't deserve it. He bent and replaced the old flowers with the new. When he was done, he took a chance and issued his earlier invitation once again. "How about that coffee? You can tell me if my skills have improved."

She pushed herself up in one swift movement, the crumpled, crying mess he'd come upon already a thing of the past. In her place, stood the determined, confident woman he'd come face-to-face with yesterday. He barely had time to get to his feet and no time at all to hold out a hand to aid her. By the time he found his own footing, she was busy dusting off bits of grass and dirt that clung to her skirts.

"As it turns out, that was my next stop. I mean to speak to Bill Yucton."

"Meredith…"

Anger spiked the color in her cheeks and her hands twitched where she'd pulled her shawl tight against her chest. "Don't you *Meredith* me, Hunter Donovan. What I do is no longer your concern. You lost that right a long time ago."

Exasperation filled him. "I'm not trying to tell you what to do," he said, but she wasn't interested in listening. She'd gathered her skirts in one hand and brushed past him, following the path back to town. "Dammit." He tossed the old bouquet to the ground and stalked after her.

"Don't try and stop me," she warned, keeping her gaze fixed straight ahead.

"I'm not trying to stop you. I'm trying to warn you!" Lord help him, had she always been this stubborn?

She stopped suddenly and he had to practically dance a jig to keep from barreling into her. "Warn me about what?"

He danced around the idea of telling her what Yucton had said to him. Could she have a piece of the puzzle without even realizing it? Maybe, but he was still reluctant to involve her.

And he definitely didn't want to tell her the whole truth. That he hadn't wanted to send her away. That he'd regretted his decision the moment the stagecoach had pulled away from the station. She had enough to contend with right now and what would it matter anyway? What was done couldn't be undone. Still, if she knew something…

"Have you ever heard of the Syndicate?"

Her nose crinkled in confusion and for a fleeting second the girl he used to know surfaced from beneath the finery once again. "The what?"

He had his answer. Guile and deception had never been a part of Meredith's makeup and though she now wore fancy dresses and had the lofty manners to match, he'd bet his last dollar her insides remained the same, even if her heart had changed. She didn't know the first thing about this mysterious Syndicate both McLaren and Yucton had mentioned and he wasn't about to inform her. Not that he had much to tell her. Either way, the less she was involved the better. Abbott might be dead but the promise Hunter had made him still stood. Whether he liked it or not.

He waved a hand. "Nothing. Never mind. C'mon, I'll walk you back to the office."

She ignored his proffered arm and marched ahead of him. He stood in place a moment and watched her walk away. Her straight spine and rigid shoulders made the gentle sway of her hips all the more enticing. Regret crept in with a sad finality as he realized he couldn't breathe life back into the embers of a fire that had gone out long ago.

Especially when he had been the one to douse those embers in the first place.

Meredith ignored the gazes she and Hunter collected as they made their way back to the jailhouse. She knew how the town worked. News of her homecoming had likely rippled through its underbelly and by sunrise this morning everyone living in close proximity of the town's core would be apprised of her return. By evening everyone on the outskirts would be aware, as well. And they would also know she had returned a woman of means.

She tried not to think of the dent the ruse put in her small nest egg. She only needed to keep it up long enough to get people's attention and enlist their help. A jury of men from this town had found her father guilty. Now she needed them to admit they were wrong. That the full scope of evidence hadn't been presented.

That he had been framed.

She would need the town on her side to do this. If there was one thing experience had taught her, it was that the more money you had, the more respect you were given, the more influence you could wield. She needed all of that now.

But first she had to feel the pulse of the town. Figure out who was best placed to help her. She thought of her old friend Rachel Beckett and wondered if she dared a visit. She had been Rachel Sutter when Meredith had left town, but had since remarried a man by the name of Caleb Beckett according to Bertram. She and Rachel had lost touch during her father's trial and perhaps her old friend no longer wished an acquaintance. She wouldn't have been the first friend Meredith lost after her father's arrest, but she had been the one she missed the most. Not that it had been Rachel's fault. Rachel had had her own problems to deal with, and Meredith hadn't wanted to burden her with hers. Besides, she'd had Hunter to lean on. Or so she had thought.

She turned to ask Hunter about Rachel, but when she glanced over at his profile, carved against the stark landscape, the words wouldn't come. She didn't want to engage with him as if they were old friends. They weren't. He had broken her heart and while seven years may have passed since then, the hurt had not healed. She'd thought it had, but returning to Salvation Falls and seeing him in the flesh had torn the wound open once again. She didn't want to ask him about Rachel. What she really wanted to do was beat on his chest in anger and ask him why. Why had he done it?

Pride stayed her tongue.

By the time they reached his office, the silence had stretched to an uncomfortable tension. He walked up the steps in front of her and rested his hand on the door handle. He stopped and faced her, his body barring her way.

"I wish you'd reconsider."

"Reconsider?"

"About staying. Settling here. Trying to change the past. Your pa is gone, Meredith, and I'm right sorry about that. I know how much you loved him. But digging all of this up again? It's just going to cause you more pain. Maybe you should think about going back to Boston."

The wound opened a little wider. It hurt her heart to think of how broken things had become. Once they had shared something beautiful, something that filled every part of her. She had believed it would last forever, was certain he shared the same feelings. She'd been wrong. All these years later and he still didn't want the reminder of her. Of the mistake he'd made.

"Boston is not my home. It never was. There's nothing left for me there."

"There's nothing left for you here either." His stern voice burned across her skin.

Aunt Erma had promised her broken hearts healed, but what she hadn't told her was that when the pieces were stitched back together they would no longer fit properly. She hadn't realized it at the time, but seeing Hunter now she understood it to be true. With each beat of her heart, the hurt pulsed deep and unforgiving, reminding her of everything she'd lost. If she'd ever really had it in the first place.

"This is my home." She fought to keep her

voice steady. "And my father deserves to rest easy in his grave knowing his name has been cleared of any wrong-doing. Wouldn't you do the same if it was your father?"

He didn't answer, but his expression tightened. "Then you're determined to stay?"

She walked up the stairs and stopped in front of him. Being this close was dangerous. The heat in her body rose to the surface and she could feel her skin tingle. A deep longing coaxed her to move closer, to give in to her body's craving to have him hold her. Would he? She shook the question off, irritated with her thoughts, the way they kept circling back to him. He was her past, and while she may need to deal with him in her present, he had no place in her future. He'd made his feelings on that matter perfectly clear.

"I am staying and I'm proving my father's innocence. Now, I would appreciate it if you would step aside and let me pass."

He ignored her request. "I don't see the point in what you're doing. Your pa is gone. It isn't going to matter to him what people think."

"It matters to me. I don't expect you to understand." His family had wealth, privilege and a good name. What had he ever struggled for?

Hunter hung his head and let out a slow breath. When he looked back up, myriad emotions warred in his dark eyes. She'd lost herself in those eyes once and the pull of them had not lessened over time.

"It isn't that I don't understand." His voice softened and only increased the potency. She struggled against it, against the small voice that longed for what he said to be true, the sense that she wasn't alone in this. "I know you loved your pa. I know you want to clear his name. I just don't want to see you get hurt—"

His words broke the spell his voice wound around her. What did he know of hurt? He had used her and tossed her aside, cutting her so deep the gash refused to heal.

"You weren't concerned with hurting me when you told me I wasn't good enough to be a Donovan."

The harsh words he'd said had carved themselves into her heart, imprinted on her soul. They had shared one passionate night together. She spent one glorious week dreaming of the life they would have together as man and wife, a much-needed respite of happiness as she struggled to come to terms with her father's sentence. It had given her something to hang on to when everything else had turned dark.

But it had all been a lie. What she had given

him meant nothing. She had meant nothing. No. Worse—she *was* nothing. Not to him.

The last image she had of Salvation Falls was seeing him walk away from her before the stage-coach had even pulled away from the livery station. He hadn't said goodbye, hadn't wished her well. Hadn't changed his mind and told her it was all a cruel joke.

"Meredith, I never meant—"

"No." She sliced her hand through the air and cut off the rest of his words. She couldn't bear to hear them. And what could he say? That he'd never meant to say he loved her in the first place? That he shouldn't have led her on and made promises he had no intentions of keeping? "It doesn't matter anymore."

Except that it did. And she hated that fact more than all the others.

She pulled her shoulders back and took a deep breath. "I have no desire to relive the past or stand here discussing it with you. If you never planned on marrying me, you should have never taken things as far as you did. Now we both have to live with the consequences. I'm sorry we have to deal with each other now, but there's little to be done about it. You can rest assured, however, once I prove my father's innocence we need not bother with each other ever again save for a polite nod if we pass on the street. Now please, step aside."

The idea saddened her. Despite everything, the hurt, the anger, the betrayal. Maybe that had something to do with the wrongness of the way her heart had pieced itself back together. She didn't know. But she couldn't worry about it now. Now she had to focus on what she'd come here to do.

Hunter looked as if he wanted to say something else, but whatever it was hovered unspoken in the silence left between them and in the end, he did as she asked and opened the door, stepping to one side to let her pass.

Chapter Five

Hunter kept silent as she passed, wishing he could tell her the truth, but what good would it do them now? So much water had passed under their bridge it was a wonder they hadn't drowned in the overflow. Would she care that the reason he had walked away from the stage before she even pulled out of the station was because he couldn't stand the thought of watching her leave? Knowing it was happening had been bad enough, witnessing it was something else entirely.

He knew without a doubt if he'd had to stand there and watch her leave, he would have hauled her off that stage without a moment's hesitation, her safety and the promises he'd made be damned.

So he'd walked away before it came to that. He couldn't put his own wants and needs first. He may not have fully understood what was going on, but instinct told him if Abbott was adamant she be kept safe, he needed to do it. He didn't have a choice.

Hunter followed Meredith into the office and stopped abruptly. Near Yucton's cell, a tall lanky stranger stood with his back to them. He reacted instantly and grabbed Meredith by the arm, shoving her behind him as the stranger turned around.

"What do you think you're do—"

Hunter held on to her arm to keep her in place, then raised his voice to drown her out. "Who are you? Jenkins!"

"Out here choppin' some wood, Sheriff," Jenkins called out, his voice filtering from around the back of the jailhouse, through the window he kept open a crack to keep the air from getting stale. "There's a man here to see Bill but I told him he should talk to you first!"

Hunter shook his head. What his deputy had in brawn he lacked in judgment. It did not bode well for the future of the town once Hunter stepped down. He gave the stranger a hard stare. "What's your business here?"

Beneath the stranger's thin moustache, a painted-on smile plastered itself across his bland face. As it did so, Hunter noticed Yucton sitting on the edge of the bed partially hidden by shadow. The outlaw made a small, swift motion with his hand and, much to Hunter's surprise, Meredith stopped struggling.

"Good day. You must be Sheriff Donovan." The man stepped forward, his hand extended. Hunter didn't bother taking it. No point makin' friendly until he knew what the man was about. Though whatever that was, he was already forming the opinion he didn't like him. Trussed up in a fancy suit, he reminded Hunter of someone you'd see peddling an elixir on the thoroughfare claiming it would cure all your ills. Men like that usually wanted something, and after his setdown from Meredith, he wasn't in a giving mood.

"You didn't answer my question."

The stranger's hand dropped and his smile grew more forced. "Of course, how ill-mannered of me. My name is Wallace Platt."

Hunter noted the Southern lilt to the man's speech. An outsider. "Not familiar. What are you doing in my jail?"

Yucton's lazy drawl drifted out from the middle cell. "Says he's my lawyer."

"That's what he says, huh?" Yucton had been taking up space in the middle jail cell for over two weeks now and not once during that time had he made any kind of move to employ legal counsel. Nor had he bothered curing Hunter's curiosity as to why that was. It was as if the man was biding his time—but for what? "Didn't know you'd hired one."

"I didn't."

Hunter turned his attention back to Platt. "Care to shed some light?"

The smile on Platt's face became pinched and a red stain tinted his pale skin. It didn't look like the man spent much time out of doors. City type, no doubt. Hunter didn't necessarily have a stringent dislike for city folk, he just didn't trust them was all. Especially not the namby-pamby type standing in front of him now.

"I'm not in the habit of explaining myself, Sheriff."

"You could always leave," Hunter suggested, nodding toward the open door.

"I'm afraid I can't. I need to speak to my client."

"Your *client* doesn't appear to return those feelings. You want to speak to this man, Yucton?"

"Can't say that I do, Sheriff."

Hunter shrugged. "See."

"Think I might represent myself."

Platt spun on his well-shod heel to face the cell again. "Mr. Yucton, it is a commonly held belief that a man who represents himself—"

"Ain't interested in your beliefs," Yucton said, cutting him off.

Frustration colored Platt's tone. "I didn't say it was *my* belief, Mr. Yucton. I said it was—"

"Then you won't mind if I ignore it."

Hunter's estimation of his prisoner raised a notch.

"I get the sense Yucton here isn't the one who hired you. Which leads me to the question— who did?" Hunter didn't like this. Yucton was allegedly one of the rustlers who had stolen his father's cattle all those years ago. Why would anyone care enough about it, or Yucton, to pay for some fancy lawyer from who knows where to represent him? It didn't sit right. There was a lot of things not sitting right lately. If this kept up, he'd find himself running out of chairs real soon.

"I'm afraid I'm not at liberty to comment on that. You see, my benefactor—and yours, Mr. Yucton—wishes to remain anonymous. Suffice to say, he is interested in ensuring Mr. Yucton receives a vigorous and skillful defense against the pending charges."

Yucton snorted. "And they sent you?"

Hunter pursed his lips together to keep his smirk in check. Behind him, however, Meredith's muffled laugh rippled up to tease him. He wished he could turn around and see it. He hadn't heard her laugh in longer than he could remember, but he hadn't forgotten the way her eyes danced when she did.

Dammit. Focus, Donovan.

Platt cleared his throat and glanced over his shoulder at Hunter. Irritation flashed in his eyes and the smarmy smile disappeared.

"I can assure you, Mr. Yucton, I have much experience in these matters and I am certain I can be of great service to you."

"Not interested."

Platt ignored the rejection. "I will give you the day to think on it and return on the morrow."

Yucton grunted in response. "Return on whatever morrow you want. Won't be changing my mind."

Platt turned away from the occupied cell and fixed his snake oil salesman smile back in place. "I expect I will be allowed to see my client tomorrow, Sheriff."

Hunter shrugged. "The man isn't going anywhere." He wasn't thrilled about Platt and his pompous attitude gracing his office again, but there was something fishy about the man, and better he keep him in his sights until he figured out what was going on and who this so-called mysterious benefactor was.

Dig deeper.

Platt headed toward the door but stopped when he reached Hunter. He looked past him to where Meredith peeked around his shoulder.

"My apologies, madam. I did not see you standing there or I would have introduced myself to you directly. Mr. Wallace Platt, at your service." Platt executed a courtly bow. When he straightened, he glanced at Hunter expectantly.

Hunter ignored him. He couldn't conjure any good reason to introduce Meredith to the likes of this dandified Southerner. Meredith, unfortunately, did not feel the same. She elbowed past his protective barrier and held out her hand. He watched in disgust as Platt bowed over it. Lucky for him, he didn't raise it to his lips. If he had, Hunter was more than prepared to plant him into next week. He wasn't sure what irritated him more—the fact that she didn't appreciate he was only trying to protect her, or this ridiculous sense of proprietorship he felt toward her. She didn't belong to him. A fact his head had accepted but failed to relay to his heart. Or other parts of him for that matter.

"You'll have to excuse the sheriff, Mr. Platt. Manners were never his strong suit. I suppose those of us who have come from away can appreciate their usefulness a bit more. Miss Meredith

Connolly." She gifted the lawyer with a smile so sweet Hunter's teeth ached.

"It is indeed my honor to make your acquaintance, ma'am. And where might *away* be for you, Miss Connolly, if it is not too impertinent of me to ask?"

He had yet to let go of her hand. Hunter gritted his teeth against the surge of possessiveness that erupted within him. Planting Platt into next week was beginning to look like a stellar idea. He curled his hand into a tight fist.

"Boston, Mr. Platt. And you? I assume from your accent you do not hail from these parts?"

"Alas, no. From the fine state of Virginia originally. San Francisco most recently."

"How lovely."

"It's positively wonderful," Hunter drawled out, unable to keep his growing irritation from lacing its way through each word. "Now if you'll excuse us, Platt. I have things to do and seein' as how your supposed client isn't interested in having you as his lawyer, I don't see much reason for you to hang around."

Platt didn't bother looking at him. He was too busy making cow eyes at Meredith. "Perhaps we'll meet again, Miss Connolly. I always feel it is nice to make as many friends as possible when one is a stranger in a new place. It would be my pleasure to count a lovely lady like yourself among them."

"I appreciate the sentiment, Mr. Platt. And I agree— one cannot have too many friends. I look forward to furthering our acquaintance."

Hunter waited until Platt closed the door behind him upon his exit, then turned on Meredith. "What the hell was that all about?"

The words were out before he could stop them. She blinked at him, her eyes pools of innocent blue. She dropped her gaze to her gloves and slowly pulled them off, one finger at a time. "I have no idea what you're talking about? I was merely being polite to a stranger."

He glared down at her. His agitation grew with her feigned innocence. For crying out loud, she'd all but swooned at Platt's pretty words. "Well you might want to learn more about the damn stranger before you start cozying up to him like he was your new best friend."

She pulled off her second glove then smiled up at him. "I hardly think one has to take a man's measure before they decide whether or not to be polite. Perhaps you should try it. Your manners could use a little brushing up. They're hardly up to the Donovan standard, now are they? Oh no, wait," her brow furrowed, "of course they are. You Donovans always had a habit of assuming money meant you didn't need manners, if I recall?"

The barb hit its intended mark. "My manners are just fine, thank you."

She offered him a dubious look then brushed past him and walked to Yucton's cell her hips tormenting him with their gentle sway. Her dismissal and low opinion left a gaping emptiness inside of him. Is this how she'd felt when he'd jilted her? No wonder she disliked him with such intensity.

"Good morning, Bill. It is lovely to see you again."

Yucton stood and held his hands out through the bars that separated them. She grasped them like an old friend.

"Still able to charm any gentleman that crosses your path, I see."

Meredith laughed and took the older man's hands in her own. They were warm and rough, a lifetime of hard living worn into them. "I may have learned a thing or two while navigating Boston's high society." Granted, it was as their seamstress, but Hunter didn't need to know that. Let him think she was now on a social par with him, even if it was nothing more than a ruse. It would serve him right.

"That a fact? And have you given any thought to returning to Boston? Sounds like you had a nice life going for yourself there? Sure be a shame to give something like that up."

Meredith scowled at Bill. "Why is everyone trying to pack me off and send me back to Boston? I appreciate Aunt Erma taking me in, but that didn't make it home. My heart always longed for the fresh mountain air and wide-open spaces. What brought you back, Bill?"

She was thankful he let the matter drop. She didn't want to argue with him. "Figured you'd come home when you learned about your pa's passing. Thought I'd head back this way. Make sure you was all right. Your pa died an innocent man. He didn't deserve what happened to him."

She squeezed Bill's hands and pulled strength from them. Pa was gone for good. Seeing his grave marker had driven the reality of it home. She fought back the tears from earlier. There was no time for such things now.

"I'm afraid you and I are in the minority on that belief."

"It's no belief. It's a plain and simple fact." Bill smiled and his eyes creased deeply at the corners. She noted his hair was grayer than she remembered and the lines of his face had burrowed a little deeper. "He was so proud of you. Told me so himself."

Meredith's throat tightened. She took a deep breath and swallowed past it. "I wish you hadn't made the trip back. Now look at you." Guilt swept through her. Bill had always been a close friend of her father's. Steady and reliable, though he drifted in and out of their lives from time to time. She understood as she got older it was because of his penchant for living on the outskirts of the law. She always wished he'd chosen a different path, but it hadn't diminished her affection for one of the few men to be a true friend to her father.

"Don't worry too much on that. Ain't been a jail that could hold me yet."

"This one will." The conviction in Hunter's words cut through the small office. He'd moved and now sat behind his desk. Meredith couldn't help but notice he filled the space with a sense of authority. He'd been so uncertain when Sheriff McLaren had died. Unsure if he was up to the task, if he could do the job justice. Part of her had wondered if he might relinquish the role the town had bestowed upon him and instead take up the reins of running the Diamond D Ranch as his father insisted. He hadn't, though. Fortunate for the town, she supposed, though she didn't much care for the constant contact with him while she tried to clear her father's name.

She glared over her shoulder at Hunter who leaned back in his chair and propped his feet up onto his desk, actively listening to their conversation. She walked over to his desk and picked up the straight-back chair in front of it.

"Do you mind?" she said to Hunter.

"Not so much. You?"

She carried the chair back to Bill's cell and set it down with a bang. "Yes! I would appreciate some privacy." The sharp tone in her voice made her cringe. She wanted to maintain a distance from him emotionally if not physically, but somehow he managed to pluck every last nerve she owned.

"This place isn't exactly built for private conversations," he informed her, waving a hand in the air at the small open space.

"Perhaps you could plug your ears."

"Can't. I'm on duty. Never know when someone might call for help." He grinned. Damnation if that didn't pick at her nerves all over again but in a completely different way. Lord help her, dealing with him was going to turn her upside down and inside out before it was over and done. The man was infuriating. Though no more so than her body's response to him.

"You don't have to be so smug about it." She scuttled her chair closer to the bars and lowered her voice in the hopes of putting an end to Hunter's eavesdropping. "I plan to clear Pa's name, Bill. I'm hoping you can help me with that."

Bill's eyebrows raised a notch until they disappeared beneath the rim of his hat. "Can't imagine what kind of assistance I could be to you in that regard. I already told 'em your pa didn't take part in the rustling. No one cared about my opinion then. Can't imagine much has changed in that regard."

Meredith remembered the impotent rage she felt when Bill's eyewitness testimony was tossed aside by the circuit court judge. Judge Arthur Laidlow had arrived in town with his mind already made up on the matter it seemed. Truth and justice didn't sway him one iota, a fact made obvious by his rulings. Bill had escaped and disappeared shortly after that and she didn't blame him. Nor had her father.

Best he get gone and stay that way. No sense both of us sitting in this cell waitin' for the hangman's noose, Pa had told her. She'd agreed he had the right of it, but she had missed Bill's comforting presence, the feeling that someone else was on her side. She hadn't seen him since, though in his letters her father referred to him from time to time indicating they had been in contact.

She slipped one of the strings of her reticule from her wrist and opened it up, fishing inside until her fingers hit upon what she was looking for. She pulled out two folded pieces of paper and handed them to Bill through the bars.

"When Aunt Erma died, I was sorting through her things and came across a letter Pa had sent her early on, shortly after I arrived."

Bill took the papers and flipped them open. She didn't bother to ask him if he could read it. She knew him to be an educated man. His mama had run a high-end brothel somewhere in Texas, and she ensured her only son was educated, hoping to give him every advantage she hadn't had. Unfortunately she'd died of the pox when Bill was only fourteen, putting an end to her dreams.

When he finished perusing the first piece of paper, he let out a slow breath, refolded it along the crease and passed it back to her. "You know what this is?" He asked, indicating the second piece of paper.

She lifted a hand in exasperation. "It's a page from a ledger of some sort. I kept the account books for Aunt Erma, but I can't make heads or tails out of this one. The list of items on the left is a jumble of letters. It's like it was written in code. Do you recognize it? I figured it must be important. Pa's letter told Aunt Erma to keep it somewhere safe. Why else would he do that if it wasn't important?"

"Like I said," Bill told her, his voice more weary than when they first began their conversation. "I'm not sure I can be much help to you."

"But—"

Bill shook his head, cutting her off. "It was a long time ago, Meredith. My memory ain't what it used to be. Besides, you really think your pa would want you dredging all this old stuff up? I think for certain he'd rather you get on with your life. Find yourself a good man, settle down and have some babies. Bet he'd smile real proud-like from Heaven to see you bringing up his grandbabies."

Frustration rippled through her. She'd had dreams like that once, but her foolish heart and rebellious body had put an end to that. What man would want her now when she had already given herself to another? No, she had put that dream away, along with the idea of love. It was a road riddled with hurt and heartbreak and she had no desire to travel down it ever again.

"I'm sorry, Bill. But I can't. I can't live here day in and day out, seeing my father's grave and knowing people believe the man buried there was a thief."

Bill nodded and fell silent for a moment, staring at his hands. "Do you remember that ole chessboard your pa made?"

She had hoped Bill could help her, that he could shed light on the curious ledger sheet her father deemed important enough to send to Aunt Erma for safekeeping. Her shoulders drooped with disappointment. She was on her own with no idea of how to proceed.

"Yes, of course, I remember," she said, forcing a smile. "Pa taught me how to play when I was a little girl."

"Taught me, too. Haven't played in a dog's age, though. You still have that?"

"I suppose it's still out at the homestead. I haven't been back yet." Bertram assured her he'd kept an eye on it, but she had put off going there herself. Seeing the place in which she had once lived safe and happy now sitting empty and abandoned only drove home everything she had lost. Sooner or later she would have to—she couldn't stay at the Klein forever, but she'd hoped the sooner would be more like later.

"Might be kinda nice to take it up again, whittle away the hours. What do you say?"

"I can get you a chessboard and you can teach

Jenkins to play if you're hard up for entertainment, Yucton. Sitting in here keeping you company isn't any place for a lady," Hunter said, butting into their conversation again.

"I don't recall you ever thinking of me as a lady, *Sheriff*, and I certainly don't recall asking you for your opinion on the matter," Meredith stated. If nothing else, she could use the time to convince Bill to hire Bertram for his defense.

Hunter pulled his mouth into a tight line. "No one has to ask me. It's my jail."

She offered him her sweetest smile but layered her words with sarcasm. "Is it now? I thought it was the town's jail."

"Semantics."

"Well, if you are saying you're prohibiting Bill from having visitors, I'm not sure you have the right to do that. Of course, I suppose I could always check with that gentleman lawyer. What was his name again?"

"Mr. Wallace Platt," Bill supplied.

"Of course. Mr. Platt. I'm sure such a fine Southern gentleman wouldn't hesitate to help a lady in need."

A small sliver of satisfaction pierced her when Hunter shot her a dark look. "I'm not saying he can't have visitors. I'm saying I can think of better places for you to be spending your time."

"Really? And where are these *better* places?"

"Boston."

She narrowed her gaze. "Has anyone ever told you how annoyingly overbearing you are?"

"Not recently."

"I find that very difficult to believe."

Bill laughed, the deep rumble rolling around her. "Maybe I won't need that chess game after all, Sheriff. I find listenin' to the two of you jaw back and forth quite entertaining."

Hunter shifted his gaze away from her to land on Bill. "Shut up, Yucton. She shouldn't be here."

Shouldn't be around him is what Hunter likely meant. And while she would be more than happy to comply, it hurt more than she cared to admit to know he shared those feelings. Had he always felt that way, even while he played her false? She'd been such a fool, too blinded by the wonder that someone as fine and upstanding as Hunter Donovan was interested in her to see the truth.

Bill shrugged. "Can't do no harm. 'Sides, a man can get sick of looking at your mug day in and day out. Ain't sayin' you're ugly or nothin'. God knows to hear Jenkins tell it, half the single women in town get downright fluttery whenever you walk by. But I'd still rather have a pretty face and sweet disposition to keep me company all the same."

Meredith didn't care to hear how the women still got themselves all in a dither over Hunter. Obviously, not much had changed in that regard during her absence. Still, she did find it odd he hadn't found one to settle down with. Surely one of them met the lofty Donovan standards. Though a small, rebellious part of her, a part she refused to give credence to, gave a little cheer over the fact no one had.

"If you're done arguing on that account," she said. "I will ride out to the homestead tomorrow and see if I can't find Pa's old chess set. It would be my pleasure to keep you entertained, Bill. Although I'll admit, I'm quite rusty."

"That makes two of us. Guess we can relearn the game together."

Hunter waited until Meredith left the office before he gave up on his relaxed position and let his feet hit the floor with every ounce of his suppressed anger coursing through his veins.

"You mind telling me what the hell you're doing bringing her into this place every day like it's where she oughta be? This isn't the place for her! Hell, half the time we've got drunks and idiots on either side of you. Do you want her exposed to that?"

Hunter certainly didn't. Nor did he want to

be constantly exposed to her. Or rather he did, which meant he shouldn't because there was only so much a man could stand on that account before he started to lose the part of his mind that made him step back and steer clear. If Meredith was in his jail every day, there'd be no avoiding it. How long did he think he could go without declaring his feelings, making a total arse of himself and giving her enough ammunition to do him in? Not long, he guessed if his current state of thinking was any indication.

Yucton glared up at him. "Well she ain't going back to Boston that much is clear. And if you think you're going to convince her otherwise then you've forgotten she owns a stubborn streak deep enough to sink a ship in. So tell me this, Sheriff—given she's not leavin' and given you promised her pa you'd keep her safe, where do you think is a safer place to keep her if not right under your nose?"

Yucton's words stopped him in his tracks halfway to the cell. He hadn't told a soul about the promise he'd made to Abbott. "How do you know about that?"

"Who do you think he entrusted to make sure you kept up your end of things if she got it in her head to come back here?"

The truth of things settled around him. "Is that what you're doing back here?"

Yucton said nothing.

"You could end up hanging for your efforts."

The glint of determination hardened Yucton's expression making the bones of his face stand out even more. "We all gotta die sometime. And who knows, maybe your pappy will come to my defense, the way he did Abbott's."

"I wouldn't hold your breath." His father wasn't known for doing favors. The fact he had stood up in court and argued against a sentence of hanging for Abbott Connolly had been completely out of character for the man, especially when he'd spent the better part of his life trying to ruin Abbott. To this day, Hunter could not find a satisfactory reason to justify the behavior. Lord only knew his father was not inclined to give him one.

"You ever find that strange?" Yucton asked, as if reading Hunter's mind. "Your pappy hated Abbott with every breath he took. Odd, then, that the one chance he had to get rid of him, he didn't take."

"Maybe he had a change of heart."

Yucton arched one eyebrow upward, his expression echoing Hunter's own thoughts. His father didn't have a heart. The only true feeling he'd ever shown was toward Vivienne Connolly. He called it love, but Hunter had seen love, and that wasn't it. Vivienne had been his father's obsession. Vernon had wanted what he couldn't have, and not having it had turned him into a bitter and hateful man. Going out of his way to save Abbott's neck from the hangman's noose had never added up.

"Maybe he did it for Vivienne."

Yucton shrugged. "You believe that?"

Hunter let out a long slow breath. He wished he did, but truth be told the idea fit about as well as a pair of boots two sizes too small. Vivienne had died a week before Abbott's sentencing and somehow the idea of Vernon waxing sentimental over her passing and letting his emotions change his mind on what happened to Abbott… well, *sentimental* and *emotions* weren't exactly words Hunter associated with his father.

"What precisely is it Abbott thought Meredith needed protection from? Does this have anything to do with the Syndicate you mentioned?"

Yucton pulled his hat off his head and worked the brim in his hands, turning it slowly as if mulling over Hunter's question. In the end, whatever he decided didn't include imparting any more information than what Hunter already had. Which amounted to diddly-squat.

"You just make sure that little lady has you for a shadow."

"That's it? You don't think it would help me out if I knew exactly what it was I'm supposed to be watching out for?" Yucton said nothing. "Hell, I'm the last person she wants dogging her every step."

Yucton smirked. "Maybe you oughta try changin' her mind on that."

Hunter sat on the edge of his desk and folded his arms over his chest. The man was obviously a few birds short of a full nest if he believed that could happen. "You think you know so much, yet you don't even know who's bankrolling your defense."

Yucton leaned back on his bed. "I have a good idea."

"Enlighten me."

Yucton placed the hat he'd been turning in his hands over his face. "Been to see your father lately?"

The ground shifted beneath Hunter as the conversation swerved in a direction he hadn't been prepared for. "What does my father have to do with anything?"

Yucton lifted his hat. "You really that clueless, boy? Or are you just pretendin' because maybe you got something to do with it and you jus' don't want no one to know?"

"Know about what?" The old man had an irritating habit of talking in riddles.

"You think on it a bit," Yucton said. His sharp eyes probed and stared and willed Hunter to pay attention, to read between the lines. But Hunter didn't like the story he found there. He didn't like it one bit.

Chapter Six

Meredith walked from the hotel to the livery at the far end of the street. It wasn't a long walk, but she took her time, perusing the storefronts, some faded, others newly painted. Many of the businesses she recognized, having been there since she was small, but sprinkled throughout were newer businesses. It was nice to see the growth in the town, its prosperity. She took it as a good omen that her business, once established, would do well. It had to.

The nest egg she had inherited from Aunt Erma wouldn't last forever, especially not if she stayed at The Klein for much longer. But for now, it was necessary. She had learned from Aunt Erma that part of the secret to success was appearing successful. It had worked, though the competition in Boston for business had been fierce. Aunt Erma had been stuck in her ways near the end and it had fallen to Meredith to try and grow their clientele. She had done so by introducing new patterns, ones she had designed herself. But by then her aunt's health was failing. Meredith couldn't keep up with the orders on her own, yet Aunt Erma refused to pay out funds to hire another seamstress. In the end, they had to shut their doors.

Now, Meredith was ready to open them again in Salvation Falls. But, in keeping with Aunt Erma's advice, she first needed to show the townspeople she had changed her circumstances, she had made something of herself. And maybe...well, more than maybe, she wanted to show Hunter. She wanted him to see that she was every bit as good as a Donovan.

She paused in front of an empty window and peered inside. The store was empty, but from what she could see through the dusty pane it possessed a main area and a back room, as well as a set of stairs leading to a second story. It was perfect for what she had in mind. She backed up and looked at the sign swinging from above the door. Hattie's Hats.

She lifted an eyebrow. Hardly the most original of names. She would try to do better.

"Meredith?"

She recognized the voice the instant she heard

it and turned to find Rachel Beckett standing a few feet away. "Rachel…" The name trailed off and left an awkward silence between them. All the things she'd wanted to say rushed through her head but too quickly for them to take hold. "I—I was hoping to call on you."

"I was hoping you would when I heard you'd returned, but I thought I might give you a day or two to get settled." Rachel smiled, and the motion took Meredith by surprise. When she'd left, Rachel had been going through a hard time of her own with her husband, Robert, prone to gambling and debts mounting. It had been a long time since she'd seen Rachel happy and when she did, lingering behind it was the weight of all she carried on her narrow shoulders. But this smile, this was real and genuine and—

"Oh!" Meredith covered her mouth before she let something inappropriate fly out of it, but she couldn't take her eyes off the rounded bump of Rachel's belly. "Are you…?"

Rachel's smile grew. "I am."

Meredith wanted to hug her old friend but it had been so long and she wasn't sure she had the right anymore. She'd been the one to let their friendship lapse. She'd thought of writing her after she reached Boston, but due to Rachel's close friendship with Hunter, she'd feared the return letters would contain information her heart could not bear.

"I heard about Robert's passing. It was dreadful what you had to go through."

Rachel's expression turned somber, though a light still played in her eyes. Even her hair, a mass of dark curls she had never managed to tame, had a particular bounce to it. "Thank you for saying so, but I guess we shouldn't be all that surprised. I wish he could have taken a different path, but if he had, maybe I wouldn't have found the one I'm on with Caleb. He's a good man." She touched her belly and sunlight glinted off the thin gold band on her left hand. "But enough about me. I was sorry to hear about your pa. We had a nice memorial service for him when Hunter brought him home."

"Hunter?" Bertram hadn't mentioned Hunter had been the one who had transported her father from the prison when he wrote to tell her about his passing.

Rachel nodded. "The prison contacted him when your pa took a turn for the worse. I think he'd asked them to. He'd been up to visit your pa a time or two when he heard his health was failing. He wanted to be sure he was receiving proper care. But I expect you know all that."

But she hadn't. In truth, she hadn't even

thought of it. The news that her father was gone forever had been so overwhelming, she hadn't thought about the details. She'd assumed it had been Bertram. She'd been wrong. The truth found the crevices in her heart and seeped inside. Why had her father never mentioned it in his letters? And more importantly, why had he asked Hunter to do it when she would have been more than willing to leave Boston and come home to tend to him?

"Are you on your way somewhere?"

Rachel's question pulled her out of her tangled thoughts. "Oh…yes. To the livery. I'm going to rent a wagon and check on the old homestead." Her words drifted out on a whisper, the rest of her trying to absorb what Rachel had told her.

"I'll walk with you. I have a little time before Caleb finishes up at the bank." Rachel looped her arm through Meredith's and guided her along the planked walkway in the direction of Abe's Livery. "Personally, I think Hunter always regretted that you'd had to move away. He was pretty sweet on you. I half expected him to propose, but I guess during the trial was hardly the time, and then maybe he figured it was better for you to get away from everything for a while."

Their footsteps echoed on the wood of the raised sidewalks, beating in tandem with her heart, though the latter seemed to hold more ferocity. She tried to marry Rachel's words with what had actually happened, but there was a deep abyss between what her friend believed and the truth.

"I'm sure he got over it." She tried to keep the bitterness from her voice. Rachel and Hunter were still good friends.

"Are you?" Rachel tilted her head to one side and the morning sunlight danced along her glowing skin. "I'm not so sure. He'd never talk about it afterward. Closed right up on the subject. And he's never taken up with anyone else, not seriously. Not that there haven't been plenty of mamas practically throwing their daughters at him. A handsome sheriff with a family fortune waiting in the wings is a potent combination. But he's avoided the matchmaking. I always wondered if he wasn't carrying a torch for you."

"I'm sure he isn't." No man rejected a woman in such a horrendous fashion, then pined for her afterward.

"Well, either way. When he received word your pa had passed on, he rode to Laramie to bring him home. He and Bertram arranged the burial and made sure he rested next to your ma like he wanted." Rachel stopped at the corner in front of the mercantile and nodded toward the door. "This is me. I promised Ethan I would bring him back a peppermint stick."

"Ethan?"

Rachel laughed. Meredith marveled at how her friend's face lit up as the sound filtered around them like music. "Oh, Meredith. There is so much to catch up on. I took Ethan in a few years ago after his ma died. Promise me you will let me invite you out to the Circle S. You can meet Caleb and Ethan and you wouldn't believe how much Brody has grown."

"Good heavens. Your brother was just a little boy when I left. And Freedom?" Meredith asked, referring to Rachel's housekeeper.

Rachel shook her head. "Still trying to teach me how to cook. She'd love to see you. Tell me you'll come?"

A strange sense of belonging rooted Meredith to the spot and for a brief speck of time all she could do was stand there and let it wrap around her. It had been so long since she'd felt it. She'd feared coming back to Salvation Falls she wouldn't be able to find it. Just another thing she'd lost along with her family. But she hadn't. It was still there waiting for her to grab hold.

"I would love to, Rachel."

"Great!" Rachel hugged her hard, the tiny baby growing in her belly brushing against Meredith's own. A strange longing bloomed deep inside of her but she shook it off. The hope of love and family were lost to her now. She needed to accept that. "How about this coming Sunday? After church. We can make a day of it," her friend suggested.

"I'm looking forward to it."

They said their goodbyes and Meredith continued on to the livery, her step lighter than it had been, the ruffled edge of her skirt bouncing at her ankles. For the first time since arriving in Salvation Falls she felt certain she had made the right decision.

She still had friends here. People who cared. She wasn't alone.

Hunter opened the door to his father's house, taking in the shabby state of the once grand home. The house had been in decline since his mother had left them over fifteen years ago.

For a little while, Hunter had made an obligatory effort to keep the place up, certain it would just be a matter of time before his mother returned. But weeks passed into months then into years and eventually he stopped believing in such things. He packed away his hopes in that regard and shelved them along with the few belongings she hadn't seen fit to take with her.

Shy Waters, his father's latest housekeeper, did her best to keep the place clean, cook meals for his father and see to his basic comforts, but time insisted on having its way. Curtains and quilts faded, cushions flattened, surfaces dulled and dust collected.

At some point, Shy Waters had decided that covering a large portion of the house in sheets and closing the doors made it easier to deal with. It gave the cavernous house an abandoned feel to it.

He guessed, in a sense, that's what it was. His mother had abandoned it, and so had he, spending most of his time between the sheriff's office and the room he'd cleared out in the attic above it. He came home weekly to check in on his father, playing the dutiful son. Not that his father noticed. As far as he was concerned, Hunter should be here full-time; anything less was reneging on his responsibilities. Soon, his father would have his wish. It was not a day Hunter looked forward to. He kept making up reasons to put it off but time was running out. He told himself he didn't owe his father anything—God only knew he'd never got anything from him—but duty and honor and some misplaced hope that he could still build a relationship with his father would not die. He longed to experience the type of closeness he'd witnessed between Meredith and Abbott. It was foolish, he knew. His father was nothing like Abbott Connolly, but he was the only blood Hunter had left.

When he had accepted the position of Sheriff of Salvation Falls, he thought it would help his father see him as a man in his own right. It hadn't. Vernon had taken it as a betrayal, a slap in the face to everything he'd built.

Hunter stepped farther into the house. A mixture of stale air and cooking spices greeted him. He turned down the hallway leading to his father's study, hoping he could make this visit a short one. He didn't relish sitting through another strained conversation filled with undertones of accusation and recrimination about what a disappointment he was as a son, turning away from the family heritage. But his encounter with Yucton, and the insinuation he'd left hanging in the air, had him agitated and out of sorts. He wanted to ask his father about it, clear up the matter and leave. Maybe he'd stop by The Seahorse and share a shot of whiskey with Kincaid, provided the man hadn't already drunk himself under one of the tables. He wanted to know what the bounty hunter was hiding. There was more to the story than what he was getting.

"Vernon?" He'd stopped calling him "Pa" a

long time ago when he realized his father's interest in fulfilling the role was minimal at best. Vernon hadn't wanted a son for any other reason than he required an heir. He couldn't stand the idea of the fortune he had built going outside of the family to a distant relative he didn't know.

"Over here." His father waved a hand from the tall wing back chair facing the fire. Low flames licked the hearth doing little to chase out the cold in the room. Hunter pulled off his hat and set it on the narrow table next to the door.

"How you been?" He took the chair opposite his father.

"Well enough." Vernon didn't bother looking up from the newspaper resting in his lap.

His father's health had been in decline since last year. He'd suffered a small stroke and though he had recovered mentally, a little weakness on one side of his body remained. It made him even more difficult to deal with, as Vernon Donovan was not a man given to showing weakness of any kind. As such, he rarely left the house now save for the occasional town council meeting. Hunter suspected his pride wouldn't let him. The town knew him as a robust and domineering man. To be felled by something he had no control over was a slight he had no desire to share with others. Best they remember him as he used to be, not as he was now.

Hunter looked for a way to open the conversation he dreaded having. Vernon didn't like being questioned and Hunter worried he may not like the answers. "Big trial starting in town soon."

Vernon made a grunting sound and pointed at the paper. Ollie Mathers had reported on little else ever since Bill Yucton had arrived back in town and the event was announced.

"Turns out someone hired some high-falutin' lawyer to defend Bill Yucton. Man by the name of Wallace Platt."

His father appeared nonplussed by the news. "Can't imagine it will do the man any good. Guilty is guilty."

Hunter's sense of fairness bucked at his father's words. "Pretty sure that's for the judge and jury to decide."

Vernon shrugged and fell silent, more interested in his newspaper than Hunter's opinions on justice. Nothing new there. His father never did have time for him unless it was to criticize or argue or try to run his life in the manner he saw fit. Was it any wonder he'd left?

Hunter leaned forward in his chair. The low heat from the fire warmed the side facing the flames. "Thing I can't figure is, who is bankroll-

ing Platt. He says he has an anonymous benefactor." There were few men in town who could
afford to bring in a fancy lawyer from away.
Fewer still who'd had a vested interest in the
original trial seven years ago. But why would
Yucton suggest it was his father? Vernon had
been the victim of the crime Yucton was being
tried for. It didn't make any sense. Yucton had to
be mistaken. "You know anything about that?"

"Can't imagine why I would."

Vernon continued to read his paper, but he was
still on the same page and appeared to be staring
at the same paragraph since Hunter sat down.

"So you have nothing to do with it?" he
pressed.

"You deaf, boy?" The sharpness of Vernon's
voice lashed out at Hunter. *Boy.* His father had
called him that for as long as he could remember.
Sometimes he wondered why Vernon had even
bothered giving him a name. He never used it.

His anger spiked and he pulled out the one
thing he knew would get a rise out of Vernon.
"Meredith Connolly is back in town."

Vernon's fingers crumpled the edge of the
paper where he held it, his pale eyes finding
Hunter's. A seething bitterness radiated outward
from his father and curled around them like an
acrid smoke from a long-smoldering fire.

"To what end?" Each word was bitten off at the end before being released into the tension-filled air.

Hunter shrugged, feigning a nonchalance he hadn't felt since the moment Meredith had arrived. When Abbott had died, he thought she might return to visit his grave and he'd tried steeling himself for the possibility, but the idea of her coming, and the actuality of her staying were worlds apart.

"She's moved back to settle." He debated telling him the rest of it, but he was bound to hear eventually. "And she's intent on clearing her father's name."

The newspaper was quickly forgotten. Vernon turned in his chair, giving Hunter his full attention for the first time since he'd arrived. He jabbed a finger in his direction, his cheeks florid with anger. "You make sure that doesn't happen. You get that girl on the next train back to Boston. You did it once, you do it again, boy. You hear me?"

Hunter heard him just fine. Each word Vernon spoke cut into his flesh like a jagged knife. He didn't need the reminder of what he'd done. He'd lived with the guilt every day. But why did his father care?

"She's not a girl any longer, Vernon. And she's

not without means. She won't be pushed around and she sure as hell won't be letting anyone send her anywhere she doesn't want to go."

"How do you know? You been sniffin' around her skirts again? You mind what little sense you got. I won't have you mooning over that bastard's daughter again and dragging the Donovan name through the dirt with her."

Hunter's muscles stiffened. He didn't cotton to being treated like an imbecile who couldn't make his own decisions. And he sure as hell wasn't taking relationship advice from a man who couldn't keep one wife and spent his life obsessing over someone else's.

"Think I can keep my own counsel in that regard."

His father's lip curled into a snarl. "Like you did before? Worked out fine for you then, didn't it? The girl isn't worth the dirt her house was built on, just like her father before her."

The pain of losing Meredith, always close to the surface no matter how hard he tried to bury it, raged forward. He had thought he'd done the right thing at the time, but time had a funny way of changing the colors of one's memory. Now he wasn't so sure and that uncertainty burrowed deep inside of him and refused to let go.

"Meredith is nothing like her father." It was

a lie, though. Even he could see she'd inherited her father's energy, his sense of faith that truth would prevail. His goodness. He'd spent a lot of time talking to Abbott as he sat in his jail cell during the trial. Never once had he wavered in his proclamation of innocence. But unlike his daughter, he seemed to know the way things would go, to understand the deck was stacked against him with a judge that cared little about fairness or the law.

"Blood is blood," Vernon said, spitting the words out like poison.

If that was true, Hunter wasn't sure what it said about him. Nothing good, for sure.

"Then she has as much of her mother in her as her father. And as I recall, you were always particularly fond of Vivienne."

He threw the accusation out, stones meant to hurt. They found their mark. His father fell silent and stared into the fire. Hunter didn't wonder if the anger in his gaze wasn't enough to fuel the flames all winter.

Perhaps he should feel guilty, but he didn't. He'd spoken the truth. Vivienne Connolly had been a beautiful woman with the same delicate bone structure inherited by her daughter. But where Vivienne was dark, Meredith favored the lighter coloring of her father with the same brilliant blue eyes that cut through all the barriers you put up and saw what lived at your core.

Hunter cleared his throat and tried to shake the vision. "Just tell me one thing. Did you hire Platt?"

"I got better things to spend my money on than some beaten-down outlaw sittin' in your jail waiting to hang."

"You kept Connolly from hanging. You hated every breath that man took, yet you stood up for him in court that day and made a case that kept Judge Laidlow from putting a noose around his neck. Why?"

His father glared at him, not an ounce of affection anywhere to be seen. "You know what your problem is, boy?"

"Do tell."

Vernon jabbed a finger in his direction again. "Your problem is you don't know when to leave well enough alone. As far as Yucton is concerned, your only job is to keep him locked up until the time comes for the judge and jury to make a decision on what happens to him. If you know what's good for you, you'll keep it that way. That Connolly chit wants to mess around in it, that's her business. My guess is she'll regret it. But you keep your nose out. This business isn't any of your affair. Keep it that way."

A chill washed over Hunter. He wasn't sure if his father was warning him, or threatening him. And why?

"What do you know about a group called the Syndicate?"

His father's expression darkened. Shadows from the flames flickered across his aged face and for the longest time he said nothing. "Are you stupid, boy? Did you not hear what I just said?"

Hunter's heart stilled. "What do you know about them? Who are they and what do they have to do with Yucton or Abbott Connolly?"

His father leaned back into his chair and picked up his newspaper, each movement slow and deliberate. "Never heard of them."

"You're lying." He'd bet his gun hand on it. But his father had fallen silent, the only sound in the room the logs crackling and crumbling within the fire. A sick feeling coiled in Hunter's gut.

"Think maybe it's time you left. You've outstayed your welcome."

Hunter stood and stared down at his father. This whole mess was becoming a jumble of puzzle pieces that didn't fit together. But one piece he was certain about. He needed to keep a close eye on Meredith Connolly. Vernon's veiled threat echoed inside of him. Seven years ago, he'd made a promise. He'd thought sending Meredith far away would mean the end of it. It didn't. It was becoming a bit clearer just how deep the threat went. Just not clear enough.

Yet.

Whoever the Syndicate was, wherever they fit in this puzzle, he needed to find out—and he needed to make sure Meredith didn't become tangled up in it.

Chapter Seven

The muscles in Meredith's arms pulled against the tension of the reins as the wagon jostled over the rutted road. She hadn't driven a wagon in a long while; there'd been no need in Boston with cabs at the ready to take you where you needed to go. It had made her soft, but that would change, she determined. Until it did, however, she was more than happy to see the small cabin on the horizon.

Pa hadn't owned a lot of land, but what he had owned was, in her estimation, the prettiest spot in all of Salvation Falls. Surrounded mostly by trees along one side and the back, the cabin was tucked into a little alcove that had protected it from the elements and left it shaded in the summer. The creek ran a short distance away along the other side and on still evenings she remembered lying in her bed with the window open listening to its babble as the water rushed past, gliding over the rocks as if it was in a hurry to get somewhere.

She pulled the wagon up to the cabin and sat for a moment staring at her old home. Bertram had done an excellent job seeing the place tended to. It looked exactly as she had left it for the most part. The trees were taller and the garden her mother kept had become overgrown. None of that mattered. In her mind's eye, she could see Mama standing in the doorway, one hand on her hip and a gentle smile spread across her face. The years and the hardship had done nothing to diminish her mother's beauty, and though she could have chosen an easier life by marrying Vernon Donovan, she'd told Meredith shortly before she passed on that she hadn't regretted her decision to follow her heart for one minute. Meredith wished she could say the same thing.

She blinked back the tears at the memory and took a deep breath. "Enough of that," she said, giving herself a shake.

She pulled the brake and climbed down from the wagon. She'd been careful to dress more appropriately today, wearing one of her less elaborate dresses. The cream-and-navy-striped cotton silk had a small bustle but no lengthy train. The ruffle along the hemline brushed her ankles and made it easier to maneuver the wagon and rougher terrain.

She made a mental note to ensure the next dress she designed had similar features. She wasn't in Boston any longer and she needed to adapt her designs to fit the lives of the women in Salvation Falls.

Despite her happy memories of her old home, it looked lonely and forlorn, left behind and forgotten. "I told you I'd come back," she whispered, as if the wooden logs piled atop one another to create its structure were living, breathing things. She touched them with affection as she stood in front of the door.

She closed her eyes and leaned her head against the rough wood. Oftentimes her mother would hang dried herbs and flowers on the front of it, but any hint of them was long gone. Meredith pushed down on the door latch and opened it, holding her breath.

The interior was smaller than in her memories. She marveled at how the three of them had lived comfortably within its confines without constantly bumping into each other. But then, when you filled a house with love, perhaps its dimensions expanded to accommodate you and you didn't notice the cramped quarters quite so much.

She stood in the doorway and let her gaze roam the main room. Some of the furniture was slightly out of place, or had she simply remembered wrong? The bed where she had slept was tucked into a corner against the wall opposite the large stone fireplace, though the mice had chewed at the mattress and straw now poked out haphazardly in several directions. The quilt her mama had sewn was gone from the bed, and the chest where she stored her belongings was now situated at the footboard instead of against the wall. Maybe Bertram had sent someone to clean the interior—it did look rather tidier than she recalled.

The small kitchen lined another wall, the table where they'd eaten doing double duty as counter space. Pa had always promised to build Mama a larger cabin with a kitchen fit for a queen once his fortunes turned, but he'd never been given that opportunity. Vernon Donovan had made certain of that, thwarting every effort her father made to find proper work to support his family. They'd talked about leaving from time to time, starting over somewhere else, but they had both loved the little town where they'd fallen in love and neither wanted to be chased out of it conceding defeat.

So they had stayed, and they had struggled.

And they had loved and laughed and dreamed of better days. Those days never came. Her mother fell ill and Pa was arrested for rustling cattle from the Diamond D Ranch. Despite needing money for her mother's medicine, Meredith never once believed her father had returned to a life of crime. He'd made a promise to his wife he would never walk that path again, and Abbott Connolly was a man who'd put a lot of stock in promises.

For all the good it did him. He'd lost everything in the end anyway. His wife, his freedom, his home, and eventually his life. Even through the worst of it though, their little family stayed strong. But then Mama died, Pa was taken away and the ties that bound them frayed and broke.

There was no going back. No chance to redo all that had been done.

Bitterness welled up in Meredith's chest with such force she thought it would burst. She crossed the room to the trunk at the end of her narrow bed and knelt next to it. The top creaked as she opened it, the hinges rusty from disuse. The chessboard her father had made rested on top of her mother's quilt. Someone had put it in the chest for safekeeping. She reached inside and pulled the chessboard out, along with the cloth bag that held the pieces.

Pa had crafted it himself out of a thick slab of oak. She remembered the hours he spent next to the fire, whittling away until the pieces took shape, then staining one half red with a paint Mama had made from berries and such. It was nothing fancy, but it meant the world to her. She'd forgotten it when she'd left, hustled out of her own home and shipped off to Boston, to a new life.

She turned the smooth oak box with its checkerboard top over in her hands. The painted squares had faded a bit with time until they appeared more brown than red. Pa had hollowed out the inside of the thick slab of oak with the intent of housing the pieces there, but the space had not been large enough. Mama sewed up a cloth bag instead while her father looked on, a sheepish grin on his face.

She stood and hugged the board to her chest to hold the memory close, Pa's voice drifting back to her with one of his riddles he loved so much.

Two kings and two queens standing still as stone, their subjects all like ice; one move and only one is needed to start the fight. Where is the battleground, Merry? Her father had smiled, his bright eyes twinkling in the firelight. He pointed a finger down at his newest creation. *On the chessboard. And chess, Merry, is all about strategy, one move at a time. But you need to think ahead, get inside the mind of your opponent. Figure out what they'll do before they actually do it.*

She'd been small at the time, but his words had stuck with her. As did his smile and the way his eyes danced with delight as he taught her the game. She missed him so much her heart broke anew with every sunrise. She would never see him again, never hear the laughter in his voice, or be subject to his riddles and rhymes. It was too much.

Memories pummeled her from every angle and robbed her strength. She sank back to her knees on the dusty floor. Once again, the tears she had tried so hard to hold off had their way and she let them come. She'd prided herself on being strong, on leaving the tears to others, but Heaven's bells, she'd cried more since arriving back in Salvation Falls than she had in the entire seven years she'd been gone. She couldn't seem to help herself.

Being back made all she'd lost feel like a fresh wound. In Boston, she could imagine things were fine. Pa was not in prison, Mama was still alive and they carried on with their lives. No one had died; no one had been torn away from her, leaving her all alone in the world. One day, she would go home and rejoin them. Boston was just temporary. It helped her make it through, helped stave off the loneliness. But it wasn't reality. This empty cabin was reality. The two grave markers resting beneath the shady branches of the old oak tree were reality.

Being left alone in the world was reality.

"Meredith?"

The sound of Hunter's voice slid into the room and past her memories. She turned. He stood in the doorway, and for a brief moment, it was like a memory come to life. It had been eight years ago, after the Autumn Festival where he'd asked her to dance several times, causing some tongues to wag. He came to their home the next day to ask her father's permission to court her proper. He had wanted Pa's blessing, given their families' history.

Her father had been impressed and agreed to allow it, making Hunter promise to treat her with dignity and respect. He'd humbly agreed, standing in the doorway with his hat in his hand, a solemn expression on his handsome face.

Much as he stood there now.

But when she blinked away her tears she saw it wasn't a memory. Sun from the open door turned his dark brown hair a warm mahogany. Its rays bathed one side of his face. Time had only made him more handsome, etching lines and refining edges. The deputy's badge he'd worn had been replaced with a sheriff's star. And the promise he'd made to her father lay broken and scattered in the space between them.

Meredith swiped at the tears on her face. "What are you doing here?"

"I, uh…" He searched for what to tell her, preferring to avoid the truth. To be honest, he wasn't even sure what the truth was. He saw the wagon outside her old home on his way back from Vernon's and knew it had to be her. He should have kept riding, but he didn't. He couldn't. She had a strange pull on him. She always had. And it had not lessened in the time she'd been gone. He'd tried to move on, but it was no use. He couldn't shake her memory and now with her here in the flesh, he kept coming up with reasons to be near her. It was more than the warning from Yucton to watch over her or the promise he'd made to her father to keep her safe. It was even more than the need to atone for the hurt he'd caused.

It was her. Pure and simple.

"You're staring."

"You're beautiful." The words escaped before he could hold them back. A crimson stain spread across her cheeks and she looked away. Her gaze skirted around the corners of the room.

The cabin had been ransacked shortly after she'd left town. At first, Hunter thought it was drifters looking for anything of value they could find, but anything the Connollys had of value wasn't measured in dollars and it didn't appear as if anything was missing. Now he wasn't so sure. Had it been drifters? Or had it been the Syndicate? And if so, what could Abbott possibly have had that they'd wanted? Either way, a second attempt had never been made. Hunter had set the room back to rights afterward and it had remained untouched since then.

He wondered if, after a while, Meredith would wire instructions to Bertram to sell the land and the cabin, but she never had. Instead, it became a shrine of sorts. He'd stop by after each visit with his father, step inside the cabin and sit in the straight-backed chair next to the door. There were happy memories here, ones that didn't torment him quite as deeply as the ones that held sway in his room above the jailhouse.

What would she think if she knew? There were some days he'd stop by for only a few minutes, breathe it in and leave. Other days, he would sit for an hour or more, absorbing as many of the memories as he could. Happy memories of sitting by the fire with Meredith while her ma and pa talked quietly to themselves at the kitchen table. Neither of her parents had ever judged him harshly or blamed him for the hardships brought on them by his father. He'd always respected them for that. He wasn't sure if he would have been as gracious had the circumstances been reversed. But their acceptance had given him something he'd never experienced before—a sense of home, of family and a place to belong. He'd longed to build the same with Meredith, dreamed of a different life than the one he'd grown up in.

He longed for it still.

Meredith patted the last of her tears away with the back of her sleeve. She was dressed more simply today, and yet she was still more beautiful than every other woman in town. Then again, the same had been true when she was dressed in hand-me-downs the church had doled out.

"Seems you're always coming upon me when I'm at my worst." Her words were quiet, devoid of recrimination, as if the tears had bled it dry.

He offered her a half smile and, after a brief hesitation, decided to join her on the floor. He sat next to her and rested an arm on one bent knee.

"I guess homecomings can be bittersweet even under the best of circumstances. You expect things to be just the way you left them. It must feel a little strange when they aren't."

She sniffed and gave a small nod. "It feels a little bit like a betrayal that time marched on without me. But then I came here, and time hasn't touched this place and I think that makes me even sadder. Like it got left behind and forgotten."

"No one's forgotten, Mere." The shortened form of her name slipped off his tongue like a gentle caress. How long had it been since he'd spoken it, whispered it in her ear. He wanted to do that now, to haul her over onto his lap and hold her close, rock the sadness out of her and make her whole again. Make them both whole again.

"Don't be nice to me," she whispered. "You'll make me start crying again if you do. And we both know you don't mean it."

Her simple statement took him aback. He'd meant every bit of it. She deserved nothing less from him, and God help him, he wanted to give her so much more. "Why wouldn't I mean it?"

She ran a hand over the red-checkered board resting in her lap. "It's just a game you play, I think. You're sweet to me, make me think you mean it, and then it changes like the wind. Isn't that what happened?"

Her question sliced into his heart driving deep and the guilt he lived with every day bled through him like a poison. How he wanted to tell her the truth. But what good would it do now? It wouldn't take away the hurt. Instead, it would tear open an old wound with no hope of healing it.

"I never meant to hurt you."

Her mouth twisted to one side. "Well, you did all the same." She took a deep breath and let it out in a huff. "Anyway, that's over and done with. And so is the crying. I've shed more than enough tears."

"Seems to me you haven't shed enough. The whole time your ma was sick, when your pa was on trial, even after he was sentenced, I kept waiting for you to break down but you never did."

"I couldn't." Her chin trembled but she quickly regained control. "I was afraid if I started I wouldn't be able to stop."

He knew the feeling.

He decided to change the topic. It did neither of them any good to sit here and bemoan all the things Fate and stupidity had cost them. "What was on the piece of paper you showed Yucton yesterday? You said it was a ledger?"

She looked at him, sizing him up. He could see it in the narrowing of her eyes, the set of her enticing mouth. "You know, it's very rude to eavesdrop on other people's conversations."

"They teach you that in Boston?"

She shot him a hard look. "There's nothing wrong with manners."

"There's nothing wrong with asking questions either. What was the ledger from?"

She shrugged. "It doesn't matter. Bill didn't recognize it, so it's a moot point."

Hunter had questioned enough people in his day to recognize when someone was skirting his question. He switched tactics.

"Just how is it that you plan on proving your father's innocence?"

She hung her head. "I'm not sure."

"No plan?"

She sighed. "I thought if I came home, it would come to me. I'd see something, or think of something I had missed. I had hoped time and distance would offer a better perspective, but…" She looked at him and desperation turned her eyes a darker blue, as if storm clouds had scuttled in and leeched their brightness. She shook her head and defeat slumped her shoulders. "I know he's innocent, I just don't know how to prove it."

Abbott's guilt or innocence had been something Hunter wrestled with since the accusation was first made. The man he knew would never have committed such a crime. But the woman Abbott loved was dying. She needed medicines he couldn't afford and more care than he could give her. Before Meredith, Hunter wouldn't have thought that reason enough to break the law. But afterward he understood just how far a man in love would go. If it meant saving the woman he loved, there wasn't anything he wouldn't do. No pain or consequence he wouldn't suffer. Had love driven Abbott to take part in the rustling?

If it had, Hunter couldn't blame him. In the end, hadn't he done the one thing he swore he would never do to save the woman he loved?

"Help me up," Meredith said, interrupting his thoughts. He pushed himself to his feet and took the chessboard from her before taking her proffered hand. It looked small clasped in his and once on her feet, he didn't immediately let go. They stood close, the musty air of the cabin surrounding them. He waited for her to pull away, surprised when she didn't. He could see the pain in her eyes, the loss. The need to comfort her proved too strong to resist. He stepped closer. His free arm slipped around her back and pulled her to him until she rested lightly against him.

Every nerve in his body read him the riot act, but he ignored each one. He ignored everything save for the warmth spreading through him.

Despite the layers of fancy fabric, he could feel the length of her pressing into him. She still clutched the cloth bag, her arms curled between their bodies. The wooden edges of the chess pieces dug into him, but he didn't care. Nothing had ever felt this right, this good. How had he ever let her go?

Abbott had been adamant he send her away, but what if there had been another way to keep her safe? How many nights since she'd left had he tormented himself with that question? Especially after what they had done. He'd never known being with a woman could be like that. It was as if someone had set off fireworks throughout his body, waking him up fully for the first time in his life. The memory of what they'd shared that one night above the jailhouse when they'd given in to their passion still had the power to rock him to his core. To give it up, to let it go... it had almost killed him.

"I'm sorry, Mere," he whispered, his lips brushing the hair at her temple. The words were woefully inadequate, falling short of ever making up for what she had suffered at the hands of others.

At his hands.

He breathed her in one last time and then released her. He'd given up his right to hold her when he'd broken her heart and destroyed any tender feelings that had grown between them.

"I'll take you back to town," he said.

She nodded and pulled away. Her absence left a gaping hole inside of him and the loneliness he'd nurtured since she'd left for Boston rushed back in to fill the space.

Chapter Eight

Meredith glanced over her shoulder to the back of the wagon where Hunter tied his horse's reins, his head bent to the task. The brim of his hat shielded his face as he looped the leather straps through a metal rung on the back of the wagon. She couldn't help but wonder what might have been had he truly loved her as she once thought. Would they be here now as husband and wife? Would children fill the empty house and laughter replace the quiet loneliness that had sunk into its walls?

Those were the thoughts that had sustained her through Pa's trial. In her darkest moments, she'd held her dreams of a future with Hunter tight and wrapped herself in them like a protective cloak. She had thought Hunter shared the same dreams. He'd seemed so earnest, been so loving. She'd had no inkling he'd only been toying with her affections to get what he wanted.

And yet…

And yet here he was now, being so kind again, acting the man she'd once believed him to be, and Heaven help her, she was glad he'd happened upon her today. She knew she shouldn't rely on him in such a way. She'd done that once and it was a road littered with regret. He'd made it clear to her then, he didn't want a life with her. What he'd wanted, he'd already taken.

No. That wasn't entirely true. If she was being honest, anything he'd taken she had freely given. One thing Pa had always taught her was to take responsibility for her own actions.

Your actions belong to you. You need to own up to them. Good or bad, right or wrong. It's just the right thing to do.

Her father had never balked or glossed over the things he'd done in his past. But he'd turned his life around when he met Mama. He'd admitted to her once that when you found that kind of love, you did whatever you had to in order to hang on to it and never let it go.

Meredith had found that kind of love once, and she'd taken Pa's advice, but it turned out Hunter didn't share her feelings. She'd discovered the hard way you couldn't always hold on

to something if it didn't want to hold you back—
a lesson easily forgotten when Hunter had taken
her in his arms.

It hadn't always been that way. During the
worst of it, when her father's sentence was passed
and there was no recourse left, being held in
Hunter's arms had made it a little less overwhelming. A little less scary. It had felt the most
natural thing in the world to seek comfort in
the most basic of ways. He was her forever. The
marriage vows had already been spoken by their
hearts, the actual ceremony a formality. She had
truly believed that. She could lean on him and
know he would always be there for her.

Until the day when he wasn't. Until the day
when she woke from one nightmare only to realize another had begun.

Even so, she hadn't regretted what they had
shared. She had gone into it with her heart wide-
open. She only wished her eyes had been open,
as well. Maybe then she would have seen a hint
of what was to come. She'd been quick to believe
he loved her, never once doubting the strength
of his feelings. She had never considered their
different circumstances, never thought he would
place his family name and his father's expecta-
tions over what they had shared. She thought she
knew him better than that, but she hadn't.

He'd turned cold and harsh, uncaring. He'd made it clear a Donovan could never marry a Connolly. He needed to choose a woman of a certain caliber, and she simply didn't measure up.

The hurtful letdown had lacerated her heart, buried itself in her soul. Where was that man now?

This man—kind, warm, supportive—this was the man she had fallen in love with. Seeing him resurrected made resisting him that much harder.

Hunter finished tying the reins and glanced up. She didn't bother to look away.

He leaned against the side of the wagon and tilted his head to one side. "You're staring," he said, repeating her words of earlier.

"I'm trying to figure out who you really are."

He hesitated. "I'm the same man I've always been."

But who was that? The man who placed flowers on her mother's grave, visited her father in prison and ensured he had a proper burial next to his wife—*that* was the Hunter she had known, the man she'd fallen in love with. Or the man who had broken her heart, who had been a stranger to her? That man had yet to resurface since her return, but she waited and looked for signs, afraid to let her guard down.

"Maybe I just don't know who that is."

He bowed his head and pulled on his gloves, avoiding her gaze. "I guess that's fair." It was the only answer he gave her and it left her unsatisfied.

"Why don't you tell me then?"

He walked up the length of the wagon and climbed into the seat next to her, taking the reins. He leaned forward and rested his forearms on his thighs. His gaze remained fixed on the horizon. "If I told you I regretted like hell the hurt I've caused you, would you believe me?"

She paused, giving it some thought. Her heart wanted to open up, but the bad memories barred the doors that kept it locked up safe. "I want to, but—"

"But any trust you had in me is gone." He looked at her then, his mouth tight. Pain kindled in his eyes. Her heart lurched and she had to bite the inside of her cheek to keep from blurting out something stupid like she forgave him, or what he had done was water under the bridge. It would be a lie, and they both knew it. He nodded, as if reading her thoughts. "Maybe, in time, I can change that. You think that's possible?"

She longed to trust him now, while hating herself for the weakness. "I don't know."

He nodded. "All right then." He let the reins fall on the back of the horse. "Git up!"

The wagon jerked as it pulled away, leaving the tender moment they'd shared in her home behind with all the other memories. That part of her life was over.

There was no going back. Was there?

Meredith regretted accepting an invitation to join the Bancrofts for lunch. The family dynamic was a mishmash of awkwardness that left the food unsettled in her belly. Mr. Bancroft's large presence overpowered the others, though he said little. Mrs. Bancroft, in stark contrast, was filled with nervous energy, her insistent chatter running in all directions. Charlotte took after her father, it seemed, and had barely said a word or looked in Meredith's direction since she'd sat down.

"How long do you intend to stay in Salvation Falls?" Meredith asked, slipping a few words in while Mrs. Bancroft stopped briefly to take a bite of the apple pie she'd ordered for dessert. She had ordered one for Charlotte as well, though her daughter had only picked at the crust, leaving it crumbled on her plate.

"Oh, well, you never know. Mr. Bancroft has his sights set on a piece of property, but there's just no telling. I don't try to understand the business of men, oh no, dear me. Too taxing on my poor mind."

Meredith turned her attention to Mr. Bancroft, hoping to steer the conversation away from the silly topics his wife continued to fill the air with. Did anyone really care about the array of spices carried in the mercantile? If they were planning on living in Salvation Falls, perhaps she could gain the Bancrofts' friendship, their allegiance aiding her in her efforts to start over. "What is your business in, Mr. Bancroft? Where is it you traveled from to come here?" They had been less than forthcoming about themselves, preferring to ask her about herself.

"San Francisco," Charlotte answered, at the same time her mother blurted out, "Colorado."

"Oh…" Meredith glanced from one to the other but Mrs. Bancroft was busy burrowing into her pie, and Charlotte was busy glaring at her mother. After a moment of silence, Mrs. Bancroft's chatter began again, though it sounded more nervous than ever, the words coming in rapid fire.

"And what of you, dearie, are you settling here for good or just passing through? Such a pretty little town, but I'm so used to a bit more of a metropolitan area. Was it Boston you came from? I've never been that far east. Is it nice?"

Meredith wondered if Mrs. Bancroft bothered listening to anything she said. She had asked her the same question twice now, and both times Meredith had given her the same answer.

"Mother, Miss Connolly has answered that question already." There was a sharpness to Charlotte's voice. "She grew up here and has returned. She plans to open a dress shop."

"Oh, dear, yes you did. Yes, you did." Her tittering laugh nipped at Meredith's nerves. "How silly of me. So forgetful at times, aren't I. Just like not knowing where we came from." She giggled and shook her head. "Silly, silly, silly."

"You mentioned you had grown up here," Mr. Bancroft said, his deep baritone smothering his wife's words.

"Yes. I left seven years ago."

"And why was that?" Mr. Bancroft set her on edge, his cold eyes and brusque manner difficult to warm up to.

She chose her words carefully, finding the question intrusive and not something she cared to discuss with strangers. People had a habit of hearing the story's end and making their own judgments based on that alone. "My circumstances changed."

Mr. Bancroft took a sip of his coffee, staring at her from over the rim of his cup with a flinty gaze. He set the cup back in the saucer, his attention unwavering. The scrutiny made her uncomfortable. *He* made her uncomfortable.

"I heard your father was tried and found guilty of cattle rustling. Would those be the circumstances you refer to?"

Heat climbed up Meredith's neck. She found his question rude and his tone mocking, but she refused to be cowed by it. Her father had been innocent. She would not feel shame over what he had gone through.

"My father was indeed sent to prison, Mr. Bancroft, but he went an innocent man."

"Innocent men don't usually find themselves tried and convicted."

Mrs. Bancroft made a noise as if the tension that settled around their small group strangled her. Meredith set her fork down, afraid if she took a bite of her own dessert, she would choke on it.

"They do if the judge presiding over the case refuses to allow all the evidence to be heard."

Mr. Bancroft took another sip of his coffee, again studying her with his unrelenting gaze. A chill tripped down her spine and the urge to run made her legs fidgety. She quickly changed her mind about counting him as an ally. He was a most unpleasant man. Wherever he was from, be it San Francisco or Colorado, apparently manners were not held in high regard there. He grunted at her, a dismissal of the conversation he had begun.

Meredith pushed her chair out and set the checkered serviette over her half-eaten dessert. "If you will excuse me," she said, standing. Mr. Bancroft found enough of his manners to join her. "I have a meeting with Mr. Trent I do not wish to be late for. Thank you for the invitation to join you for lunch. It was very thoughtful of you to include me." She stopped short of claiming to have enjoyed the experience. She wondered now if the intent had been as friendly as she originally believed. Mr. Bancroft seemed on a fishing expedition, though whether he'd caught what he wished for, she had no idea. Her father's arrest and subsequent trial were common knowledge in town. He certainly hadn't needed to invite her to lunch to determine the details. And why should he even care, stranger to the town as he was?

"Oh, my dear. Yes, of course. You're quite welcome. We must do it again soon, of course, of course," Mrs. Bancroft twittered.

Meredith didn't answer. She had no desire to repeat today's experience. Instead, she offered Mrs. Bancroft a tight smile and Charlotte a brief nod. Mr. Bancroft she gave her shoulder and felt his gaze boring into her spine as she left the restaurant.

She gulped in the cool afternoon air, thankful to be away from the company of the Bancrofts. She turned in the direction of Bertram's office, her head high and her shoulders back. She would not allow Mr. Bancroft to think he had rattled her, though in truth, he had, and she hated that she'd allowed him that much power over her.

Hunter wished he could force himself to stop constantly glancing out the window of his office, watching for the telltale blond hair and whatever fancy outfit Meredith had decided to dress herself in that day to visit Yucton. He hadn't paid much attention to ladies' fashion in the past and figured he'd lost part of his mind if he was doing it now. Maybe that loss would explain why he was entertaining the idea of somehow working his way back into Meredith's good graces.

For a moment yesterday, being back inside her childhood home where so many good memories were stored, the possibility surfaced with a vengeance. She hadn't resisted when he'd pulled her into his arms. Her body had moved against his as if it belonged there and in that instant, he had believed in miracles. Reality had quickly reinserted itself, however, when she admitted she still didn't trust him. He couldn't blame her. From her perspective, his treatment of her had been despicable. Unforgiveable. She didn't know he'd had no other choice. What he'd done, he'd done with the best of intentions, though in hindsight his execution had been flawed. But how did he tell her that, and would it make a difference now?

"You waitin' on someone?"

"Huh?" Hunter turned from the window and folded his arms across his chest, embarrassed at being caught. "No, why?"

Yucton shrugged. "Jus' seem pretty interested in staring out into the street every few minutes. Figured you might be waitin' on someone to arrive."

"Well, I'm not," he growled and purposely walked away from the window to the coffeepot sitting on the woodstove. The strong stench of burned coffee did nothing to improve his mood.

Yucton chuckled, the sound enough to send Hunter reaching for his hat. "Jenkins!" His deputy came running from the storeroom down the hall where he collected blankets for the cooler nights. "Watch the prisoner. I'm heading out to find Kincaid." It was time he tracked down the wayward bounty hunter and questioned him about whoever paid the private bounty for Bill Yucton's arrest and return to Salvation Falls.

Hunter made his way down to The Seahorse Saloon and found Kincaid sitting at a table by himself. He motioned to Franklyn behind the bar. "Coffee. And bring me some of Del's baked beans."

Kincaid glanced up briefly then returned his attention to the shot of whiskey in front of him. Given the bottle at his side was still mostly full, Hunter judged Kincaid as passably sober.

"Kincaid," Hunter said, pulling out a chair. He didn't wait for an invitation. The bounty hunter didn't seem the type to seek out company.

"What do you want?" Sober, but not friendly.

Del appeared to his left and set the coffee and beans in front of him. "Thought I'd join you for lunch."

"Don't recall issuing an invite and don't much care to share a meal with you."

Hunter put a hand over his heart. "I'm wounded by your rejection."

"Guess that explains the sour look on your face."

"Maybe my mood would improve if you'd tell me what you know about who paid the bounty on Yucton."

"Nothing to tell. The poster said to bring him

to Salvation Falls—dead or alive. That's what I did."

"Given Yucton's penchant for escape, why did you choose alive?"

Kincaid shot him a hard look. "I'm no hired killer if that's what you're askin'. If I've got to kill someone because it comes down to me or him, then so be it, but I ain't doin' it just because someone offers to up the ante. I've got some humanity left."

The last bit was grumbled under his breath and Hunter wasn't sure if it was meant for his benefit or Kincaid's. He didn't ask. That Kincaid wrestled with his own personal demons was obvious, but it was none of Hunter's affair. He had enough to deal with. And near as he could tell, whatever humanity Kincaid might possess, he was doing his best to drown it in a bottle of cheap whiskey.

"You never wondered who it was offering the bounty?"

Kincaid downed his shot then poured another one. "None of my business. They don't want to be known—fine by me. I got my money like I wanted and Yucton got brought in alive, just like he wanted."

Hunter's fork stopped partway to his mouth.

He slowly lowered it back down to the bowl. "Yucton wanted to come in?"

Kincaid shrugged. "Didn't put up a fight over it."

"And you didn't find that odd?"

"Didn't much care. Said he was on his way back here anyway. Figured if I wanted to collect a bounty by assisting him in that regard, no harm done." Except harm was done. Yucton was sitting in a jail cell and would likely hang.

"Did he say why he was heading this way?"

Kincaid pursed his lips and slid a glance in Hunter's direction. He hesitated a moment and a strange tension slithered in the air between them. But before Hunter could ascertain its origin, the tension shifted and disappeared. "Said a friend had passed and he meant to pay his respects and take care of some business."

One of the girls from the saloon plunked down in front of the piano and banged out a lively tune. Or it would have been lively if the damned instrument had been in tune. The sound grated on Hunter's nerves. He needed to make a case to the town council to implement a law that outlawed such things.

"And he didn't seem put out your taking him in meant he'd have to answer to charges of cattle rustling?"

Kincaid rolled the empty shot glass between his finger and thumb. "I didn't ask."

Hunter sighed and rubbed a hand over his face. He was running in circles and getting nowhere fast. "Why do I get the feeling there's more to this than meets the eye?"

Kincaid turned the shot glass over and pushed it away. "Maybe if you can't see something it's because you're not looking hard enough."

"What's that mean? What more do you know?" He was getting damned sick of riddles and innuendos.

Kincaid stood up and threw a few bills on the table. "I'm not leavin' town because Yucton asked me not to. Said he'd make it worth my while. That's all I got to say on the matter. Now you think you can stop doggin' my every step and leave me in peace?"

Hunter didn't answer and Kincaid didn't wait around. He stared at the back of the bounty hunter as he walked from the saloon, far steadier than a man who'd downed a quarter of a bottle of whiskey in a short period of time ought to be. But it wasn't his steadiness that held Hunter's attention, it was his words.

Why would Yucton pay Kincaid to stay in town? What was the outlaw up to?

Chapter Nine

"I want to purchase the shop that used to belong to Hattie's Hats," Meredith said, sitting across the large oak desk from Bertram. Papers were scattered over its surface in disarray and piled a foot high in other areas. How the man ever found anything was beyond her. "It's the perfect spot from what I can see peeking through the window. With a little work to the interior to spiff it up, it will suit a dress shop perfectly."

"Hmm." Bertram leaned back in his padded chair, the leather creaking beneath his ample weight. One hand lifted to stroke his snow-white beard. He was a bear of a man, more wide than tall, yet he gave off an air of joviality that endeared him to others. Until he stepped into the courtroom that was. Sharp and witty, with more knowledge of the law than anyone she had ever met, he became a force to be reckoned with. Yet

it still had not been enough to save her father. She
didn't hold Bertram responsible, though. He had
done all he could, but every attempt he'd made
had been shut down by Judge Laidlow. The lop-
sided trial and the judge's rulings had infuriated
both Meredith and Bertram, but there had been
no getting around them.

"If it's a matter of money, I can afford it. I
have a small nest egg." One that grew smaller by
the day the longer she stayed at The Klein. She
should move out to the homestead but she wasn't
ready yet. Especially after yesterday.

She blamed her memories and sense of loss
for softening toward Hunter and allowing him
to console her. Being back there in her old home
and him behaving so much like the man she had
fallen in love with made it hard to remember the
man who had tossed her aside because she wasn't
good enough to bear his family name. That man
had been nowhere in evidence. In fact, she hadn't
seen hide or hair of that man since she'd arrived
back in Salvation Falls. If the memory of that
fateful day weren't so god-awfully vivid in her
mind, she'd wonder if she hadn't dreamed up the
entire incident. But a dream hadn't exiled her to
Boston for seven years. And no nightmare, no
matter how awful, could place such scars upon
her heart.

Bertram waved a hand at her mention of money. "It isn't a matter of finances, my dear."

"Then, what?"

Bertram leaned forward in his chair and rested his forearms on his desk. Pensiveness dulled the sparkle in his eyes but not the warmth and affection radiating from him. "As you may recall, the town council must approve all businesses first."

Meredith sat up straight. "I remember."

"Vernon Donovan is still a prominent member of the town council."

Her heart sank. "Still?"

Bertram nodded. "And most of the members are reluctant to vote against him."

The breath went out of her, and along with it her hopes of building a new future. "He will never allow my proposal to pass, will he?"

Bertram pointed a finger at her. "Now, don't you go getting yourself defeated before we even start the fight. I said he holds sway, and it will be an uphill battle, but there are a few of us on the council who can argue in your favor."

"Like who?"

"I will," Bertram told her. "And Caleb Beckett, Rachel's new husband, has a good head on his shoulders and doesn't cotton to bullies."

Two. Two men out of seven. The odds were not in her favor, no matter how much respect

Caleb Beckett commanded or how convincing Bertram was. If going against Vernon would have a detrimental effect on the other members who had businesses of their own in town, no amount of convincing testimony in the world would bring them around.

Vernon Donovan was more than a bully. Bullies were full of hot air. They blustered and bluffed but in the end they were cowards who backed down if confronted. Not Vernon. He'd meet you blow for blow and not feel a bit sorry if he left you in a bloodied heap. And she should know. She'd spent her whole life witnessing his vindictive nature as he tried to ruin her father.

She'd always found it suspect Vernon had argued with the judge against passing a sentence of hanging and instead fought for prison time for her father. She had no idea why. Perhaps her mother's death had caused him to have a change of heart, to realize the vendetta he carried on against Pa no longer mattered.

Maybe if she appealed to him, she could convince him to let bygones be bygones. She needed this. She would never have a husband or children. She'd forfeited her rights to that when she gave herself to Hunter. Besides, idleness did not suit her. It gave her too much time to think of all the things she wanted but would never have.

She mustered up her determination. Her father hadn't raised a quitter. He'd raised a fighter. If he hadn't been afraid of Vernon Donovan, she wouldn't be either. "What do I have to do to convince the town council to let me buy this building and open my business?"

"Rachel tells me we're expecting a guest after church on Sunday."

Hunter arched an eyebrow but said nothing. He'd come to know Caleb Beckett as a man of few words, and when he had something to say, he said it in his own time without need of prompting.

They sat in silent camaraderie, legs outstretched and chairs tipped back against the exterior wall of his office enjoying the fresh air and hot coffee. He shrugged farther down into the collar of his sheepskin coat to keep the cold from biting at his skin. It was a quiet time of the day and Hunter was pleased to share the company of a man who didn't try to change that. It allowed him time to drink his coffee and enjoy the view as the morning sun burned the horizon orange and painted the mountain peaks in broad strokes where they thrust their jagged edges into the sky. God help him, he loved this place. How could he blame Meredith for longing to come back when he was determined to never leave?

And how did he go more than five minutes without her entering into every thought he had?

Caleb continued after a time. "Seems my wife has decided to renew an old acquaintance."

"You don't say?"

"Likely you know her." Caleb took a swig of the steaming liquid then peered down into the mug's contents. "Good coffee."

Hunter shook his head. No one had ever described his coffee as anything close to good. "You've been eating too much of your wife's cooking if you think this constitutes *good*. And I assume you're referring to Meredith Connolly."

Caleb gave a quiet chuckle. "We try to avoid Rachel's cooking as much as possible. And yes, I do mean Miss Connolly."

"Guess it's good she's renewing old friendships."

"Has she renewed yours?"

Hunter glanced at Caleb and wondered how much of the story Rachel had imparted to him. He and Rachel went way back, growing up together as children. She knew his relationship with Meredith had ended badly but he'd kept the particulars to himself.

"We didn't exactly part on the best of terms."

"Mmm." Caleb took another sip of coffee. "Well, I'm supposed to invite you to supper just the same."

"Rachel trying to play matchmaker?" If she was, he should probably tell her she had a better chance of scaling the mountains in the middle of a snowstorm and reaching the highest peak.

"Maybe. Either way, you're supposed to say yes, then I'm supposed to tell you I can't make it into town to pick her up, and so you're to do the gentlemanly thing and bring her out to the ranch yourself." Caleb glanced over and grinned. A rare event. "You can arrive by noon."

"And if I say no?"

"Don't believe Rachel stipulated that as an option."

Hunter rubbed his forehead, dislodging his hat a bit. "Fine. We'll be there. Guess I've got to keep an eye on her anyway."

"That a fact? She prone to accidents or something?" his friend asked.

"Not so near as I can tell."

"Guess there's more to that story than you're telling."

Hunter rested his coffee mug on his thigh and let the warmth seep through his denims to help ward off the morning chill. He debated telling Caleb, but he sure could use another perspective.

"Things just aren't adding up," he admitted with a weary sigh. He leaned forward and let the legs of his chair touch down on the raised porch. "Before Abbott Connolly was sent to the prison in Laramie, he made me promise to do whatever I had to in order to get Meredith out of town. He had an older sister in Boston willing to take her in. Claimed it was for her own safety, but I couldn't get him to budge when it came to telling me why. Either way, I kept up my end of the bargain."

"Take it that's why things ended badly?"

Hunter stared across the street at The Klein Hotel. "I did what I had to. It wasn't pretty, but it got the job done."

"You think she's in danger now that she's back?"

"I don't know. Yucton seems to think so. He won't say as much, but I think that's why he came back. He mentioned something called the Syndicate."

"That mean anything to you?"

"Sort of. It was one of the last things Sheriff McLaren said to me when he lay dying. I've tried every which way to Sunday to find information on them, but I keep hitting a brick wall. I'm sure it's somehow tied to the private bounty Kincaid collected on when he brought Yucton in.

Now he tells me Yucton is paying him to stay in Salvation Falls."

"Why?"

Hunter's frustration mounted and he tossed what was left in his coffee cup over the porch rail. Caleb's horse snorted at him, though the contents had fallen several feet short of where the horse stood hitched to the pole. "Your guess is as good as mine."

Caleb shook his head and let his gaze wander toward the mountains. "Any way to figure out who this Syndicate is?"

Hunter shrugged. "Nearly everyone who was involved in the rustling is dead, save for Yucton and Vernon. Depending on how Yucton's trial goes when the judge finally gets off his backside and shows up, he could be the next to go." Leaving only Vernon. His stomach recoiled at the thought of his father being involved in any of this. He was supposed to have been the victim of the crime. Was it possible Kincaid was right, and he wasn't looking hard enough? Hunter shied away from that line of thinking, at least until he had more information.

Caleb stood and handed Hunter his empty mug before stretching his arms out and taking in a deep breath of mountain air. "Rachel mentioned Yucton spent some time working the ranch back in her pa's day."

Hunter nodded. "McLaren said he had questioned Foster and a few of the other men but came up empty. I'd like to take another crack at it." Foster had been a fixture on the Circle S Ranch for as long as anyone could remember. He had started as a ranch hand before Hunter was born and when he became too old for the rigors of the position, he'd taken up manning the chuck wagon. Hunter hoped the old man's memory hadn't faded with time and age. If he'd worked with Yucton, maybe he'd recollect something he hadn't thought to mention to McLaren all those years ago. It was worth a shot.

Caleb readjusted his hat, the merest hint of a smirk pulling at the corner of his mouth. "Then I guess we'll be seeing you after church on Sunday."

"I'll be there," Hunter said. He had no choice but to escort Meredith out to the Circle S. He couldn't let her ride out without his protection and he needed to speak with Foster. Likely the old coot had nothing of value to help him, but he was willing to grab whatever thin thread he could find.

"Good." Caleb stepped down off the porch and undid Jasper's reins from the hitching post.

"Maybe you can spend the ride out filling Miss Connolly in on what's going on. Trust me when I tell you, women don't like being kept in the dark. There'll be hell to pay if you try."

The idea curdled in his gut. He preferred to keep Meredith out of it, but if she started digging into things to clear her father's name she could find herself up to her elbows in it. He needed to convince her to let him take the lead on this and keep her own nose clear.

She wouldn't like it, of course, but there was no other option. He'd promised her father he would keep her safe, and he meant to honor that promise whether she liked it or not.

Meredith fidgeted with the tiny buttons lining the front of her cream-colored cape and hesitated on the church steps. She scanned the crowd of people that had filtered out at the end of the service and now mingled in front of the church in small clusters. She had been nervous about coming, but did so anyway. She needed to integrate herself back into the town and show the women of Salvation Falls her talents. Maybe they could then convince their husbands to sway the vote in her favor. It was a long shot, but she had to take it.

She'd worn one of her favorite outfits to the

service, one she'd designed herself. The upper portion was a rich navy-and-gold pattern, the skirt a soft sage green with a fringed trim midway that swept across her thighs where the material hugged against her. From behind, the navy and gold flowed down from the bustle. The color flattered her ivory complexion and set off the blue in her eyes. She had received numerous compliments on it and made certain to let them know she hoped to soon open her own business.

The hum of conversation and occasional laughter drifted around her. Mr. Beckett should be here by now. Meredith had yet to meet the man, but Rachel had given her a lengthy description of her new husband in the note she'd sent to make arrangements. Given Rachel's praise, Meredith was certain she should expect the most handsome man in four counties. As it was, that is exactly who arrived. Unfortunately, the most handsome man in four counties was Hunter Donovan, and not Mr. Beckett.

Her heart leaped inside her chest. She scolded it mercilessly to no avail. There had to be some mistake. He had to be here for some other reason.

The wagon he drove stopped in front of the church. He pulled the brake and jumped down. Her heart pounded harder with each step he took in her direction until she feared it would shake the ground beneath her.

She had hoped to avoid him, at least as much as possible. The more time she spent near him, the more his warmth and kindness charmed her all over again. It was foolish on her part to allow such things. She didn't want to fall for him. Yet, with each moment she spent in his company, he became harder to resist and the only weapon she had to use against it was to conjure up the pain of his rejection. Not something she cared to relive, but the only defense she had.

"Mornin'." He leaned against the balustrade at the bottom of the steps and took off his hat. The cold November sunlight silhouetted his lean frame and highlighted shades of chocolate and mahogany in his dark hair.

"Good morning." Her fingers gripped around the prayer book she'd brought with her. It had been her mother's. "I didn't see you in church."

"Nope. Had the morning watch." He'd told her the other day the jailhouse was being manned around the clock to prevent Bill from escaping as he had seven years ago.

"I see." An awkward silence dipped between them.

Her gaze drifted back to the wagon. Not his usual mode of transportation. She scanned the crowd once again, looking for a man who fit Caleb's description. She came up empty. "You're not—?"

"I have some business at the Circle S," he said. "I told Caleb I'd give you a ride out. Save him the trouble. Hope that's okay."

Her nerves tightened. It was a two-hour ride to the Circle S Ranch, but what choice did she have? It would be impolite to Rachel, who expected her, and she had looked forward to catching up with her old friend all week.

"I suppose so." She drew the words out, doubt dancing around them.

"Try not to sound too excited. I might start thinking you like me if you keep that up." His wry tone was offset by the hint of a smile. A smile that let loose a barrage of fluttering in her stomach as if she'd eaten an entire nest of butterflies for breakfast.

He walked up the few steps and offered her his hand to assist her down.

She hesitated before taking it. Even the smallest contact with him had the ability to set her insides ablaze. The kid leather gloves she wore provided little protection against the strength in his hand as his fingers curled around hers.

It was going to be a long two hours.

Chapter Ten

If he hadn't needed to speak with Foster, Hunter would seriously question his motives in agreeing to this charade. All morning he'd kept eyeing the pocket watch he kept in the top drawer of his desk, counting the minutes until he had to fetch Meredith from church.

It was flat-out ridiculous how much he had missed her yesterday. What was even more ridiculous was the unmitigated thrill that had rushed through him as he'd pulled up in front of the church and seen her standing on the steps in all her Sunday finery. She was a beautiful woman, always had been, though her edges had been refined in Boston, smoothed down and tucked into the seams of her fancy dress. But as the days passed, he realized the sparkling, youthful woman wasn't gone. Now and again, he caught a glimpse of her in the flash of her blue eyes, the determined set of her mouth. She had simply matured, going from the brash, spirited young woman who had once run unbidden into his arms, into the strong, confident woman he saw now.

Meredith arched one eyebrow skyward, her tone dry. "Can I assume Rachel had a hand in this?"

"In part." He offered his hand and assisted her down the steps, slipping it through his arm when she reached the ground. To his surprise, she didn't pull away. Her closeness sent a riot of pleasure through him and he slowed his pace as they walked to the wagon.

"People are staring," she whispered and when he glanced down he could see a soft blush that had nothing to do with the cool air, coloring her cheeks.

"Let them. It'll give them something to talk about other than the trial for a change." Part of him wondered what would happen if the folks in this town rallied behind the idea of the two of them renewing their courtship. Would she consider it, as well? It was crazy, and a long shot, but as each day wore on the idea of living without her became harder and harder to reconcile. The idea of her being with anyone else utterly impossible.

"Have you heard anything on when the judge is set to arrive?"

Tension pulled the fair skin over her cheekbones taut. He knew she worried over Yucton and it bothered him no end to see her getting wrapped up in this all over again. Yucton was doing nothing to help his cause, still refusing Platt's daily requests to defend him. Hunter couldn't figure out what Yucton's intent was, but if he didn't do something to save himself soon, the trial would be under way and he would find himself swinging from the end of a rope or becoming a permanent resident of the nearest prison.

He hadn't wanted to talk about the trial today and ruin her chance at having an afternoon away from it all, but he didn't want to lie to her. Not if he could avoid it.

"I received a wire last night. The new judge is set to arrive within a week."

"Then the trial will start soon."

It was more of a statement than a question, but he nodded anyway. They reached the wagon and he moved to help her up into the seat. It staggered him how featherlight she was in his hands, despite the fancy layers of silks and satins or whatever it was that made up the construction of the dress she had on. It reminded him that while she may possess the internal fortitude of a hundred men, she was still vulnerable and in need of his protection.

It scared him a little, the responsibility. Perhaps it would be different if he had a better handle on just what he was up against. As it was, he was still shooting in the dark, and the only way he could think to keep her safe was to glue himself to her side. A prospect filled with a host of dangers of a different sort.

They rode in silence for a bit, until the town fell away and the trees that filled the space between Salvation Falls and the Circle S Ranch swallowed them up. The sun fought its way through the thick forest, tossing rays of light onto the path and into pools along the way, illuminating the dew where it had collected on the leaves and moss.

Hunter had forgotten how comfortable silence was with her. He never felt as if he had to fill the space with mindless chatter or struggle for words to gloss over a quiet awkwardness. He toyed with the idea of telling her his plans to speak with Foster, but decided against it for now. McLaren had declared it a dead end and he didn't want to raise her hopes when he didn't hold out much of his own.

They were well along the path before anything was said. "I had lunch with the Bancrofts the other day."

He glanced over at Meredith. Despite the jostling the wagon took over the rutted path, she managed to keep her back straight and her hands folded on her lap. Though when his gaze traveled the length of her legs, he saw her feet braced against the front of the wagon boards.

"Did you?"

She nodded. "It was rather unpleasant. And odd."

He didn't care for Anson Bancroft. He found him to be a bit of a cold individual not given to friendly overtures. He couldn't imagine sitting through an entire meal with him trying to make conversation.

"Odd how?"

"When I asked where they had traveled from, I received two different answers. Mrs. Bancroft said Colorado, but Charlotte said San Francisco."

Hunter sat up straight and pulled on the reins, slowing the wagon to allow a lazy porcupine to amble across the path a little ways in front of them. "Did they give any reason for it?"

"No." Meredith shook her head and confusion marred her delicate features. He loved the way her nose crinkled when she was deep in thought. Made him want to lean over and kiss the tip of

it. He checked himself. He needed to stop that.
"That was the odd part. Mrs. Bancroft corrected
herself in her usual dithering manner and then
Mr. Bancroft interrupted her and turned the conversation to questions about Pa. I couldn't help
but feel…"

Her words drifted off.

"Feel what?" The hackles on the back of his
neck tickled against the collar of his jacket.

Meredith let out a short breath. "That he was
doing it as a warning of sorts."

Hunter stiffened, his hands inadvertently
pulling the reins taut until his horse shimmied
against them, forcing him to release his hold.

"What did he say?" If the man dared to
threaten her, the law be damned. He'd run the
bastard so far out of town he'd never find his
way back.

"Oh, nothing specific, really." She waved her
hand in the air. "Just his opinion on Pa's guilt or
innocence."

"How would he know about your pa?"

She slid him a look. "Hunter, anyone who
spends more than one day in this town eventually gets around to hearing about the trial.
The fact that I'm back in town and Bill is about
to be tried probably has tongues wagging all
the more."

As much as he hated it, she spoke the truth. "I'm sorry you have to go through that all over again. It was hard enough the first time."

He'd lost count of how many times he'd held her in his arms trying to comfort her and tell her everything would be all right. What a hypocrite he must have seemed when her father was sentenced and he rejected her. How he wished he could have that moment back. To do it differently. He'd been young and desperate and so, so stupid to think the only way to keep his promise to Abbott was to hurt her so deeply she would welcome the chance to get as far away from him as possible. He'd been too immature at the time to realize the wound would run so deep it would last forever. That once gone, she would never come back to him.

"I'm a lot stronger than I was the first time."

He didn't doubt it. When a body went through something like that it either broke them down or built them up. Looking at her now, it wasn't hard to see which side of the coin Meredith had ended up on.

She pointed to the path in front of them. "The porcupine has crossed. Were you waiting for something else? A raccoon? A bear perhaps?"

He smiled past the pain in his chest. "No. Guess I just like this."

It had been a long time since she'd teased him and the light smile that played upon her full lips brought every last one of his senses to stand on end and lean toward her. He loved the easy conversation between them, the quiet moment where everything they had once been bloomed in front of them as if it could be reclaimed. It was a pipe dream, but for that one moment he wanted to sit there and enjoy it.

"This?"

"Us. Just talking. I've missed it."

She glanced away, deep into the forest. He worried he had ruined things, but then she looked at him and he saw the same hope reflected back in her eyes. Something inside of him loosened and the walls around his heart crumbled. One more smile and he knew they'd turn to dust and that would be it.

"It is nice." She smiled and there it was. Dust. He was a goner. There would be no moving on from this. Not that he ever really had. He'd claimed to be too busy for marriage and family but it had been a lie as big and bold as they came. In truth, he simply couldn't imagine sharing his life with anyone other than Meredith. Marrying someone else, knowing they'd be playing second fiddle to a memory, hadn't seemed fair. His father had done that and it had ended in disaster.

But what if he could have a second chance?

"You think it's possible for us to be friends after all that's happened?"

She looked at him, her expression giving no hint to her own feelings in that regard. "Is that what you want?"

No. He wanted so much more. He had from the first day he danced with her at the Autumn Festival and she had bowled him over with her beauty, inside and out. He'd been determined to never let her go. He saw in her the future he'd always dreamed of, not the one his father had mapped out for him. He'd marched to her father's house the next day and promised he'd love, honor and protect her until his dying day if only Abbott would overlook Hunter's parentage and give them his blessing.

He had, and in the end, Abbott had called him on that promise. It had been their undoing.

"I'll take what I can get," he told her. He didn't have the right to ask for more, but he hoped. God help him, he hoped.

She smiled at him and the warmth inside of it wrapped over his exposed heart and made it whole again. "Maybe we can try. We're going to be living in this town together, after all. We should try to get along."

It was a far cry from throwing herself into his

arms, but, like he'd said, he would take what he could get and go from there. He tucked the image of her smile away and kept it safe, knowing he would pull out the memory a hundred times over in the next few days.

"All right then," he nodded and slapped the reins. The wagon jolted and they started along the path again.

"Is it true what I heard?"

"Is what true?"

"That you'll be resigning as sheriff soon."

Was that disappointment he heard? "It is."

"But I thought you loved being sheriff?"

"I did. I mean I do." He'd never had a job he'd loved more. Certainly nothing at the Diamond D Ranch appealed to him as much as his current occupation. When the town had pinned the star to his chest after McLaren's death, he'd been overwhelmed by the responsibility of it, but their trust had humbled him and he set about ensuring he was the best sheriff the town had ever had. And along the way he'd discovered he loved it. In time, he discovered he was pretty good at it, despite his father's opinion to the contrary.

"Then why are you resigning?"

He stared down at his gloved hands. "Because I have a duty to my father. I'm his only son and heir. He's getting on in years and his health has been failing. The ranch has been in the family for three generations. What other choice do I have but to take it over?"

"There's always a choice. Is it what you want?" Her question whispered across the quiet of the forest and wound its way around the thump and creak of the wagon wheels to sink deep into his heart. He'd been asking himself the same question day in and day out since he'd finally agreed to do his father's bidding.

"No, it isn't," he admitted. Not even a little.

"Then don't do it."

He let out a short laugh empty of mirth. "Maybe you'd like to explain that to Vernon. Anyway." He sighed. He couldn't help but sigh every time he thought about it. "It's what needs to be done." It was a road he'd traveled before. Its familiarity didn't make it any more pleasant the second time around.

"I can't imagine you not being sheriff."

He had no answer to that one. Truth was, he couldn't much imagine it himself. They lapsed into silence once again and kept it until they reached the Circle S Ranch.

Rachel came out of the house to greet them, an apron tied around her waist, accentuating the bump growing beneath it. It filled him with relief to see her glow with such happiness. Hunter set the brake and jumped down from the wagon, coming around to the opposite side to assist Meredith. She set her hands on his shoulders and he lifted her down. Her body glided against his, setting off a riot beneath his skin. Lord have mercy, he wanted to hold her against him and never let her go, but Rachel was already on the doorstep calling their names in greeting. He closed his eyes, savoring the last few seconds of contact before he let her go. Maybe it was his imagination, or wishful thinking, but he was sure she hesitated before turning away.

Rachel pulled Meredith into a warm embrace. "I'm so glad you came."

It was strange to see Rachel so demonstrative. She'd been like that once upon a time, before her first marriage, but he'd almost forgotten. "Hunter, thank you so much for bringing her."

He gave her a look, the one that told her he knew exactly what she was up to. Not that he minded. Despite the tentative peace growing between himself and Meredith, he could use all the help he could get mending the broken pieces of their relationship.

The interior of Rachel and Caleb's house was warm and inviting. It had changed significantly since Caleb had moved in. He had completed the unfinished work Rachel's first husband had left undone. A plate of fresh-baked cookies sat on the counter and filled the room with the scent of spicy goodness. His stomach growled. The pot of coffee he'd had for breakfast had done nothing to fill his belly.

"Place is looking good, Rachel."

"Thank you. Caleb's a fine carpenter, among other things." Her hand went absently to the growing bump on her belly before she gave him a stern look. "You should visit more often."

"Would that I could, Mrs. Beckett. Unfortunately, I have a guest staying with me who, if you'll recall, managed to excuse himself from our jail once before. I'd like to avoid that particular embarrassment again now that he's returned." Although, the more he got to know the outlaw, the less inclined he was to see him swinging from the end of a rope. He wondered if that was why McLaren had never mounted a posse to chase after him all those years ago.

"Sit down, you two." Rachel waved at the long table cutting through the middle of the room as Freedom Jones stepped out of the pantry, her arms loaded down with supplies.

"Oh, as I live and breathe!" She dumped the supplies on the kitchen table and breezed past Hunter and his open arms to gather Meredith into hers. "Miz Rachel told me you was back in town but I said I wouldn't believe it till I saw with my own eyes." She stepped back and held a grinning Meredith at arm's length. "Land sakes, jus' look at you child! All dressed up in your fine clothes and whatnot. You is just a vision. Just a vision!"

Freedom pulled her in for another hug. Hunter knew Meredith had never erected the boundaries many in town had simply because Freedom's ebony skin was a different shade than hers. Like anyone close to Rachel, himself included, Freedom was part of the family. He guessed Meredith more than most knew what it was like to be set apart by something you had no choice or control over. "It's good to be home again, Freedom."

"Awful pity about your pa. I was right sorry to hear the news. But the sheriff here made sure your papa got hisself a proper burial. Nice ceremony, too. We's all made sure to go."

Hunter winced. He hadn't said anything to Meredith about arranging the ceremony for her pa but the news hadn't appeared to shock her. Had someone else already told her? And if so, what had she thought?

"Thank you, Freedom. It makes it a little easier knowing he came home to such a welcome. I'm sure he was smiling down knowing the good people of Salvation Falls hadn't forgotten him."

"Oh, we's never forget your papa. He was a

good man that one. Sorry to hear about poor Bill, though. Remember when he worked out here for a bit quite some years ago now. Nice man. Good man, too, despite appearances. You been to see him?"

"I have. He's doing well." Meredith slid her fingers down the buttons of her cape and shrugged off the wool garment. Freedom took it from her and hung it on a peg next to the door. Hunter pulled out a chair for her to sit in, and Freedom followed it with a cup of tea.

"Sit down, Hunter," Rachel said, pulling out the chair next to Meredith, a clear indication of where she expected him to sit, and set the plate of cookies from the counter onto the table in front of them. Freedom followed with a steaming mug of coffee for him.

"You trying to teach me what good coffee tastes like?"

Her strong hand patted his shoulder. "Given that muck you drink, I'm not sure you have any tasters left in your mouth that'd be able to figure it out." She waved a hand at the untouched plate in front of him. "Have y'self a taste. Dinner won't be ready for a bit yet. Don't you be worryin' about those cookies neither. I baked them myself with no help from Rachel."

"Freedom, are you besmirching my cooking

abilities?" Rachel pressed a hand to her chest as if wounded, but the spark of humor gave her away.

"I wouldn't refer to your skills in the kitchen as anything close to ability, Miz Rachel. Thank sweet heaven me and Foster are here or you's all would starve to death. Now, tell me, is there any word on ole Bill's trial?"

Meredith reached for a cookie. "Hunter received word the judge is set to arrive in a week. An anonymous benefactor has hired a lawyer named Wallace Platt to represent him, but Bill has refused to accept his counsel."

"Mmm." Freedom picked up the supplies she'd dumped on the table and transferred them to the counter. "Well, Bill knows his own mind from what I remember of him. I 'spect he has his reasons. This Wallace Platt, he from around here?"

Meredith shook her head. "No. He said he hails from Virginia originally, but San Francisco most recently…" Her voice trailed off for a moment and she glanced over at Hunter. "Just like the Bancrofts."

Chapter Eleven

Rachel leaned a hip against the counter and crossed her arms. "I thought I heard the Bancrofts were from Colorado?"

"Depends on which one of them you ask," Hunter said, reaching for another cookie. All of the so-called coincidences were building and none of them were sitting well with him. He looked at Meredith. "Maybe we should have a conversation with Mr. Platt."

She arched an eyebrow. "We?"

He nodded. "Guess if you're bent on proving your pa's innocence, you could use some help."

"Two minds do think better than one," Rachel said.

"Can't argue the truth of that." A deep voice filtered through the door seconds before Caleb opened it and walked through, nine-year-old Ethan slung over his shoulder like a sack of potatoes. "Found this out in the front yard. You wanna keep it?"

"You have to keep me, Pa. I'm gonna be the best cowpoke you ever done saw."

"Did see," Caleb corrected as he set the giggling boy down. His hand rested on top of the blond head. "And I guess you're right. Wouldn't make sense to let a good cowpoke go, now would it? Say hello to Uncle Hunter and Miss Connolly, then go clean up for supper. You smell like the barn."

Hunter wasn't sure when he had attained the status of Uncle, or who had first started referring to him as such, but he had to admit it touched him, gave him a sense he belonged to a family, even if just on the periphery. And it did a body good to see Ethan thriving. It had been touch and go there for a while when Rachel had rescued him from the brothel after his ma passed away. Her first husband had never made any secret over his resentment of the boy's presence, but Ethan and Caleb had forged a strong bond. Both knew what it was like to be unwanted.

Caleb crossed the room and gave Rachel a quick kiss.

"Caleb, this is my friend, Meredith Connolly I told you about."

"Pleasure to meet you. Rachel has spoken of

you often." Caleb nodded. "Those fresh-baked cookies I smell?"

Rachel laughed and gave him a playful shove. "Sit down," she said and he didn't hesitate, pulling out the chair at the end of the table. He set his hat next to him, brim up and reached for a cookie, but before he took a bite he shot Freedom a questioning look. She answered with a quick nod. Caleb smiled and took a large bite.

"I saw that," Rachel whispered, loud enough for the rest to hear as she set a mug of coffee in front of him and gave him a quick peck on the cheek. "Now how about you men take yourselves down to the barn and let us womenfolk have a nice catch-up? You can show Hunter how that new foal is coming along."

Caleb rose as quickly as he'd sat down and pocketed a cookie into his coat as he did so. He motioned to Hunter with a nod of his head. "Think Foster is down there. Good a time as any for a visit."

Hunter grabbed a couple of cookies of his own and his mug of coffee. Freedom made a good brew and while drinking it would likely make the next pot he made taste even worse in comparison, he couldn't pass it up.

As they made their way down toward the barn, the sun worked hard to warm the earth, but the strength of its rays was no measure against winter's intent. Snow would come soon; Hunter could smell it in the air. This was likely one of the last times he would make it up to the Circle S until spring if they received a lot of snow. As beautiful as the Colorado winters were, he found them lonely. Caleb, Rachel and their brood were the closest thing to family he had. He didn't include Vernon in the mix. He was blood, but he wasn't family. Being cut off from the Becketts for the worst of the winter months made for a long season.

Hunter shoved his free hand in his pocket and hunched against the cold. Traveling through the woods had protected them from the worst of the wind, but the Circle S was nestled into a valley closer to the mountains and the wind now swooped and swirled around them.

"Feels like it's going to be a cold winter." Caleb lifted the collar of his sheepskin coat up around his neck. "You might want to find yourself someone to keep you warm for the duration."

Hunter slid a glance to his friend. "Is that Rachel and her matchmaking talking?"

"No, that's experience talking."

"What makes you think I'm looking for someone?"

"Everyone's lookin' for someone. Just a matter of finding the right someone for you."

Hunter couldn't argue with the man on that. If ever there had been a loner born and bred, it was Caleb Beckett. Now he was happy and settled into family life as if he'd been waiting for it his whole life.

Hunter knew the feeling. And he knew Caleb had the truth of it. Problem was he'd already found his someone and he'd let her go. It would be an uphill battle on a slippery slope to convince her to come back. He'd have to tread carefully.

As they stepped into the barn and closed the sliding doors behind them, an older man, stooped and slow moving, wandered out from the tack room. His eyes lit up when he saw Hunter. "Well look what Old Man Winter blew in!" Foster's raspy chuckle echoed off the stalls. Caleb's paint, Jasper, stuck his head out as Foster approached and the old man reached into his pocket and fed him a carrot, giving him a scratch on the nose as the horse munched.

"How you been, Foster?"

"Good, good. Can't complain. Nobody would listen no how if I did." Another laugh. "Caleb says you gots Bill stayin' with you. How's that wildcat doin'? Givin' you any grief?"

"He's doing fine. Made himself right at home

in his cell. He's refusing counsel though, which has me a bit concerned. I thought you might be able to help me, tell me what you remember from seven years ago. I know McLaren already talked to you—"

"McLaren?" Foster shook his head. "That's a name I haven't heard in a dog's age. But I ain't never had a conversation with him 'bout what went on seven years ago."

"What?" The conversation he'd had with McLaren flashed through his head like an oft-told story. He clearly remembered him mentioning he had spoken to Foster specifically. "Are you sure?"

"I know I'm getting up there in years, but I'm as sure as a man gets. The old noggin ain't given up on me yet." Foster tapped his gnarled mass of white hair.

"Why would McLaren lie?" He asked the question but didn't expect an answer. It was his turn to shake his head. "You mind if I ask you about it now?"

"Ohh-wee," Foster said, walking past the two men to the stacked bales of hay closer to the doors. He waved one of the barn cats aside and waited until the tabby scurried away before he sat down, his knobby hands resting on his knees. "That was a long time ago."

Caleb and Hunter followed him and picked out their own bales to sit on. "I know, but truth is, Meredith Connolly is determined to clear her pa's name and I got a sense there's a lot more to the story than what came out during the trial. I thought, seeing as how you knew Yucton, you might be able to fill in some holes and maybe we could help Yucton and Meredith at the same time."

Foster fixed his attention on his hand and flexed the knuckles, stiff fingers bending slowly. "Not sure what I can tell ya."

"I'm curious about the relationship between Abbott Connolly and Yucton."

"Oh, that's an easy one. Like brothers those two were. Bill owed Abbott a debt in his mind. They met back in forty I guess it was. Indian scouts they were for a time. Just boys without a single chin hair between 'em. Got themselves caught up in a sneak attack. Abbott saved Bill's life, got them both out with their scalps still attached. After that, far as Bill was concerned, he owed Abbott his allegiance for life. Said that's how the Chinese did it. Don't know where he came upon that idea, but he swore by it. Can't imagine it ever sat right with Bill that he couldn't keep Abbott from being sent up river for a crime he didn't commit."

Caleb stretched out his legs and crossed them at the ankle. "You think Yucton came back to pay his final respects to a man he felt indebted to?"

Foster glanced at Caleb and shook his head, then turned his attention to Hunter, his eyes sharp despite his age and erasing any doubt he had that Foster's mind might be slowing down or growing hazy. "Knowin' Bill, he simply transferred his allegiance from one Connolly to another."

"Meredith," Hunter said.

Foster nodded. "That girl was everything to Abbott. Bill knew it. He'll protect her with his last dying breath you mark my words. And before he goes he'll make sure someone else is there to take his place."

Yucton's words came back to haunt him. *You just make sure you keep her safe.*

It appeared he'd been nominated.

"Don't suppose you have any idea what she needs protection from?"

Foster hesitated. He studied the back of his hands again before answering. "The Syndicate'd be my guess."

There it was again. The Syndicate. McLaren, Yucton and now Foster—all of them had mentioned it. "What the hell is this Syndicate?"

Foster held a hand out as if to ward off Hunter's sudden interest. "Now I don't know much and what I do know is jus' all hearsay second-hand. And don't go askin' me to stand up in a court a' law to testify 'cause near as I can tell most of the men been involved in this whole situation have a funny habit of eating dirt shortly thereafter. And I ain't got much fondness for dirt."

The air around them stilled as Hunter waited. Foster seemed reluctant to continue. It wasn't until Caleb's quiet timbre filled the empty space that he relented.

"Best you tell him what you know, Foster."

The old man stared at Caleb a moment as if sizing up the situation. If he was worried about anyone coming after him, he couldn't be in safer hands than Caleb Beckett's.

"When it became clear the judge wasn't going to allow Bill to testify on Abbott's behalf he slipped outta the jail—"

Hunter scowled. "I remember." It hadn't been on his watch, McLaren had offered to work that night instead, but he still hated the idea that Yucton had managed to get loose and disappear.

Foster smiled, showing a mouthful of tobacco-stained teeth. "Don't take it personal. Ain't been a jail made that could hold that man. He's slipperier than an eel and twice as sly as a fox. If'n he's still sitting in your jail now, it's simply 'cause that's where he's decided he needs to be."

Hunter didn't care for the implication he had little to do with whether Yucton stayed or went. "When he *slipped out* the first time, why didn't he take Abbott with him?"

"Abbott woulda never left Meredith. By then, it was clear his wife wasn't gonna make it. If he went with Bill, he'd be on the run from the law and the Syndicate for the rest of his life. It woulda meant leavin' Meredith behind unprotected. So's he told Bill to git, but to keep in contact in case Meredith ever had need of 'im."

"How would he stay in contact without raising suspicion?"

"Guess there was always someone who knew where he'd be and could wire him if he needed to."

"Bertram Trent," Hunter supplied and rubbed at the stubble sprouting a shadow across his jaw. It made sense. He'd kept in contact with Meredith and Abbott over the years. Likely he kept tabs on Yucton, as well. "How do you know all this?"

"Bill stopped by the ranch on his way out of town. I fixed him up with some supplies." Foster's eyes widened and he sat up as straight as his hunched back would allow. "That make me an outlaw, too?"

Hunter waved him off. "You're not an outlaw. Did Bill say anything to you about this Syndicate?"

"Jus' that the cattle rustlin' wasn't a random thing. Said there was a group of men runnin' some kind of ring here that stretched as far as Boulder. Bill said the Syndicate would steal 'em, transport the cattle to another ranch, rebrand them and sell them at auction. Guess it was a profitable kinda business."

"And Abbott wasn't a part of it?"

Foster shook his head. "Might have been once upon a time when he and Bill were younger, but he changed his ways after marryin' Vivienne. Can't figure out how he got himself caught up in the whole matter. Maybe one of the cattle wandered onto his property and your pa hatin' him like he did, decided to point the finger in that direction. Guess he had a change of heart, though, at least about seeing him hang for it."

Hunter absorbed the information, filling in the pieces of the puzzle. It helped, but the picture was far from complete.

"Did Abbot think this Syndicate would come after Meredith?"

"Can't say. Bill never said so exactly, but I always had the sense Abbott knew something he shouldn't have. Maybe 'cause of that he worried they might use Meredith as a means to keep him quiet."

"Why didn't they just let him hang?" No one was quieter than a dead man.

"Dunno. After Bill lit on outta here that was the last I heard on the matter. Guess I shoulda come forward, but Bill told me it was best for my own safety to keep my mouth shut and mind my own business. Figured he would know, so I did what he said. I didn't have much interest in winding up dead 'cause I shot my mouth off. Maybe I should 'ave."

Hunter shook his head. "No, you likely did the right thing." By then the die was cast. Abbott was going to prison, Meredith to Boston. Sheriff McLaren was dead and Bill Yucton had disappeared into the night.

The barn door opened a crack and a slim body slipped through the narrow opening. "Rachel sent me," Meredith said, pulling her wool shawl tightly around her shoulders. From the sound of the howling, the wind had picked up outside. "Lunch is ready." She glanced over at Foster. "Hello, Foster. How have you been?"

Foster smiled and ran a hand through the messy mass of white hair on his head. "Right as a man can be, Miss Merry. Mighty nice to see you back in town again."

"It feels good to be back."

"Well…" Caleb slapped his hands against his knees and stood. "Guess we best not keep the ladies waiting. Let's go, old man." He helped Foster to his feet and tipped his hat politely to Meredith as he walked past, glancing over his shoulder long enough to give Hunter a wink.

It appeared Rachel wasn't the only matchmaker in the Beckett family.

"The three of you looked quite intent on your conversation when I came in," Meredith said, leaning slightly against Hunter's weight where her arm looped through his. He had offered it as they set on their way up the well-worn pathway from the barn to the house and she took it without hesitation. She told herself the temperature had dropped since their arrival and the extra warmth of another body felt too good to pass up, but in truth, she wanted to prolong the tentative friendship they had embarked on during their trip here.

"Did we?"

She glanced up. "You did. What were you talking about?"

The afternoon sun caught the planes of his face. The sharp edges of his jaw and cheekbones were balanced by the sensual curve of his lips and dark intensity of his eyes. She decided she preferred the lines the years had traced into his face. The difference made it difficult sometimes to remember the pain he had caused her, breaking her heart as he'd done. And in quiet moments like this, it was easy to put it out of her mind completely, as if it had never happened at all.

It wasn't that she had forgiven him what he'd done, nor fully trusted him, but she couldn't deny how good it felt, even if just for today, to have his strength to lean on, to feel a little less alone in the world, to recapture a sense of belonging to someone. She was thankful he had offered to help her prove Pa's innocence. She was well out of her depth and had no idea where to start.

Hunter kept his gaze fixed on the path, his shadow casting a dark stain on the ground in front of him. For a moment, she thought he might not answer, but he surprised her.

"I asked Foster what he remembered about the cattle rustling. Yucton worked here during that time."

Meredith nodded, her breath catching in her throat. "I recall. Did he remember anything?"

"He did."

Meredith's heart tumbled inside of her chest. She was afraid to get her hopes up in case it was just another dead end. She'd met enough of them during her father's trial to last her a lifetime, each disappointment scarring her deep. But hope was a hard habit to break. When they reached the house, she stopped and turned.

"What did he tell you?"

The sound of voices and laughter filtered out, coaxing them inside. She ignored them, her focus on Hunter and those intoxicating dark eyes. Lord, she could get lost in them so easily. Hardly took any effort at all. Her hand had slipped out of the crook of his arm but he had captured it and held tight. Even with her gloves on, his touch flowed through her, battering back the cold and making her tingle with warmth.

The wind whipped up and grabbed a lock of her hair, wrestling it free from her pins. Before she could rescue it, Hunter reached up and tucked it behind her ear. She shivered as his calloused fingers brushed against the sensitive curve of her ear. Without meaning to, she leaned into it. Into him.

"This probably isn't the place for this conversation. They're waiting on us. I promise to tell you all about it on the way home."

She nodded but his words skimmed over her, her gaze intent on his lips, her memory reminding her heart of how wonderful they had once felt. How they had the power to blot out all the bad and make her feel only good. What she wouldn't give to feel that again. Just for a moment.

The fingers that had tucked the stray hair behind her ear had moved and now traced a gentle path down her jaw, to her lips.

"We should go inside," he said.

She nodded again, certain what he said made sense, but wanting nothing more than for him to stop talking and to kiss her. Heat pooled in her belly, then lower, urging her closer. "They're probably waiting on us."

She would have nodded yet again, but his thumb had moved to explore the outline of her mouth and she didn't want to move, afraid if she did the strange bubble they were trapped inside would pop and disappear and all of the magic that made her remember the good and forget the bad would evaporate with it. She didn't want it to end. It would soon enough, but for now, for this moment, she wanted what she'd once had, even if it was only an illusion.

Hunter must have wanted the same thing. His hand slid around her neck and urged her closer. She let him, knowing it was crazy, knowing she would regret it ten times over when she thought back with a clearer head. But as his lips touched hers, all those thoughts rushed out and caught the wind and all that was left was the gentle coaxing of his kiss and the sense of how right it was. How right it had always been.

She breathed him in. The masculine scent of cold air and leather mingled around them and for the first time since arriving in Salvation Falls she felt as if she'd finally come home. For one reckless heartbeat, she wondered if they stood a chance, if the broken pieces could be stitched back together and made stronger for having been torn apart.

"Land sakes, you two, you'll catch your death. Now quit makin' sweet on each other and git yourselves in here afore you freeze."

Freedom came and went from the front door before Meredith had time to gather her wits about her. Her face burned and her gaze flitted from one thing to the other avoiding Hunter's. She released the hold on the front of his jacket, surprised to even find her hands there. When had that happened?

Hunter cleared his voice. He'd dropped his hand away from her neck and the traitorous lock of hair that had started it all let loose once again and threw itself across the bridge of her nose. He moved to address the problem but Meredith held up her hand, stopping him.

"No…no, I'll get it." She tucked it back behind her ear. "We should…ah…we should go inside."

"Maybe we should talk about what just happened?"

She shook her head. That was the last thing they should do. Besides, how would she even find the words to explain it? She could hardly admit she wanted his kiss. Had wanted it since the moment she opened her hotel door and found him standing on the other side demanding to know why she had returned. No. Absolutely not. She could never admit that.

"There is nothing to talk about. It was just a…a moment of madness." Fueled by foolish hope and old memories, but she left that part out. "We should go. Like you said, they're waiting on us."

She stepped away from the warmth of his body. Cold air rushed in to take his place and fill her with regret, though whether it was regret over what she couldn't have, or regret over what once was, she couldn't say.

Likely it was best she not even try.

Chapter Twelve

The luncheon went wonderfully. Brody, Rachel's young brother, joined them and Meredith was shocked by how much he had grown. He'd been only a boy of seven when she'd left. Now here he was, almost a man. Bertram had filled her in on what Rachel and her family had been through in the past six months with Robert's passing and Shamus Kirkpatrick's attempt to steal Rachel's land. The scandal that Shamus was Brody's true father had only just begun to settle before she reached town. Meredith guessed Brody had earned his manhood the hard way. He seemed more weathered and serious than most boys his age. But despite the wonderful company and the chance to catch up with Rachel, Meredith could not stop thinking about the kiss.

What had she been thinking?

She hadn't. That was the problem. She hadn't

thought at all. Her head tried to warn her, but her silly heart and complicit body conspired to silence it. Worse still was the humiliating realization that she wanted to do it again, making her a fool twice over.

The wagon wheel hit a bump and jostled them, bumping her body against Hunter's hard, lean frame. They sat close together sharing the blanket Rachel had provided to keep them warm.

The comfortable silence they had shared on their trip up had been replaced with an awkward tension; the kiss stretched between them like an open wound both were too afraid to bandage. At this rate, they would reach town and she'd be no more the wiser about what information Foster had imparted to Hunter than when she first stopped him on the step to ask.

Hunter cleared his throat. It was about the third time in the past five minutes and it grated on her last nerve. Finally, she couldn't stand it any longer.

"If you have something to say, say it, but if you're going to apologize for what happened, save your breath. I take full responsibility."

From the corner of her eye she saw him turn to stare at her, his eyebrows lifted in surprise. "You do?"

She gave a curt nod. Pa had taught her to

own up to her mistakes. "Of course. You said we should go inside and I didn't listen. I just stood there and…and…" Her face flamed anew.

"Looked so damn beautiful I couldn't help myself."

"Yes. No! No, that's not what I did."

He grinned and turned to face forward. "Beg to differ on that account."

She had no words to defend his claim. She cleared her throat that only made his grin grow wider. Tarnation, this isn't what she wanted to talk about. "Maybe you could just tell me what Foster said."

She chose to ignore the chuckle that echoed off the trees surrounding them. The thick forest cut out much of the fading afternoon light and shadows layered the path ahead. By the time they reached town, it would be dark. Hunter had rigged a lamp to the front of the wagon to help light the way.

Hunter relayed the conversation he'd had with Foster and as the tale unfolded Meredith's belief that proving her father's innocence would be a simple matter of finding a missing piece of evidence shriveled.

"You asked me about this Syndicate when I first arrived. What is it?"

"Some kind of outfit, near as I can piece together. McLaren knew about it. Or suspected, at least. And Yucton, too."

"And Pa thought they would hurt me?"

Hunter nodded. "To get to him, yeah."

Fear spoiled the delicious lunch Freedom had served them. "And you think they're still a threat?"

"I'm not sure what to think. Whatever evidence your pa had against them is still out there. It's what kept him safe and alive."

"I thought your father speaking on his behalf is what kept him alive." She hated feeling indebted to Vernon Donovan for anything, and she didn't now. The way she saw it, it was the least he could do for all the grief he'd caused them.

"Maybe," Hunter said, but she heard the doubt beneath it. "Bottom line is your pa was trying to protect you."

"He shouldn't have done that." Impotent frustration filled her. "He should have taken whatever evidence he had and used it to prove his innocence and gain his freedom!"

Hunter looked across his shoulder at her, his expression a mixture of pity and finality. "Do you think he would have enjoyed his freedom if it had cost you your life? That he would have thought the price worth it?"

She didn't respond. They both knew the an-

swer. And the answer only made her more determined than ever to give something back to her
father who had given up everything for her. No
matter what the cost.

"Then you think the evidence is still out
there."

"Possibly."

"Then I guess we best find it."

"Anything go on while I was gone?" Hunter
closed the office door behind him, shutting out
the relentless cold. Snow had started falling,
swirling around in tiny whirlpools as the wind
caught the flakes and tossed them about.

Jenkins stood and stretched. "Kincaid stopped
by."

"Willingly?"

"More or less." He nodded toward the far cell
where a lump beneath a gray wool blanket snored
contentedly.

"Sober?"

"No more than any other day."

Hunter sighed and shook his head. "All right.
Go get yourself some supper. Have them fix
something up for our guests, too. I'll stay here
'til you get back." He wanted to talk to Yucton.
He'd tried to talk Meredith out of digging for
the missing evidence but it was like trying to

convince a salmon not to swim upstream. It just wasn't happening. Which left him no other alternative but to find it first.

"Sure thing, Sheriff." Jenkins left, letting in another burst of cold air. If this kept up, there would be a blanket of white covering the town by morning. He shrugged out of his coat and rested his hat on the peg by the door. Jenkins had thankfully stocked the woodpile inside, saving him having to go out into the cold yet again. He stoked the woodstove and held his hands out over it, warming them and trying not to think about the day. Much as he loved visiting Rachel and Caleb, when he returned to town he couldn't avoid the inevitable emptiness that came with him. An emptiness only enhanced by the piece of heaven he'd tasted while there.

It had been a huge risk kissing Meredith like that, even if the invitation to do so had come from her. He knew she was caught up in the pull that always occurred whenever they stood too close to one another. To his credit, he had suggested they go inside, knowing she would regret any action she took that didn't include walking away from him. But he didn't pat himself on the back. Not as though he fought all that hard when the pull became too great and she was standing so close and, hell, what was a man to do but lean in and—

"Any chance a man can get some coffee?" Hunter had been too deep in his thoughts to notice Kincaid's snoring had stopped. The bounty hunter had tossed half the blanket off and sat up in the bed rubbing his haggard face. Though he'd pegged the man to be about his own age, he looked far worse for wear, ragged around the edges as if he'd been through a storm and barely made it out alive. Then again, if he kept up the way he was going with the drinking, Hunter figured they'd be digging a hole in the ground for him before he ever made it out of town again.

"You've confused this place with the hotel across the street, Kincaid. You want some coffee, get up off your behind and make it yourself."

Kincaid threw him a scowl but didn't argue. Though his body appeared to protest the movement, he roused himself out of bed, holding a hand to his head as he stumbled out of the unlocked cell and over to the stove where Hunter stood warming his hands.

"Seems a bit unfair," Yucton said, "that he gets to just waltz out of his cell whenever he wants to and my door stays locked. Rather inhospitable, I'd say."

Kincaid grinned, peeling some of the haggard

away until what might have been a handsome man appeared beneath. "Well, I haven't committed any crimes, old timer."

"That a fact?"

Kincaid picked up the coffeepot and peered inside. "None they've arrested me for."

Yucton chuckled, reset his hat over his face and readjusted his position on the bed. "That sounds a bit more likely."

Hunter watched the exchange with curiosity. The relationship was an odd one. Kincaid was responsible for Bill's current incarceration, yet had hired him for reasons unknown. Added to that, the two men seemed to be on rather friendly terms.

"There's nothing in it." Kincaid turned the pot over and shot Hunter a glare as if he was somehow responsible. A few drops dripped out of the pot and sizzled when they hit the stove.

"Pump's out back. Feel free to go fill it up and make some more."

Kincaid scowled but didn't argue. He went outside, leaving his coat behind. Hunter walked over to Yucton's cell and leaned against the bars. "Had an interesting conversation with an old friend of yours today. Foster from out at the Circle S."

If the news had any impact on his prisoner,

he didn't show it. Then again, between the blanket and the hat, it was difficult to tell what he thought. "That old coot still alive?"

"Alive and chatty as ever. Told me a few things I didn't know."

"That a fact?"

Hunter figured he could dance around the issue, but he only had a few minutes before Kincaid coaxed enough water out of the pump and made his way back. He wanted to have the conversation without an audience, unsure of how Kincaid fit into the picture yet.

"Who is in this Syndicate? Foster mentioned what they did, but I need to know who they are."

That seemed to catch Yucton's attention and he sat up. He let out a sharp breath. "All you were supposed to do was keep Meredith safe. Abbott didn't want you caught up in this. Either of you."

"Well we're in it now and Meredith isn't stopping until she proves Abbott was innocent. She plans on finding whatever evidence he had and nothing I say is going to change her mind. So I need to know what I'm up against. Who are they?"

Yucton shook his head. "I've got a few ideas, but Abbott was the only one I know who'd figured it out and he wasn't sharin' the information.

One thing I do know, they're more than willing to do whatever they deem necessary to keep their identities from being known."

Hunter heard Kincaid's boots on the porch outside. Time was running out. He knew the minute Kincaid set foot through that door Yucton would stop talking. He raised his voice. "Kincaid grab a few sticks of wood on your way in!" He heard the bounty hunter grumble but the footsteps faded back down the steps. "Is that why they didn't kill him?"

Yucton nodded. "He had evidence to expose them. Kept it hidden so they couldn't find it."

"Where?"

"Don't know."

"Why didn't he expose them, then?" But Hunter knew the answer before Yucton could say it. "Because of Meredith. That's why he wanted her out of town."

The door burst open ushering Kincaid and the cold air inside. "It's snowing like hell out there! Next time you want coffee and wood, you can get it yourself." Kincaid set the pot on the stove. He shot Hunter a glare as the wood he brought in tumbled off the top of the full box.

Yucton moved closer to the bars. "You make sure you keep her safe," he warned, his voice low and dangerous. "I can't do it from in here."

"Then you think she's still in danger? That the Syndicate is still active?"

"If they think she can expose them, there ain't nothin' they'll stop at to make sure that don't happen." Yucton gave him a look that made his insides coil. "This ain't over by a long shot."

Meredith rolled over in bed for the umpteenth time and punched at her feathered pillow as if it was somehow to blame for the sleep that eluded her. Every time she closed her eyes, all she could see was Hunter's face, each fine line scratched in by weather and time, the inviting warmth of his brown eyes, the sensual curve of his mouth. She could still taste him on her lips, feel the pressure of his kiss, his hand on her neck. She relived the moment over and over again until every part of her traitorous body ached for more.

With a frustrated huff, she turned over again and reached for the lamp next to her bed. A sudden scratching sound at her door followed by a soft rattle of the doorknob froze her midreach. Her hand hovered near the lamp. The sound filtered through the stillness of her room, driving a stake of fear into her heart. She opened her mouth to call out then clamped it shut, Hunter's warning of earlier silencing her.

He had offered to post himself outside of her room if it would make her feel safer, had almost insisted, but she thought he was overreacting and refused to set tongues wagging by such a blatant display. Was that Hunter out there now?

The doorknob rattled again.

No. Hunter would never scare her like that. He would knock or silently position himself outside her door without telling her, but he would not stand outside and try to gain entry without her knowledge.

Possibilities shot through her like wildfire, her brain processing each one and discarding it as she slipped quietly out of bed and tiptoed over to the armoire where her boots were. She shoved her feet into them and laced them as quickly as possible, missing a few hooks along the way but not caring.

The rattling had increased. Whoever was on the other side was having trouble with the lock and she issued a prayer of thanks The Klein had spared no expense to ensure their guests and their valuables were well protected.

Her heart pounded in her chest as she opened the armoire quickly. She grabbed her long black cape and threw it around her shoulders, securing the buttons near her throat. With one last glance at the door, she made a beeline for the window then stopped.

The piece of paper from the ledger.

She rushed back and grabbed her reticule then returned to the window, carefully sliding it upward far enough to allow her to slip out onto the staircase lining the side of the building. A fire had ravaged the town years before she was born, destroying most of the buildings and killing several left trapped inside on the upper floors. Since then, the town council deemed it necessary that each building over two stories have outer staircases for escape. Likely this wasn't the kind of escape the council had in mind, but Meredith was thankful for it nonetheless. She closed the window behind her and slipped out into the snowy night.

Fat snowflakes littered the air and blanketed the ground in white. She kept close to the buildings and hoped the shadows hid her. The wind tugged at the ruffle of her nightdress and cold air nipped at her bare legs.

She bolted across the street to the jailhouse but ignored the front door. Given her state of dress, she could hardly burst in through the doors seeking protection. Anyone could be in there— drunks from the saloon, the bounty hunter, Jenkins. She veered off and slid along the side of the building to the back staircase and quickly climbed the steps.

Her heart pounded with each step. What if whoever had tried to gain access to her room witnessed her escape? Would they see her footsteps in the snow and follow her here? For a brief moment, she hesitated.

She took a deep breath and reached for the knob. She didn't bother knocking, afraid in the few heartbeats it would take for him to answer she would come to her senses and realize seeking shelter with Hunter was anything but safe.

She opened the door wide enough to slip through, cringing as the latch hitched behind her. The snow from outside created an eerie light that spilled through the small window and chased the darkness to the four corners of the room where it collected in heavy pools. The small, sparsely furnished room looked exactly as she remembered it. The walls sloped upward on either side reaching a high peak in the middle. A small table on the other side of the room held a porcelain washbasin and ewer.

She took several quiet breaths, her eyes skirting the room. She didn't know why she felt the need for stealth. She did not come here to sneak about. But the room was still and silent. She feared moving. Feared stirring up the memories hiding unbidden in secret places.

She turned her gaze to her right. The narrow bed was placed against the wall, tucked under the slope of the ceiling where it had always been. A pair of boots rested near its head, a hat hung off the simple post. A dark form lay beneath the thin blanket. Her hands shook.

She opened her mouth to whisper his name into the darkness, but never got the chance.

"You lost?"

Meredith jumped swallowing a gasp. "Don't scare me like that!" Her fingers tangled in the cape still wrapped around her shoulders. "And no, I'm not lost."

How long had he been awake? From the moment she walked into the room? But yes, he would have been, wouldn't he? He'd always been a light sleeper, his senses on high alert even as he dozed.

Her heart picked up speed as he pulled the blanket around his hips and swung his bare legs over the edge of the bed. He was naked. Dear Lord, the man was naked. Could this night get any worse?

He reached for the lamp by his bed and turned up the wick allowing a weak light to penetrate the room. She tried to keep her focus elsewhere, to save herself the embarrassment of staring at his bare torso, but she couldn't resist a shameful peek.

He'd filled out significantly from when she'd seen him in such a state seven years ago. Hard muscle stretched sinewy lines across his chest and down his ribs. Broad shoulders flexed as he rolled them and stood. Her body responded immediately and she quickly looked away.

He tossed her a brief glance as he walked past her to the table and the washbasin. "You want to tell me what you're doing here? Or did you wake up in the middle of the night and think it would be a great idea to ruin your reputation by being seen coming to my room."

"The whole town is asleep and besides, I was careful." At least as careful as one could be when they were making a mad dash to safety. She didn't appreciate the highhanded tone. "Besides, I don't recall you being overly concerned about my reputation the last time I was here."

Her accusation stopped him cold, the water he scooped into his hands from the basin slowly draining between his fingers. For a moment, he didn't move. She waited for him to mount a defense, but he didn't. Instead he left her harsh words hanging in the air between them until she wished she could take them back.

He reached for the towel and wiped the water from his face, then turned to face her. "You still didn't answer my question. What are you doing here?"

"I need your help."

Chapter Thirteen

The towel Hunter used to wipe the water from his face stopped midstroke as he stared at her.

I need your help.

He'd heard those words before, from her father. They were seared into his heart, burned into his conscience that had been blackened with their soot. Those words had been the end of him and Meredith. The end of everything he imagined they could become.

"With what?" He had already agreed to help her track down the evidence her father had against the Syndicate. What else did she need from him that necessitated a trip to his room in the middle of the night?

"I need somewhere to stay?"

"Stay?"

"Just temporarily."

"Because…" He drew the word out, trying to

make sense of what she was saying but coming up empty. She fidgeted, her fingers worrying the buttons of her cape.

"I think someone was trying to break into my room tonight."

His blood stilled in his veins. Yucton's warning of earlier echoed in his head. *This ain't over by a long shot.* The towel fell from his hands and he strode toward her and gripped her by the shoulders, looking her over head to toe. "Are you hurt? What happened?"

He had hoped Yucton had it wrong, that it wasn't as bad as all that. No such luck.

She held up a hand and it landed on his chest, sending a sizzle of heat straight to his core. "I'm fine. I escaped out my window and ran straight here."

Here. Not up the street to Bertram's, or even back into the front entryway of the hotel where Reggie manned the desk, but here. To him. His heart soared even as his stomach dropped to the hardwood floor he stood on. Images of what could have happened to her rushed through his head in vivid, horrific detail. Why was she so calm?

"Did you see anyone?"

She shook her head. "I only had time to get my boots on and grab this." She held up her reticule.

"You stopped to grab your…whatever that is? For crying out loud, Mere, why in the hell—"

She cut him off with a huff of what he could only identify as exasperation. She pulled the small bag from her wrist and opened it, reaching inside to retrieve a folded piece of paper. She handed it to him.

He stared at it but didn't take it. "What is it?"

"It's the page from a ledger I showed to Bill."

Their fingertips grazed as he took it from her setting off a deep want into areas of his body he had no business considering right now, but damnation if her presence in his room didn't conjure up memories he'd never been able to bury.

He walked over to the lamp near his bed, to get away from her and the effect she was having on him as much as to better see what was on the paper. He tipped the page toward the light. It held columns of numbers and symbols, none of which made any sense to him. Nothing else.

He shook his head. "It's written in code."

"I know."

He took a closer look. A sick feeling bloomed in his gut. He had to be wrong. He had to be. Besides, even if he was right, it didn't necessarily mean anything. The paper itself could mean nothing.

"There was no indication of why Abbott sent this to your aunt?"

"Not really. Pa sent her a note and asked her to keep it in a safe place."

He looked up at her. Something in her tone caught his attention. "And that's it?" Her fingers picked at the buttons of her cape again. She dodged his gaze. "Mere?"

She took a deep breath and finally looked at him. "Can I trust you?"

As much as he deserved the question and the uncertainty behind it, it hurt nonetheless. She could trust him with her life, but she didn't know that, and he didn't know how to tell her, afraid whatever words he used would sound empty when balanced against his past actions.

"You can trust me," he answered quietly, willing her to believe him, afraid she wouldn't. They stood on a tremulous high wire and he feared at any moment she would decide it wasn't worth the risk, jump off, and he'd lose her forever.

He watched emotions wash across the fine bones of her face—uncertainty, desperation, need—that one caught his attention and hit him hard.

"He claimed there was more, but that he had hidden it somewhere else. He wanted to keep it spread around. I didn't understand why at the time. It made no sense to me why the page was so important. Now it's clear. He worried this Syndicate might find it. This way, even if they found one piece, there would still be more hidden somewhere else."

"Any idea where that somewhere else might be?"

"No. But it has to be somewhere in Salvation Falls. I had hoped Bill might know."

"He doesn't." She gave him a sharp look. "I spoke to him tonight. He knew your pa had evidence, possibly the identities of the individuals involved in the Syndicate, maybe more. He wasn't certain."

"I think my father stumbled onto something, something he shouldn't have—and that's why he ended up being framed. Whatever he had on them, it was significant enough to keep him alive." Her hand lifted to the buttons again. A nervous habit. There was more.

"What?"

She raked her teeth over her bottom lip and held it there, staring at him with those big blue eyes. "I wonder if… Did it ever seem strange to you, your father coming to Pa's defense? Or Vernon's cattle conveniently being found on our land? Do you think there's a chance that maybe your father is somehow—"

"No!" The denial shot out of him hot and fierce. She flinched. "No," he said more softly. "I already asked him about it. He said he had no part in it."

"And you believed him?"

He nodded his head, shaking off her doubt as it tried to find purchase with his own. "I know my father well enough to know when he's lying." But did he? His father had shut him down every time he'd tried to question him on what had prompted his sudden defense of Abbott Connolly, a man he had hated for longer than Hunter had walked this earth. He glanced down at the ledger sheet again. His father couldn't be involved. He was a bastard but he wasn't a thief. Or a murderer.

He just couldn't be.

"He's not involved," he repeated.

He handed her back the piece of paper and walked to the bed. He sat down and leaned his forearms on his knees then lifted one hand to rub at the tension bunching the muscles in the back of his neck. This week had gone from bad to worse. He had a town bursting at the seams waiting for a trial, a prisoner refusing counsel and a counselor hired by an anonymous benefactor, and now someone was trying to break into Meredith's room driving her into his. If this kept up, leaving his position as Sheriff and taking up ranching might end up being the best thing that ever happened to him.

"Sit down." He motioned toward the straight-backed chair near the door.

Meredith grabbed the chair and plunked it down in front of him. Even with the space separating them he could feel her. Her presence sank into the marrow of his bones. He realized then in that moment he would never escape her. She could move to Boston, hell she could cross the ocean to parts unknown, and still she would live inside of him, a constant reminder of what might have been. It was enough to kill a man.

He kept his gaze fixed on the toes of her boots where they peeked out from the hem of her night-dress. Droplets of melted snow dotted the black leather.

"Yucton warned me this whole thing wasn't over yet."

He revealed to her what Yucton had told him. She listened without interruption. When he was finished, she remained silent. He glanced up to gauge her reaction. Her expression had stilled to such a degree she reminded him of a stone statue.

"You okay?"

She shook her head. A fat tear pooled near the corner of her eye before she blinked and sent it trailing down her cheek, racing the one on the other side. No sound came out of her, just silent tears. It was more than he could take but she had placed herself too far away for him to reach. He pushed off the bed and knelt in front of her, taking her hands.

"Mere...?"

Her question came on a whisper. "Tell me the truth, did Pa ask you to send me away?"

For a moment, Hunter couldn't speak. For so long he had wanted to tell her the truth. Now that he had the chance, he hardly knew where to begin.

"It was the best thing, Meredith. Abbott didn't think you would be safe here, but he wouldn't tell me why. He made me promise to send you away, to stay with your aunt in Boston. He wired her ahead and once she agreed to take you in, it was up to me to make sure you went."

The revelation stabbed into Meredith like a hundred tiny needles, sliding beneath the skin awakening emotions until they ran rampant through her body wreaking havoc everywhere they went.

The more pieces of the puzzle that came to light, the more the question grew inside of her. At first she ignored it. It was just her foolish heart and its silly notions. But the more she learned, the more time she spent with Hunter, the more the idea took root until she couldn't ignore it any longer.

And she had been right.

Hunter and her father had conspired to send her away.

Her mind reeled as she tried to process what had up until now been nothing more than a hope. The truth she'd lived with these past seven years had been a lie, one designed to protect her. She wondered if either her father or Hunter had understood their solution had hurt her far more than whatever danger they thought threatened her.

Her breath hiccupped in her throat. "Why did you let him do that?"

"Meredith, I…" His hand reached up and wiped at tears she hadn't been aware had fallen. His fingertips, cool and calloused, grazed her skin. "I'm sorry."

"But why?" He had told her he loved her. They'd planned a life together, even if they hadn't gotten down to the details of an actual proposal. It had never been needed between them. They had understood it as a simple formality. In their hearts, they were already joined. And soon after, their bodies had followed. It had felt the most natural thing. And then it was gone, broken by harsh words seared into her soul. Even now, she could recall them with such clarity it was as if he spoke them yesterday. She shook her head, her lips pursed as she wrestled with her emotions. "You were so cruel. It was like you were suddenly someone else."

He moved closer and rested his forehead against hers. She didn't move away, ashamed of how much she needed his comfort.

"I hated myself for hurting you. You have to believe that." He spoke with such urgency, his grip on her hands tightening.

"Then why did you?" She wanted to believe him. With each touch, each word she could feel the walls around her heart crumbling. But she had been so long without him and she needed to understand. Needed it to make sense, to make up for everything they had lost.

"Sheriff McLaren had just been killed and the trial had been a farce and I…" He pulled away and she could see the story of his pain etched into every inch of his skin. "Your father said you weren't safe here and I needed to send you away. I argued with him, said I would protect you, but he was adamant. He wouldn't tell me why but swore if I kept you here your blood and his would be on my hands. He said if I truly loved you, I would do whatever was necessary to keep you safe. So I did. I didn't mean to be so cruel, but I was afraid if I wasn't, if you thought there was a chance that you could change my mind, you wouldn't leave."

He was right. She wouldn't have. She had believed in him—in them—and she never would have left it behind if she had any thought his rejection was a lie.

"Then you..." She stopped, afraid to ask, afraid the answer would be another truth she wasn't prepared to hear. But she needed to know, and her need overrode the fear. "You did love me?"

His throat worked as he swallowed. He didn't answer her for the longest time. Her heart stilled, her body held its breath. The fear returned until she wanted to fold in on herself to protect her heart.

His fingers trailed across her cheek, brushed her lips, his gaze traveling in their wake as if he were trying to memorize her.

"I love you still. I never stopped." Pain darkened his eyes and when they found hers, she could feel it like a palpable, living thing. She hadn't been alone in mourning what they had lost.

He loved her. He had always loved her. Everything she had secretly wished for welled up inside of her and threatened to spill out. How many nights had she lain awake and replayed the scene in her head when he had spoken those cruel words of rejection? A hundred? A thousand? Her head had told her to forget him. Her heart had refused. Maybe somehow it had known the truth.

"I don't know what to say." She wasn't ready to admit the truth to him. She still loved him, too. She had tried not to, but she couldn't help it. Her heart wanted what it wanted, and it wanted him. It always had. But could she afford to make herself that vulnerable again? The danger was still out there. Would he hurt her again in the name of protecting her?

"You don't have to say anything. I don't deserve your forgiveness, I know that." He smiled at her, but it was a sad smile and it broke her heart a little to see it. "But it doesn't stop me from wanting it just the same."

She opened her mouth to offer him something, anything to erase the pain in his eyes. There was a desperation to it that cut straight through her. But he shook his head, refusing her comfort before she could offer it.

"We need to find you a place to stay. Somewhere safe."

"I'm safe here."

The words came easily, released from somewhere deep inside of her where years of hurt feelings had never reached. Staying was dangerous. If she stayed, it could change everything. Or worse, it could change nothing.

"Meredith, we can't…I won't put you through that again."

She smiled. If she recalled, and she did in vivid detail far more than a proper lady should, he'd hardly put her through it the first time. She'd come to him willingly, wantonly. And she had longed to do it again every minute since, to experience the joy of joining with someone body, heart and soul. She had never felt more connected to Hunter than in the hours they had shared in this room, exploring each other, learning things about each other on a level so intimate no one else would ever know.

If she stayed now, their emotions laid bare, neither of them would be able to hold back. Even now, with him kneeling before her, touching her, she wanted to throw caution to the wind, just as she had that night seven years ago, and to slip off the chair and into his lap. She wanted to feel his embrace encompass her and shut the rest of the world out. She needed him to make her forget the past, put the present on hold and leave the future where it belonged.

"Would you kiss me again?" The one they'd

shared at the Circle S had not been enough. If anything, it had stoked the embers kept alive by hope and set them ablaze all over again.

His gaze roved her face, searching. She remained still, afraid to move, worried if she did good sense would rain down upon them and they would realize the madness of what they were doing, what she was asking. There were consequences that could come from this. She cared about none of that right now. All she cared about was that the thin thread of a dream she'd harbored for years on end had come true, and she wanted to grab it before it escaped like wisps of smoke caught on a breeze.

Hunter shook his head. "I can't. Not because I don't want to. God knows, it's all I've been able to think about since the moment you came back. But I don't trust myself to stop at a kiss, and I won't hurt you like that again."

Her heartbeat resurrected, bringing with it a dose of courage, a sense of strength she'd held in reserve until it was aged to perfection. "You won't."

Chapter Fourteen

Hunter knew he needed to be the sensible one, but every fiber of his being screamed to ignore sense, toss it out into the storm and give her what she wanted. What they both wanted. But it wasn't that easy. He had hurt her horribly, regardless of the reason. He didn't deserve to put her in such a vulnerable position again. They got lucky the first time and she hadn't been with child, but there was no guarantee their luck would continue in that regard. Not that it mattered to him. If she was willing, he'd run down to the church now, rouse the reverend from a dead slumber and make her his wife before the sun rose over the mountains.

But he couldn't do that. He couldn't make her any promises until he knew he could keep her safe from harm, to eradicate the threat hanging over both their heads.

Meredith lifted her hand and touched his cheek, her fingers trailing downward to the bones of his jaw, brushing against the stubble he hadn't bothered to shave since two days before. He closed his eyes, taking in the sensations one by one as they coursed through him, drove into him.

God, how he wanted this woman. Not just to kiss her, not just in his bed. He wanted her in his life. He wanted her to be the woman lying next to him each morning when he woke and each night when he went to sleep. He wanted their lives to stretch into forever, to be so entangled there was no separating them. He didn't want to lose her ever again.

But he didn't know if he could make that happen.

She moved, the soft scent of wild roses tickling his senses. Then she kissed him, tentative, searching. One touch of her mouth on his, barely there, was all he needed to shove doubt into a dark corner, smothered by passion and beaten into submission by need. He should be ashamed of his weakness, how easily his good intentions crumbled, but in that moment the only thing he regretted was the years they had missed out on. The Syndicate had stolen those from them and he would be damned if he would let them take one more minute.

Hunter slipped his arms around her and pulled her from the chair until her body was flush to his. His mouth searched hers, tasted and teased until she whimpered and pressed into him and he cursed the layers of cape she still wore and the nightdress beneath it that kept him from feeling her skin against his own. His hand tangled in her hair where it flowed down her back, wild and free and continued the kiss until his lungs screamed for air.

He broke away suddenly, filling his senses with her sweet scent, both their bodies shaking from the intensity of their passion. Her beauty in that moment staggered him. Tousled and in disarray, a fire lit in her from within, shining in her pale eyes and spilling over her rosy cheeks. It was as if time had erased itself.

"If you kiss me again, I can't trust I'll be able to stop." He owed her the truth at least.

She smiled, shy at first, then one corner of her mouth tipped upward a little farther with an impishness that turned his heart over. "I don't recall asking you to."

Caution went the way of the wind, howling down Main Street, whipping around houses and dancing with the snow. It didn't matter any longer, or at least not for now, and maybe that was all he had, but it had been more than he'd had since he'd sent her away and he'd be damned if he'd let it slip through his fingers now. He would deal with the consequences later. For now, in this moment, he was happy. He'd forgotten how intoxicating that could be.

He pulled them both to their feet and undid the buttons of her cape, letting it pool on the floor behind her. Then he dipped and lifted her into his arms, placing her gently on the narrow bed. With slow deliberation that prolonged the agony and the pleasure, he covered her body with his. He kissed her again, more slowly this time, to tease and taste, to savor her for as long as he could. He kissed her mouth, her eyelids, the tip of her nose and the line of her jaw. He trailed his lips down the length of her neck and made her arch her lithe body against him until he could stand it no longer.

He found her mouth again and reached for the line of buttons that lined the top half of her nightdress. He wrestled each one from its moorings, his fingers clumsy and impatient until Meredith's hand brushed his away to do it herself. When she finally reached the last button the thin cotton fell open and he slipped his hand inside to cup her breast.

"In case I forgot to mention, I truly appreciate the lack of clothing this evening," he murmured against her lips. A fire raged within him and he didn't think he'd have the patience to deal with the layers of clothing that made up her new fancy dresses.

"My rather hurried exit didn't allow time to dress properly," she said. A rush of protectiveness swept through him.

"You're safe now." He would protect her with his life if it came to that.

She shifted beneath him, pushing at his chest. For a brief second he thought she had changed her mind, that his reminder of what had brought her here had doused her desire, but then she rolled over him, careful not to hit her head on the slanted roof above them. Her nightdress slipped from her shoulders

His hand slid over the smoothness of her belly, upward to cup her breast. It filled the palm of his hand, soft and pliable. He pushed himself into a sitting position, careful not to dislodge her, and kissed the taut nipple, drawing it into his mouth and flicking his tongue over it.

Meredith arched against him, pushing her weight against his groin while her hands threaded through his hair and held his mouth in place. Lord help him, she was a glory to behold. Pure and passionate, sweet and sensual. Maybe a stronger man could resist the temptation, but he wasn't that man. He fell back onto the bed and brought her full against him before rolling with her until she was beneath him once more. He didn't know how much longer he could survive without feeling her skin against his.

"Pull it off." She pulled at her nightdress, her voice filled with the same impatience he felt. He was more than happy to oblige, pulling the soft material up over her head. He sat up and tossed the garment to the floor.

"Lord have mercy," he managed to utter, but that was all. Speech eluded him as need and desire overtook him.

She lifted one leg and pressed a booted foot against him. "My boots."

He blindly undid the laces, his gaze never leaving her body. He tossed one boot aside, then the other until her legs fell one to either side of him. God, she was beautiful. The lamplight flickered over her smooth, pale skin and he swore she was even more beautiful now than in his memories. She let his gaze roam over every inch of her body and though her cheeks were flushed red, she did not try to hide herself from him.

She nodded her chin toward him. "You're horribly overdressed for the occasion."

* * *

Meredith missed the heat of his body when Hunter left the bed and shucked off the blanket around his waist with one swift movement. He stayed there a moment, hovering over her, so close she could feel the heat pulsating off his body, but not close enough to feel the deep satisfaction of his skin against hers. The dim light slicked over his body like liquid shadow caressing every edge and contour. She reached for him, letting her hands glaze a brazen trail over lean, hard muscle. A deep ache pulled inside of her and begged for release.

God help her, she loved this man. Despite everything that had happened between them, the truth, the lies, the hurt—she loved him. She had tried to deny it for so long, to bury it with feelings of anger and betrayal, but it had lived on, cocooned in memories of better times where it remained shielded from his parting words.

Words he had spoken for no other reason than to keep her safe. He had done what her father asked of him, and they'd both paid the price. But no more. She would not let the Syndicate rob her of anything else.

Her heart opened and embraced freedom, relegating the hurt and resentment into dark corners where it belonged. Later, she would excavate it completely, glad to see the end of it, but for now this was enough.

Outside, the wind howled a mournful tune against the walls and windows. Hunter pulled her hands from his body and pressed them into the pillow above her head as he nestled himself between her legs, his hardness resting against her, taunting her until she couldn't stand it. She squirmed against him and smiled as his breath caught in his throat.

"Evil wench."

She pressed her hips upward in response. With something that fell between a growl and a laugh, he let her hands go and kissed her with a fierce passion that left her breathless and wanting.

"Don't make me wait." She didn't think she could stand it if he did. She needed him. Now. Always. Forever. They could take their time later, but right now she needed release. She needed him to become a part of her.

He kissed her again, this time with such gentle sweetness she thought she might expire then and there, but it was nothing compared to what came next.

Hunter sighed into her, as if he'd finally come home. And she understood. In that moment, it all made sense. He was home. And so was she.

She pressed her knees against his hips to hold

him there for a moment, to take in the wondrous sensation of their bodies joined as one. But the moment was fleeting, the urge for more impatient and demanding. She loosened her hold just enough to allow him to move against her in a slow, torturous rhythm. Their tongues dancing as their bodies moved.

Pressure built inside of her, insistent. She met each of his thrusts, reaching for something she couldn't name, mindless with the need for it. She sensed Hunter's need as well, his eyes closed, thick lashes feathered against skin pulled tight across his cheekbones.

Every nerve in her body sang with fierce release as the storm broke inside of her, crested over her as Hunter found his own release, a guttural sound coming from deep within him before he collapsed upon her, his arms saving her from his full weight.

She hugged him to her, not ready to let him go, to remove herself from this moment of ecstasy and wholeness. She knew once she did, she would have to face the reality of what had happened here, but for now, she simply wanted to enjoy it. The rest would still be there waiting for her when she was done.

They lay like that for several long moments before Hunter moved to rest beside her, his arm across her belly, his leg entwined with hers. Though her passion had been temporarily sated, she was thankful he did not leave. She needed his comfort and his warmth. He reached down and pulled the blankets up around them.

She wanted to say something, but she didn't know where to begin and she was reluctant to break the tentative harmony that existed between them.

"We probably shouldn't have done that." He whispered the words next to her ear, then gently kissed her temple as if to soften their effect.

"You said that the first time we found ourselves in this predicament." He'd been torn up the first time, feeling he had taken something from her too soon, without the bonds of matrimony she deserved. She had been less upset. She'd given herself willingly, already married to him heart and soul.

"I should have married you straight away. Argued harder with your father. Hell, I should have gone with you."

"To Boston?" She shook her head. "You would have hated it." Hunter was wide-open spaces, rugged and wild. City life would have suffocated him more than it had her.

He leaned up, bracing himself on his elbow and brushed away a wayward curl where it dipped near her eye. "We'll have to be careful." The elation he'd experienced bled from his face replaced by a potent mix of determination and concern. "Whoever these people are, they obviously think you have the evidence that can put them away. We need to find somewhere for you to go—"

She arched one eyebrow. "Why is it, every time we make love you try to send me away afterward?"

"Maybe so I know you'll stay alive so we can do this again."

"Well, I'm not going anywhere. I promise to take every precaution, but I'm not leaving Salvation Falls."

"Meredith, please. I'm serious."

She sat up, dragging the sheet with her. "So am I. I came home to prove my father's innocence. And I'm not going to let this Syndicate stop me. If they are so brazen as to break into my room at night, we must be close to something. We'd be foolish to stop now!"

"I promised your pa I'd keep you safe. He might not be here any longer but I plan to honor that promise."

"Then honor it some other way. I'm not going anywhere."

"Have I ever mentioned what a stubborn woman you are?"

"Several times." She smiled and nestled against him. "Now stop scowling."

"Give me a good reason not to."

She let her hand drift over the ridged muscles of his stomach, down farther until his breath caught and his body stiffened. "Reason enough?"

He gave a swift nod and after a moment of torment, grabbed her and pulled her on top of him. She straddled his hips and this time it was she who held his hands to the side, captive as she arched her back and rode them both to oblivion.

Sometime late into the night, Hunter awoke. With careful movements, he extricated himself from the warmth of Meredith's embrace and slipped out of the bed to where her reticule and cape lay on the floor. The cold air prickled his bare skin. The fire in the woodstove had dwindled to embers. He should stoke it and add another log but he didn't want to wake Meredith. Not yet.

He picked through her clothes until he found the reticule, carefully extracting the ledger sheet. With quiet footsteps, he walked over to the lamp still burning low on the table next to the bed and stared at the numbers and symbols again.

Their meaning remained as elusive as when Meredith showed him the paper earlier, but there was something else. He stared at the writing on the paper as the light flickered over it.

This time, he couldn't deny what he saw.

Chapter Fifteen

As the sun started to creep over the edge of the horizon, Meredith awoke, stretching her body against Hunter's warm length. She wished she could spend the day here, the two of them getting reacquainted, burrowing in and forgetting about the Syndicate, the trial, everything that conspired to tear apart their budding happiness.

But real life refused to be ignored, and she still had to slip out of Hunter's room and make it across the street to The Klein without being noticed. Surely it was safe to return now, though she knew Hunter would not let her make the trip alone. Another hurdle. If anyone spied them together, with her in nothing but her nightdress and a cape, her reputation would be destroyed and any hope she had of convincing the council to grant her business proposal at tonight's meeting forever lost.

"Wake up." She nudged Hunter's arm. "I need to get back to my room."

A slow groan escaped him as he rolled onto his side and gathered her against him. "That's not a good idea."

"It isn't an idea, it's a reality. My proposal is there, as are all my belongings. You can follow behind me, but I need to go."

He lifted his head. "Proposal? What proposal?"

"I'm addressing the council tonight at the town meeting. I want to open my dressmaking shop in Hattie's Hats' former building."

Hunter pinched the bridge of his nose. "I'd forgotten about that. Do you have to do that now? Can't it wait until after?"

After. After they brought down the Syndicate. Except they didn't know how long that would take and as each day passed her nest egg dwindled.

"No, it can't." She took a deep breath and sat up. "I'm not as well off as I may have made it seem."

"What do you mean?"

"I mean I need to open my business soon, or what money I do have saved is going to be gone." She explained to him Aunt Erma's belief you had to look successful to be successful, but she carefully left off the hope that she would show him, too, and make him regret having thrown her over. None of that mattered now that she knew the truth.

Hunter shook his head. "I just think putting yourself out there could make you more of a target."

"Well, I can hardly hide out in my room. They've already come after me there." Hunter's face tightened at the reminder. She reached out a hand and touched his arm. "I'll be fine. I need to do this. I'm not going to let the Syndicate rob me of one more day. I'm presenting to the town council this evening."

He was silent a moment. "You know my father is on the council?"

"I do." She pushed out of the safe cocoon of his arms and dropped her feet over the edge of the bed. The floor was cold. She shivered, the pull to dive back between the covers with Hunter strong. She resisted.

"Do you want me to speak to him?"

"Do you think speaking on my behalf would help my case?" She smiled at Hunter's scowl. "No, I didn't think so. But thank you for the offer."

She picked up her nightdress and glanced over at Hunter who had propped himself up on his elbow and was staring at her.

"Are you getting up?"

"Yes." But he didn't move and Meredith realized from the foolish grin on his face he meant
something else entirely.

She laughed. It felt good. "Beast." She dropped
her nightdress over her head and let it slither
down her body covering his view of her backside. Behind her, he let out a dramatic sigh. Meredith bent and tossed his denims and shirt at him.
"Hurry. The sun will be up soon."

Hunter went first, entering the hotel from the
front door. Meredith followed shortly behind,
going up the stairs she had escaped down the
night before. By the time she made it to the top,
Hunter was already in the room, pushing the
window open for her to crawl through with his
assistance.

She wasn't prepared for what she saw. The
room was in complete disarray. Clothes had
been pulled out of the armoire and strewn about.
Drawers were opened everywhere, their contents
littering the floor and bed. Nothing had been left
untouched, including the bolts of expensive cloth
she'd brought with her from Boston.

Hunter dragged a hand down his face and
looked around. He looked even less pleased than
she did. "Thank God you got out," he muttered.

She agreed with the sentiment, although part

of her wished she had waited long enough to at least get a glimpse of the perpetrator. She hated being in the dark over the Syndicate's identity.

"I should try to straighten up and see if anything is missing." Though she was certain nothing was. She had little of value to a thief, unless the thief was into dressmaking, and she had even less of value to the Syndicate. The only evidence she possessed she'd taken with her.

"I'll help," Hunter offered, but Meredith shook her head.

"No. It's better if you return downstairs before anyone is the wiser."

He turned on her, fire blazing in his eyes. "I'm not leaving you alone."

"You don't have a choice. We can hardly march about town attached at the hip without raising suspicion." She walked over and rested her hands on his broad chest. "I promise I will be careful. I have a meeting with Bertram. I won't be alone. Besides, they've already searched my room and found nothing, so there's no reason for them to return."

He touched her face, his fingertips trailing across her jaw. "Promise me, you won't go anywhere without an escort?"

She smiled up at him, keeping her tone light in

the hopes of erasing the worry pulling his mouth into a tight line. "I promise."

His gaze swept the room one last time, uncertainty coloring his expression. "When you're done with Bertram, come over to the jailhouse. I have an errand to run first, but I'll meet you there."

She agreed and let herself be swept up in one last kiss, filled with the passion of last night and the uncertainty of today. The need to expose the Syndicate grew more urgent with each passing day with not only her father's innocence riding on it, but their future happiness, as well.

"I wish I could say it's going to be easy," Bertram said. Meredith's spirits sank and she slouched in the deep leather chair in the lawyer's office. "Now, don't give me the long face. Just because it's uphill doesn't mean you can't climb it."

His words bolstered her somewhat, but doubt remained. Even Hunter hadn't sounded positive earlier this morning. Not that she'd mentioned that to Bertram. She didn't want to have to explain to him what she was doing with Hunter in the wee hours of the morning.

An hour after he'd left, Reggie had showed up indicating the sheriff had given instructions for him to bolster the lock on her door by adding a secondary bolt she could latch from the inside. Thankfully, she had started cleaning the sitting area first, leaving no evidence of what had occurred last night that could set Reggie's tongue wagging. If Reggie wondered why Hunter had made the request, he'd given no indication. She was thankful for Hunter's thoughtfulness, though she wondered if she would ever be able to get a good night's sleep in this room again, preferring the idea of sleeping curled up in Hunter's arms instead.

But she couldn't risk another night. Her reputation wouldn't withstand the scandal it would create if they were found out.

"What if the council denies my proposal?"

Bertram leaned back in his chair and tapped his thick fingers on the arms. "If they deny it, you have the option to reapply three months hence. Or you can open your business somewhere other than the main core of the town. The council only concerns itself with that area. So long as they don't have to look at it, they don't much care."

But she needed her business to be in the main core, to be front and center to drive in the customers. If she tucked her business away in some little corner outside of town she would never make the profits she needed to be successful.

"Have they ever denied a claim before? Excluding my father, of course." She remembered how angry Pa had been when they'd denied his proposal to open a hardware goods store where the butchery now stood. Vernon Donovan made certain the council voted against him. Two months later, Mick Ronson had opened a hardware store on the opposite side of the street. The Diamond D Ranch had benefited from a lifelong discount from Ronson's Hardware ever since. "One of the girls from The Seahorse Saloon proposed a brothel. Council shot that down, though I think there were some members that were sad to see the claim die."

Meredith stood and walked to the window, peering down the street to the jailhouse. It was difficult to keep her mind on business today. Her body still sang from the pleasures Hunter took it to last night. It hadn't been her intent when she'd gone over there. She had simply sought a safe place. Funny that he was the only one she'd thought of to provide that. Maybe even then her heart knew she could trust him.

"Meredith?"

"Hmm?" She turned around, embarrassed to

be caught woolgathering. "I'm sorry, Bertram. I guess my mind is on something else today."

The old lawyer's gaze drifted to the window, his sharp eyes missing little. "Something or someone?"

She kept her lips pursed and tried not to grin like a fool. They still had much to overcome before there was anything worth celebrating. She needed to remember that and not get ahead of herself.

"Hunter said the new judge is expected to arrive this week?"

Bertram's expression turned grave. "Yes, I heard the same thing."

She let out a slow breath. "Bill's running out of time, isn't he?"

"I'm afraid so. I expect the trial will begin on Monday."

Her happiness from last night dimmed. "Maybe that will jolt him into hiring counsel."

"Don't hold your breath on that account. I stopped in to see him earlier this morning. He hasn't budged in that regard."

"Why is he being so stubborn?"

"I've no idea what that fool has up his sleeve."

Meredith crossed her arms and hugged herself. "You think he's going to slip away in the night, don't you?"

Bertram smiled and lifted one shoulder in a shrug. "Wouldn't be the first time."

Meredith didn't share Bertram's optimism, however. "I don't think Hunter's willing to let that happen." He'd had men on watch around the clock since Bill's incarceration. Maybe if they could expose the Syndicate before the trial began, Bill would stand a better chance of getting off. Otherwise, chances of him getting out of this alive were slim to none.

Time was running out.

"What you doing in here, boy?"

Hunter glanced up from the ledgers he'd splayed across Vernon's desk. His father stood in the doorway, leaning heavily against his cane.

"Trying to convince myself you're not the bastard everyone believes you are." As much sway as Vernon held in Salvation Falls, it was not wrought from respect. He simply bullied people into doing his bidding, supporting his opinions. If they complied, they profited. If they didn't... well, Abbott Connolly was a cautionary tale.

"Can't imagine how that gives you the right to rummage through my things. You want to explain that?" His father's voice held a sharp edge.

"How about you explain to me what these

are?" Hunter waved his hands at the hardbound red ledgers resting on top of the desk.

Before striking out on his own, Hunter had helped keep his father's books. But these weren't them. These were kept in Vernon's hand and dated back ten years. Each book serviced one year, the last one dated the year before Abbott Connolly's trial. None appeared to have a page torn out of them, but all were written in the same undecipherable code as Meredith's page.

The page he had taken without telling her.

It was the handwriting that had caught his attention. He'd recognize his father's scratchy penmanship anywhere, but still, he hoped he'd been wrong, that he would find something to refute the growing certainty in his gut.

He'd turned his father's study inside out, looking in every nook and cranny. It wasn't until he noticed one of the desk drawers didn't run as deep as it should that he'd discovered a false bottom, and the stack of ledgers hidden within. Ledgers that had nothing to do with the business of the ranch.

His father was involved with the Syndicate.

Hunter wanted to reject the idea. His father was no saint, of that he had no doubt. He'd spent the better part of his adult life obsessed with a woman he couldn't have and making everyone else around him miserable in the process. He'd lashed out at Hunter's mother for not being Vivienne and tried to destroy Abbott for having won her love. But this...this was so much more.

This was a hanging offense.

"Those are none of your business. You walked away from this, remember?"

"I'm not here as your son," he said. "I'm here as the sheriff. What do these ledgers pertain to?"

Hunter had suspected from his last visit, but he'd dismissed the idea, not wanting to believe it. Now, he had no choice. But nor did he have any solid proof. The ledgers on their own meant nothing and Vernon knew it.

His father walked farther into the room. "You think to question me? Am I accused of a crime?"

"Not yet." Hunter watched his father's uneven gait. He had been a big man once, but the stroke had struck him low. He'd lost weight and his once erect posture had grown hunched. But the illness had not diminished Vernon's ego.

"And just what crime do you think I've committed?"

Hunter held his tongue. His father was a smart man. If he was involved in the Syndicate, he'd try to glean as much information out of Hunter as he could without giving any in return.

"Hmm," his father grunted. He reached

across the desk and gathered the thin ledgers in his gnarled hand. Arthritis had taken over the knuckles, twisting his fingers into an unnatural shape.

"Are you part of the Syndicate?" He threw the question out there, watched his father carefully for any telltale signs, but his father wasn't some greenhorn intimidated by a badge. He didn't flinch. Didn't do anything. His face remained implacable. That in itself told its own tale. "You need to mind your own business, boy."

"And I need you and whoever else you are working with to leave Meredith the hell alone. She's been through enough."

"When someone insists on nosing around and stirring up dirt, they find themselves six feet deep in it. That's just the way it is." His father had a cryptic way of speaking volumes without ever incriminating himself.

"Are you threatening her?"

"You want that girl left alone, you do what her daddy did seven years ago. You get her gone."

"She's not leaving. She has plans of settling here and setting up a dress shop. She won't be run out of town again." And he had plans of his own. Plans that included making her his wife, raising a family, finally having a home filled with love and laughter and a place to belong.

"You'll find a way. You did before."

"Steer clear of Meredith, do you hear me? Anything happens to her and it won't go well for you." His hand rested against the Colt at his hip. It would be a hell of a thing if it came down to using it, but he would if he had to.

"It's not me you have to worry about. Now, from what I hear, the town council thinks her little dress shop is a grand idea. You need to change their way of thinking."

"You want me to tell the council to vote it down? They're never going to vote against you. They never do."

Vernon sneered. "Seems their wives are all in a dither about it, insisting they vote to pass it. You want her left alone then you best convince the council their wives are wrong. The way I see it, if they are convinced, it doesn't leave her much reason to stay, does it? Because if she does stay…" He shrugged and a thin smile played about his lips. "Abbott saw the wisdom in my advice. If you know what's good for you, and for that Connolly chit, you'll heed it, as well."

Hunter stared at his father, words escaping him. Is this how Abbott had felt? Backed into a corner with nowhere to turn. He'd been desperate when he'd enlisted Hunter's help all those years ago, his insistence that of a father who would do anything he had to in order to protect his child. It was Abbott's desperation that made Hunter act, even without knowing the particulars. It had hit him at an instinctual level, bleeding through him until Abbott's need became his own.

And now here he was again, only this time he had a better idea of what the threat was and how many people had paid the price for it.

How could he let Meredith pay it, too?

The hopes he'd allowed to grow since her return to Salvation Falls withered and died, just as they had seven years before. But this time a small ember kindled in the remnants. He could go with her. They could start over somewhere new where the Syndicate would never find them.

The idea of tucking tail like a coward and running away stuck in his craw, but the idea of Meredith out in the world with no one to protect her... He couldn't countenance it. Could he swallow his pride? His honor? Hell, he'd choke both down along with the oath he took as Sheriff to protect the people of this town from the likes of the Syndicate if it meant Meredith got out of this alive. He would live with the shame easier than he could live without her.

"If I do this, you need to swear the Syndicate will leave her alone."

"On one condition."

"What?" It was like bargaining with the devil. Every time he thought he'd given enough, the devil wanted one more strip of flesh.

"You'll retire that badge pinned to your chest immediately thereafter and come back home where you belong."

The idea of returning home to work with his father, knowing now who he was and what he'd done, sickened him. He couldn't do it. Nor did he have any intention of turning in his badge and leaving this town at the mercy of people like his father.

There had to be another way, but for the life of him, he could not think of one. Yet.

"Fine. But if I do this then Meredith leaves Salvation Falls and no one bothers her again. Got it?"

"I'll do what I can," Vernon said, but the lack of conviction in his father's voice crawled over his skin like a blanket of ants. "Now why don't you let yourself out? I believe you have some town council members to speak to."

Hunter stepped away from the desk and headed to the door. He stopped where his father stood and pressed a finger into Vernon's sunken chest. "If anything happens to her, I'm coming back for you."

"If anything happens to her, you have only yourself to blame."

Vernon's words nipped at his heels as left the house. He hesitated a brief moment on the other side of the door and stared at the drifts of snow the wind had blown up overnight.

His hand went to the deep pocket in his sheepskin jacket and pressed against the hard outline of the ledger he'd slipped in there before Vernon had entered the room. His father could hide or destroy the others if he wanted, but Hunter was not walking away empty-handed.

He mounted his horse and pressed his heels in, bringing his mount to a swift gallop. The betrayal his father suggested left a hollow pit in his gut that grew larger the closer he came to town. Let his father think he'd been cowed by his threats. If it bought him some time to figure a way out of this mess then he'd play the part of the obedient son. But he'd keep digging. He wasn't giving up. The meeting wasn't until this evening. Maybe, just maybe, the old notebook in the file cabinet at the office would give up its secrets. Perhaps what he knew now would make the words on the pages look different. It was a long shot, but it was the only one he had. He'd exhausted every other avenue.

And he knew without a doubt, if he was going after the Syndicate, he had better have enough ammunition before he pulled the trigger.

He wouldn't get a second shot.

Chapter Sixteen

"The judge will be arriving soon," Meredith said, the chess game in front of her forgotten. It had been a lost cause. Her concentration was not in it. Her nerves were tangled into knots over this evening's meeting. "You're running out of time, Bill."

She glanced over at Hunter who was sifting through paperwork on his desk, silently imploring him to look up and help. But whatever he was looking at had him thoroughly engrossed.

"Judge was bound to arrive sooner or later," Bill said, reaching through the bars and pointing at one of her pawns. "You can move that one over here."

She did as he suggested without studying the board to determine why. She didn't care. Right now, all she cared about was convincing Bill to hire himself a good lawyer. Even if that lawyer was Wallace Platt.

"It has been said on numerous occasions that I could charm the feathers straight off a bird." Mr. Platt had entered the office only five minutes before, eliciting a dark glare from Hunter, the only time he looked up from his desk. The gentleman lawyer wasted no time pulling up a chair to the small table where she and Bill were playing chess and began listing each and every attribute he possessed, whether it pertained to his lawyering or not. By the end of the five minutes Meredith was exhausted from listening to him, but if it convinced Bill to hire him, or Bertram for that matter, she would bite her tongue.

She leaned forward, the edge of the small table set between them pressing into her. "Please, Bill. Perhaps you should avail yourself of Mr. Platt's services. Or at the very least, speak to Bertram. I'm sure he'd be willing to—"

Bill shook his head. "Bertram's done enough for me. And I can't pay him. My money's tied up elsewhere." How much money Bill had Meredith had no way of knowing. He owned no property that she was aware of, had never settled in any one place for long. The sum of his possessions filled two saddlebags with room to spare.

"Then it only makes sense that you take me up on my offer, Mr. Yucton, as my services come free of charge."

"Well, that ain't quite the truth, now, is it?" Bill gave Mr. Platt a hard stare and held it until the other man squirmed in his chair. It did not bode well, in Meredith's estimation, that the lawyer could be so easily rattled. Perhaps the abilities he spoke of only existed in his own mind.

Hunter's chair scraped across the hardwood, cutting into the conversation. He walked across to the stove and stoked the fire, the sound of his boot heels striking the floor and echoing through the office area. When he was done, he came over to their small group and leaned against the bars of Bill's cell. The man made lounging look like a bona fide art form and she could not help but react to it. Heat flushed her body and it took her a moment to recollect her thoughts.

"Who is it exactly that has hired you, Mr. Platt?" Meredith asked.

"Well, now don't you worry your pretty little head over that Miss Connolly." Mr. Platt let out a little laugh, its condescending nature skidding over Meredith's nerves.

"Pardon me, Mr. Platt, but Bill is like family to me. To tell me not to worry about him would be akin to suggesting I stop breathing. It simply isn't going to happen. Now, if you want me to assist you in convincing Mr. Yucton to take you up on your offer, I suggest you start by giving us a little more information on who this anonymous benefactor so concerned about his future is."

Mr. Platt blinked at her.

Hunter's deep chuckle filled the room. "Believe the lady asked you a direct question, Platt."

"As I am well aware, Sheriff. But I am sorry to say, my benefactor wishes to remain anonymous and as I am but his employee—" Platt pressed a hand to his heart as if this pained him greatly to say "—I am bound by his wishes and cannot provide the information you request."

Meredith itched to slap the pandering expression on his smarmy face, as if his pretty words were enough to douse her interest. The man was as foolish as his fancy suits. "Then can I ascertain from your inference that you know the identity of your employer?"

"Oh," Mr. Platt sat up straighter. He had obviously not been expecting the question. He blinked at her again several times.

Hunter's smile widened. He seemed to enjoy watching Mr. Platt squirm.

Meredith pulled her attention back to Mr. Platt. "Is that a yes, Mr. Platt?"

"Uh…yes. To a certain extent."

"That's a half-assed answer if I ever heard one," Hunter said.

Bill grunted. "True enough."

"And not one I understand the meaning of," Meredith added. "Either you know your employer or you do not. Which is it?"

Mr. Platt crossed then uncrossed his legs. He looked at Hunter and Bill, but if he hoped to find any assistance there he was to be disappointed. "I have met my benefactor on one occasion only. The meeting was brief and we have not spoken since. We have communicated through written correspondence."

"Then your benefactor does not reside in Salvation Falls?"

Mr. Platt swallowed, the nob of his throat bobbing up and down. "I cannot say where he resides."

The more Mr. Platt spoke, the murkier the situation became. Something wasn't right.

"You can't say or you won't say?" Hunter's gaze had grown intense and fixed directly on Mr. Platt. He sensed it, too, a fact that gave her little comfort.

"I...I..."

"You know, Platt—" Hunter glared down at the lawyer "—maybe this isn't something you want to get yourself involved in."

"And why is that, Sheriff?"

"Because," Bill answered, his lazy drawl filled with irony, "everyone who got themselves involved in anything to do with the cattle rustling out at the Diamond D Ranch is either dead or on their way there."

Mr. Platt blanched, his gaze flitting from Bill to Hunter then back to her. "I...I'm sure you're exaggerating."

"I'm sure he's not," Hunter said. "I take it your employer didn't bother mentioning that aspect of the situation to you, did he?"

"Well..." Mr. Platt slapped his gloved hands against his thighs and stood, but he seemed a little less sure of his footing than when he arrived. "That's a very interesting tale you tell, gentlemen, but I'm certain you've exaggerated its truth. Now, if you'll excuse me, I've done all I can here. Please let me know if you change your mind, Mr. Yucton. Good day, Miss Connolly. It was, as always, delightful to spend time in your company."

"Good day, Mr. Platt." She nodded in his direction but he had already turned and hurried toward the door. It slammed shut behind him seconds later. She had a feeling he wouldn't be back.

Bill chuckled. "Think you might have rattled the poor man, Meredith."

Hunter scowled after the departed lawyer. "Might be he could use a good rattling. Might be, too, it's high time I head over to the telegraph office and wire my contacts in San Francisco to see what we can learn about Wallace Platt. I've got a feeling the man doesn't have any clue what he's gotten himself into."

Bill looked up at him. "Do you?"

Hunter glanced over his shoulder and the two men exchanged a look Meredith couldn't interpret. "I'm beginning to."

It wasn't there.

Meredith pulled the opening of the reticule wider, stretching the strings as far as they would go then turned it upside down. A vigorous shake over her bed produced nothing. Had she forgotten the ledger sheet in Hunter's room?

But no. He had handed it back to her and she had...

She dropped the reticule on the bed and crossed into the sitting room. Perhaps she had stuffed it into the pocket of her cape. She searched both pockets. Still nothing.

Bile rose in her throat. It made no sense. Why would he take it? And if he did, why wouldn't he tell her?

There was a light knock on her door. She whirled around, her nerves on a sharp edge. "Miss Connolly?"

She inched toward the door. "Yes?"

"It's Kincaid. I'll be escorting you to the town council meeting."

"You will?"

"Yes, ma'am. Best hurry. It'll be starting soon."

"One moment, Mr. Kincaid."

Meredith took one last glance in the mirror. She had worn one of her favorite dresses today, a dove-gray silk with sections of lace sewn into the skirt, giving it a striped appearance. The same lace detailing had been intricately added onto the edges of her jacket completing the look. She looked competent, able. On the outside at least. Her insides were another matter altogether.

Every noise that rattled through the alleyway below jolted her. She'd lost count of how many times she'd scurried to her window to peer outside, afraid someone was climbing up the side staircase to break in once again. By the time the sun set over the mountains, she was bleary-eyed and foggy-headed. Not even the thick substance Hunter tried to pass off as coffee had perked her up.

She needed to speak with him. Confront him about the missing ledger sheet. There had to be a reasonable explanation. There just had to be. She refused to consider the alternative, but it needled at the back of her mind either way.

Did Hunter know more than he was telling her? Was he somehow involved?

He'd been acting odd all day, avoiding her. Doubts swirled like a tempest inside of her.

Another knock. "Miss Connolly?"

"Coming." She turned away from the mirror and opened the door. Mr. Kincaid appeared reasonably sober, save for the red rimming his eyes. He gave her a short nod. "Let's go."

Her escort was not the talkative sort, she realized as they made their way out of the hotel. He walked a couple of steps in front of her, looking over his shoulder repeatedly as if he half expected her to take a wrong turn and get herself lost.

She hurried her step and caught up with him. "Thank you for escorting me, Mr. Kincaid."

He shrugged. "Just a short walk. No skin off my back to make it."

"Did Bill ask you to do it?"

"More or less."

"Which is it? More? Or less?"

"Depends on your perspective."

It was rather thin as far as answers went, but she sensed it was all she was going to get. Mr. Kincaid clearly did not bother with idle conversation.

A gentle breeze made the ostrich feather in

her hat bounce in the air and brought with it the scent of whiskey from her escort. Apparently appearances could be deceiving. "You smell like a distillery."

He slid her a sideways glance. "Been inside a lot of distilleries have you?"

He had her there. She looked behind them toward the jailhouse. She needed to speak with Hunter. She needed him to tell her the doubts creeping up and taking hold were foolish notions that had no business being in her head.

"He's not here."

She narrowed her gaze. "You don't know who I'm looking for."

"You're lookin' for the sheriff. And he ain't here."

For a man who spent a good amount of time with a bottle of whiskey protruding from his face, he was annoyingly astute.

"He'll be at the meeting," Mr. Kincaid said.

"I didn't ask."

"Didn't have to."

"Has anyone told you you're rather annoying, Mr. Kincaid."

"Not sure *annoying* is the word they used."

She allowed the conversation to lapse back into silence as they approached the Town Hall. The small white building with its elaborate peaked roof was housed at the end of the block next to the church.

She dropped her gaze to the steps and lifted her skirts to climb the steep staircase to the oak doors.

"Why, good evening, Miss Connolly."

Everything inside of her froze. Her bones, her heart, even her skin. She was certain if Mr. Kincaid touched her she would break apart, shatter into a million pieces. It had been seven long years since she had heard the voice but it was seared into her memories like a scar.

She looked up into the smiling face of Judge Arthur Laidlow, the man who had sent her father to prison and made a mockery of everything that was fair and just.

"What are you doing here?" But she already knew. He was the new judge presiding over Bill's trial. It could mean only one thing.

Judge Laidlow was a member of the Syndicate.

Chapter Seventeen

"Such a delightful surprise, Miss Connolly."
The slow Southern drawl dragged over each
word and a sickening smile split his jowly face.

Meredith had always envisioned him as the
devil incarnate. Though not a big man by any
stretch of the imagination, save for the round
belly pressing against his black waistcoat his
presence was imposing and filled the air with
a fetid stench.

She took a step back, bumping into Mr. Kincaid who stood behind her. He put out a steady-
ing hand.

"I thought I heard you had tucked tail and
headed to parts unknown?" the judge mocked.

Her throat closed up, suffocating any response
she hoped to make.

"As I thought." His gaze raked over her. "It
appears your circumstances have changed since
last we met."

Mr. Kincaid pushed in front of her. "Can't imagine the lady's circumstances are any of your business, so how about you move out of our way?" The bounty hunter's rigid posture reminded her of a coiled rattler ready to strike. Despite his ornery disposition, she was suddenly glad to have him there.

"I don't believe we've been introduced, Mr....?" The judge spoke with genteel politeness, but the steely edge of a dark threat ran beneath it.

If Mr. Kincaid noticed or cared, it was not apparent. He didn't bother providing his name or attempting civility. "Believe I suggested you move out of our way. Don't think I'll be asking again." His hand lingered at the gun holster on his hip. The hard look in his eye told her he'd use it if need be. She almost wished he would.

The judge's thick lips pulled into a grin that made her stomach turn. He came down the steps, each footfall cutting through her with a stab of fear. He stopped when he reached her and Mr. Kincaid reached with his arm to push her farther behind him.

"I'm sure we'll have plenty of time to get reacquainted, my dear. I understand you'll be putting forth a proposal to start your own business, this evening. May I extend to you the best of luck? I believe you'll need it."

Meredith scrounged up what little nerve she could find. "I don't require your luck, thank you. My ability will speak for itself."

"Feisty as always, I see. Although—" he chuckled and waved a hand in the air as he walked away from her "—I don't recall that doing you much good at your father's trial, do you?"

Anger surged through her at his parting words and she took a step toward his retreating back but Mr. Kincaid caught her arm. "Don't. He's trying to goad you."

"Well it worked," she bit out, angry with herself for allowing her fear to get the better of her. She'd stood there practically cowering! Impotent rage burned inside of her and made her shake.

"Save all that for the meeting."

She turned and glared at Mr. Kincaid. "Didn't you hear him? The decision has already been made. No doubt he and Vernon Donovan have ensured everyone will vote against me save for Caleb and Bertram. They did the same thing to my father when he tried. I'm wasting my time!"

"Did your pa back down when the deck was stacked against him?"

She wanted to hit Mr. Kincaid, flail her rage

against his chest, but it wasn't his fault. And he was right.

"No."

"Then what are you gonna do?"

The question echoed in her mind. Mr. Kincaid was right. Pa hadn't backed down and neither would she. She straightened her shoulders and took several deep breaths, willing her heartbeat to slow. It grudgingly complied. The shaking of her hands, however, she could do little about.

Hunter stared down at the telegram he'd received from his contacts in San Francisco. They had never heard of a lawyer by the name of Wallace Platt, nor were they familiar with a prominent family by the name of Bancroft, or any business dealings by an Anson Bancroft.

"What do you think this means?" He looked up from the wire in his hand and glanced at Yucton who stood, arms crossed, at the bars of his cell.

"Means I don't got me a free lawyer."

Hunter twisted his mouth at the outlaw's devil-may-care attitude. "Like it would matter with Arthur Laidlow presiding over your trial."

Yucton shrugged. "Are you surprised?"

He wished he could say he was, but the way things were going, it seemed appropriate that the man who had made a farce out of Abbott Connolly's trial had arrived to preside over Yucton's. Only this time, Hunter would bet money there'd be no last-minute reprieve. Yucton would hang as certain as he was standing here. They both knew it.

"You think he's part of the Syndicate?" He already told Bill about the ledgers he'd found. About Vernon's threats, though not the promises Hunter had made to him to keep Meredith safe.

Yucton slowly arched one eyebrow. "You think he isn't?"

Hunter didn't answer. The truth was carved into the walls of Yucton's cell, the same one Abbott had spent time in. He only wished he had seen it sooner, maybe he could have saved everyone a world of hurt. But he'd never thought to look at his father. He'd been the supposed victim of the crime, after all. But he guessed that was the intent.

"Vernon, Laidlow. Maybe Platt and Bancroft, too. They showed up in town at the same time and both claim to hail from San Francisco. Unless Bancroft is from Colorado. Depends on which family member you ask. Either way, it's all conjecture. I've got no proof. I need whatever it was that Abbott had on them. The homestead was ransacked after the trial." At the time he'd thought it was drifters, now he knew better. "Where the hell did Abbott hide it?"

Yucton shook his head. "He said I was better not knowin'."

"Great." Hunter rubbed a hand down his face. "You know what you gotta do."

Hunter nodded, but it didn't mean he liked it. Fact was he hated it. But there was no other way. The old file had yielded nothing and time had run out. He needed to keep Meredith safe and Salvation Falls was no longer a safe haven. Maybe he should have spoken to the town council, but he hadn't. He couldn't do that to her. Not that it mattered now. Even if the town council voted against Vernon and approved her dress shop, he had to wreck her dreams and get her out of town either way.

Just like he had before.

"This is just temporary," he said. "Once I find the proof and take the Syndicate down, I'll bring her back. I'll convince the council to reverse their decision."

Neither of them acknowledged the ugly truth hanging in the air. Meredith would never forgive him for running her out of town a second time. The tenuous bridge of trust they had rebuilt crumbled underfoot.

"I've gotta go," he said. "The town council meeting is starting. I should at least be there."

"I don't see the need for this business. Women in this town can make their own dresses." Vernon's acidic tone raked over her.

"I don't deny many can, but there are also many who can't, or who don't have the time. Currently they must buy ready-made dresses whether the sizing is to their advantage or not, or they must order from a catalogue, never knowing if, when the item arrives, it will fit properly. The service I provide is to make a dress using quality materials and cut specifically to the woman's needs."

"For a price." Vernon sneered at her, as if the idea of her making money disgusted him.

"Yes, for an affordable price. It's a business, Mr. Donovan. Not a charity."

"Something you would know ample about, if I recall."

Her skin burned from the slight but she refused to back down. "My business will give the women of Salvation Falls choices they do not currently have at their disposal. They will be able to choose from a variety of patterns from plain and serviceable to the more elaborate designs that rival anything coming out of London or Paris."

"Fripperies," Vernon barked, reminding her of an angry dog.

Caleb spoke up before she could protest. "I don't see how outfitting a woman in the dress of her choice is a frippery. Are you going to tell me your suits aren't custom-made, Mr. Donovan? Or yours, Mayor Greggs?"

Mayor Greggs squirmed in his seat. His gaze slid down the table to where Vernon sat before quickly skidding away.

"I can vouch for the fact mine are," Bertram said. He puffed up his barrel chest. "As are the suits of many others on this council, you included Vernon."

For a brief moment, Vernon's glare left Meredith and rested on Bertram, though the old lawyer appeared far less affected by it than she. She was fighting for her livelihood and losing badly. Her run-in with Laidlow had left her shaken and, try as she might, she found it hard to regain her footing.

"Rachel would be more than happy to see a dress shop open here," Caleb said. "Between running a ranch and looking after the boys, she doesn't have the time to be sewing her own wardrobe. I'm certain she would appreciate the service."

"Perhaps we should call for a vote?" Mayor Greggs suggested.

"Can I say something?"

Meredith glanced over her shoulder. She had been so focused on the council she hadn't heard Hunter approach. He stood a few feet behind her, his hat held in his hands. The lamplight set up around the room to ward off the early November nightfall made his dark hair glisten.

"This matter doesn't concern you," Vernon said. "Lest you're planning on wearing a dress, boy."

Meredith cringed at Vernon's remark, but Hunter ignored him. He took a few steps forward, his chin raised in defiance against his father's words. "As sheriff of this town, whatever goes on in it is my concern."

He had used the same line on her, though she didn't mind it half as much when it was being offered in her defense.

"He has a valid point," Bertram said. "Let the man speak." He nodded toward Hunter. The center aisle where they stood was narrow. He stood close enough that she could smell the scent of cold air and sheepskin. A part of her longed to turn and bury herself in his embrace, but the other part remembered the ledger sheet that had gone missing, and the likely culprit who took it.

Her head and heart warred within her. She wanted to believe in his innocence. Needed to believe his reasons for taking it were just. But try as she might, she couldn't understand what such reasons could be. Or why he felt the need to keep it from her.

"The way I see it, the town can only benefit from Miss Connolly's shop. I don't know much about dressmaking, but it seems to me if a man can go get a suit made to fit in the style he chooses, I see no reason women shouldn't be afforded the same opportunity. Miss Connolly is able to provide an expertise we don't currently have available. She was born and raised in this town, and I think we owe it to her to give her a chance."

"Sheriff Donovan makes a valid point," Caleb agreed.

"Agreed," Bertram added. "The building sits empty and no one has come forth with a better use for it."

"Then we can wait until someone more deserving does come forth." Vernon banged his meaty hand on the table. "No doubt Miss Connolly has allowed him certain favors to ensure his endorsement. My son doesn't know what he's talking about."

Hunter's posture turned rigid and a collective gasp shot through the hall, including her own.

"How dare you!" She sputtered the words out.

"I don't know what I'm talking about?" Hunter left the podium and in two swift strides reached the dais where the council members sat. Both of his fists were clenched tightly at his sides and she could feel the anger and tension vibrating off of him from several feet away. "I know exactly what I'm talking about. I know you've spent over thirty years holding a grudge against Abbott Connolly because Vivienne loved him and not you."

Meredith watched Vernon's face pale significantly. She had never seen anyone, including Hunter, speak to him in such a way.

"Shut up, boy."

"I also know you went out of your way to make Abbott's life a misery and now you're trying to do the same to his daughter."

Color raged back into Vernon's face until it turned a deep crimson. "Abbott Connolly was a thief and an outlaw!"

"Was he? Was he the true outlaw, or was it somebody else? Maybe a *syndicate* of somebody else's."

"Watch it, boy," Vernon warned. "You remember our agreement."

Meredith's breath caught in her throat. Agreement? What was Vernon talking about? What agreement did Hunter have with him? Was Hunter somehow involved? No. Every part of her rejected the idea. But what about the missing ledger sheet? Her heart sank a little lower.

Behind her, the audience had fallen silent, the air brittle.

"Ah, perhaps we should take a vote," Mayor Greggs said once again. He raised the gavel in his hand but Caleb reached over and grabbed his wrist, his movements so lightning quick Meredith wasn't even sure she saw it.

Vernon stood. One gnarled hand gripped his cane and the other held the table. His voice pulsated with anger. "I wash my hands of you."

"You did that a long time ago."

Vernon stepped down from the dais and glared at Hunter. "You had your chance. Any agreement we had is null and void."

His parting words left Meredith confused, but it was all he said before he strode unevenly down the outside aisle. His walking stick struck the ground with every second step. The doors at the back of the room banged against the exterior of the hall echoing his departure.

Cold air rushed into the room. Meredith couldn't breathe. She couldn't move. What had just happened? The crowd erupted into a cacophony of voices. Mayor Greggs banged his gavel repeatedly in an attempt to restore order.

Hunter turned to Mr. Kincaid who sat on the end of the bench nearby. "Take Meredith to Bertram's offices when this is over." He looked at her then. "I'm sorry. Whatever happens, I'm sorry. Just know that."

"For what? What agreement did you have with your father?" She had to shout over the growing voices and Mayor Greggs's calls for order.

Hunter didn't answer her. For a brief moment, he stared at her hard and his gaze swept across her features as if trying to memorize her face. The thought filled her veins with a sense of dread. He leaned down and kissed her forehead. His lips lingered against her skin, sending warmth spreading through the chill that had invaded her insides. "Go with Kincaid. I'll find you. We need to talk."

She had only time to nod before he turned and fought his way through the crowd to follow his father from the room.

Finally Mayor Greggs wrested control back from the audience.

"Perhaps we should call for a vote then," Bertram said. Meredith returned her attention to the front of the room, her mind swirling in a heady mixture of confusion as she tried to make sense of what had happened. Though the council members continued to argue for and against her and her business it was obvious the argument between Hunter and his father had left everyone shaken. In the end, they voted her proposal down four to two. She had failed.

"C'mon," Mr. Kincaid said, his rough tone somewhat gentled. "I'll take you to Trent's offices."

She let him lead her from the room, following in Hunter's footsteps. The wind caught the door as it opened and sent it flying backward against the exterior wall with a snap. Snow whipped up in swirls from the scattered patches on the ground. Another snap split the air but this one was different.

Meredith froze, her body understanding the danger before her brain could make the connection.

A strong arm banded around her chest in the same instant the wood next to her head splintered. Mr. Kincaid pulled her back into the hall as her mind finally realized what was happening.

Someone was shooting at her.

Chapter Eighteen

Hunter went after Vernon, determined to stop him from implementing his threat against Meredith, but his father's wagon was nowhere to be found. He hadn't planned on confronting Vernon at the meeting, but his anger got the best of him when the man tried to damage Meredith's reputation. In that instant he knew, his father had no intention of keeping up his end of the bargain. Vernon's promise that she would remain unharmed if Hunter could get her out of town had been an empty one, just as he suspected. He needed to stop the Syndicate and he needed to keep Meredith safe until he did. There was no other way. And that meant another showdown with his father. Vernon was the only connection he had to the other members of the Syndicate. He needed to know who they were before he could figure out how to stop them.

He was halfway to his office to get his horse when the first shot rang out. He spun on his heel.

Another shot cut through the wind blowing down from the mountains. He picked up speed, his boots catching in the mix of muck and snow until his muscles screamed from the effort. As he came around the bend in Main Street, he saw Meredith being pulled back into the hall by Kincaid. Had she been hit?

His heart hammered against his ribs. Fear and exertion raced through his veins.

Let her be okay. The words chanted over and over in his head. He couldn't fathom the alternative. That she wasn't okay. That the bullet had found its mark.

He had drawn his own gun, but couldn't remember slipping the Colt out of its holster, simply felt the weight of it in his hand. His gaze swept the street, searching for the shooter. A shadow in the alley next to Ronson's Hardware caught his eye and took shape. He skidded to a stop, but the slippery street sent him past the alley. He doubled back and stopped.

"Vernon." He crouched down where his father sat propped against the side of the building facing into the alleyway. His head lolled backward and he winced in pain. A hand clutched his jacket near his shoulder.

Vernon opened his eyes and glared at him through the dark night. "This is your doing, boy." His voice was barely more than a rasp, each word infused with pain and accusation.

"Who did this?"

"Hardly matters. He's long gone. Took the wagon." He stopped after each statement, gathering his breath for the next.

"I'll go get Doc." Unless he was tending to Meredith. Hunter refused to go there. He took off again, sprinting the last fifty yards to the Town Hall. He took the steps two at a time and rushed through the door. Inside, voices rose in mass hysteria as a few of the council members tried to calm the crowd.

Hunter grabbed Caleb by the arm and pulled him around. "Where's Meredith?"

Caleb's calm voice did little to soothe his jagged nerves. "She's fine. Kincaid grabbed her and pulled her inside before any harm could come to her." Relief swept through him. "They voted down her proposal."

"Dammit." He shook his head; he would deal with that later. "I need the doc. I found Vernon in the alley. Think the shooter got him."

"Is he—?"

Hunter gave a curt shake of his head. "He's alive." *For now.* He let the words hang in the air unspoken, but believed them nonetheless. He'd seen enough death to know what it looked like when it approached.

"The shooter?"

"Gone."

"Get your father to Doc's office. I'll grab Doc and we'll meet you there."

Hunter nodded. "Bring Meredith." He wasn't letting her out of his sight from here on in.

He ran back into the cold, to his father. The tenuous hold Vernon had on consciousness had slipped away and he'd slumped against the wall. His hand fell away to reveal a dark stain spreading across his chest. Hunter hoisted the old man up onto his shoulder, struggling beneath the weight, and headed for Doc's office. He could hear the others pouring out of the Town Hall behind him.

Part of him considered leaving the old man in the alley after what he'd done to Meredith and to her family. He deserved nothing better. His own father had lied to him, played him false. He'd never had any intention of ensuring Meredith's safety and Hunter had been an idiot to think otherwise. Why he kept hoping his father would turn into the kind of man he could be proud of, he didn't know, but it stopped here. No more. Now the man would answer for his crimes, whether to a jury of his peers or his Maker remained to be seen.

The evening took on a surreal quality as Meredith found herself rushed out of Town Hall and down the street to Doc Whyte's office, surrounded by Caleb and Bertram at either side, their arms looped through hers to hurry her along. Doc Whyte flanked her and Mr. Kincaid walked in front, moving swiftly with his sidearm drawn and his gaze scanning the street. He'd done this before, she suspected, given the ease with which he moved, and a complete absence of fear. Perhaps she had used it all up and there was none left for anyone else to feel.

It didn't take them long to reach Doc's office, situated an equal distance between the jailhouse and the Town Hall. Still, the race there felt as if it took forever. Each time her foot struck the ground she waited for the next gunshot. It never came. The eerie silence only unnerved her more.

When they stepped through the door, she relaxed somewhat until Hunter turned away from his father's prone body and motioned to her, blood staining his hand.

"Stay away from the windows."

Up until that moment, she had hoped the gunshot had just been a few rowdies from the saloon who'd had too much to drink, but Hunter's instruction erased any illusions to the contrary. The bullet hadn't been a random thing.

The Syndicate had come for her.

Terror gripped her insides and squeezed. It became hard to breathe and all she wanted was to find a safe haven, crawl under the covers and hide until it was all over. But she couldn't. Her father had lived with this fear for years, had done everything in his power to protect her from it and he'd succeeded. At least until she'd come back to this town and started poking around again. Well, now it was her turn. He had been unable to take the Syndicate down. To do so would have been to risk her life. Instead he had sacrificed his own.

And scared as she was, she would not—no, she *could* not let that go unanswered.

She would finish the job. She would find the evidence Pa had hidden and hold the Syndicate accountable for what they had taken from her.

She moved to where a narrow bench lined a portion of a windowless wall. It was a small office, equipment laid out in precise, orderly rows. In the adjacent room, Meredith knew from experience, there was an exam table, shelves of books, a bed and the doc's desk. She had spent plenty of time here during the beginning of her mother's illness, until she became too ill to make the trip into town.

In front of her was a high long table Doc used for mixing his medicines and herbs. Tonight it held a bloody and unconscious Vernon Donovan.

"How's it look, Doc?" Strain pulled Hunter's voice tight. Doc had wasted little time in cutting away Vernon's shirt and jacket. Meredith only caught glimpses as Hunter and Doc shifted position, but it didn't look good. His chest was covered with blood, smeared and soaked, and his weathered skin had paled considerably. His breath rasped and labored.

Doc Whyte glanced up briefly at Hunter, then returned his attention to Vernon. "I'll do what I can."

Bertram left his position by the door and came to sit next to her on the bench. He took her hand in his and held it tight.

"The bullet's in deep," Doc said. The low tone of his voice spread across the reverent quiet of the room. Mr. Kincaid and Caleb stood sentry on either side of the door, both sets of eyes resting on the table. A sense of inevitability drew lines across their cheeks.

"Can you get it out?"

Doc shook his head. "Not right now. Don't want to risk him losing any more blood. Best thing we can do is stem the tide. Hope he regains some strength, then…well, then we'll see." There was no promise in his words, only a strange finality. Whatever he did would never be enough. Death knocked firmly at Vernon's door and it would not be turned away.

She waited for a sense of vindication to fill her, but it never came. Only sorrow. It crept in with slow deliberate steps and settled into her bones. There had been so much loss. So much anger and hurt. And for what?

Meredith didn't know how long she sat there while Doc Whyte worked to patch up Vernon as best he could. At some point, Caleb moved to turn up the lamplight. Clouds had covered the moon and stars with an unrelenting blackness.

"That's the best I can do for now," Doc said, moving back from the table and taking a small white towel from the counter to wipe his hands with. "We'll watch him for now. I'll stay. You best get Miss Connolly somewhere safe."

Somewhere safe. Was there such a place? Somewhere the Syndicate couldn't reach?

"She can stay with me," Bertram said.

"No." Her answer came swift and without compromise. Bertram was like family to her. The grandfather she had never had. "If they are coming after me, I will not put you in harm's way. You've done enough already."

He started to protest, but Caleb cut him off. "She can stay at the ranch—"

She shook her head. "I appreciate the offer, Caleb, I truly do. But I will not bring this to your doorstep either. You have Rachel, the boys and the baby to protect. This isn't your fight."

"She's right," Hunter said, his gaze never leaving his father. "But it is mine. You'll stay with me."

Bertram stood, his normally jovial demeanor nowhere in evidence. The night's events had peeled it away. "That's hardly proper. Her reputation. What will people say? Especially after Vernon's remark."

"They'll say she's still alive," Mr. Kincaid drawled, the words harsh but true.

"Mr. Kincaid is right," she said. "I'll go with Hunter. He's best equipped to keep me safe. We need to settle this once and for all." And she needed to speak with him, to know why he took the ledger sheet and what agreement his father had referred to.

Bertram turned to her, his fear palpable. "Settle what?"

Meredith stood and pressed her hands against her skirts smoothing the silk and lace beneath her palms. She had dressed so carefully for this meeting, and for what? The decision had been made before she even walked through the door. "This has been a long time coming, Bertram. I know you and Pa wanted to keep me safe and I love you both for it. But it's never going to end, not unless we put an end to it."

"This is suicide!" Bertram turned on Hunter, his face red. "Tell her this is ridiculous!"

Hunter glanced over his shoulder and met her gaze. She tried to read his expression but the dark brown eyes that often held so much had turned hard and emotionless.

"This is how it is," he said. "It's time to end it."

Hunter and Caleb carried his father to the bed in the back room of Doc's office. Hunter hadn't misinterpreted the careful choice of words Doc Whyte had chosen in describing Vernon's condition. He knew where it was heading but his mind shied away from the reality, refusing to reach the same conclusion. He found it strange he should be so affected by his father's imminent death. They were not close. Never had been. His father had never treated him with anything akin to affection or love. He'd provided no role model Hunter wanted to emulate nor imparted any wisdom he held on to. He'd gone out of his

way to make Hunter's life a living hell in ways
he was only now beginning to realize.

And yet.

And yet somewhere inside of him, the boy
who had always wanted a pa, had hoped that
would change. Had hoped his father would see
he was worth his attention. His love. He had been
a fool to hold on to that hope. Even his mother
hadn't thought him worthy enough to take with
her when she went.

The only one who had ever felt that way
about him was Meredith. She'd been the one to
make him see who he truly was, not what was
reflected in his mother's actions or his father's
cold disregard. And in turn her family had done
the same. They'd shown him what family really
meant, what a house filled with love and laughter looked like. They may have struggled to keep
a roof over their heads and food on the table but
in Hunter's mind, they were the richest people
in Salvation Falls.

He was both envious and in awe. He had
wanted nothing more than to re-create that for
himself and Meredith. Then the Syndicate had
destroyed everything. The Syndicate and his father. He had been so blind. Who else had it in
for Abbott Connolly? The Syndicate had broken the law with their rustling and murdering,

but he would bet his last breath that it was his father who had used the opportunity to try and rid himself of Abbott once and for all.

But Abbott had outsmarted him, outsmarted them all. He'd somehow gotten ahold of evidence that could bring them all down and without knowing where the evidence was or what would happen to it if Abbott were to die, he left them hog-tied.

But now they were getting desperate. Now they were gunning for Meredith and taking out anyone they saw as a liability, including Vernon.

It did not bode well.

"I'll give you a few minutes," Caleb said, pressing his hand into Hunter's shoulder as he passed.

Hunter nodded and waited until the door shut behind him. He pulled over a low stool to sit on. His father had started to come around as they were carrying him in and now his eyes were open.

"Vernon?"

His father turned his head toward him and took a minute to focus. He didn't appear to like what he saw. "Where am I?" The words came with effort.

"Doc's office. He's going to watch over you for a bit."

"No point. I'm dying." Hunter didn't argue with his father's proclamation. There was no point. Vernon took note and sniffed, wincing. "Guess you'll be happy about that."

"Not particularly." He'd never wished his father ill. He'd only wished he'd been a better man. Unfortunately, the sentiment hadn't been reciprocated.

"What do you want now? A confession?" That's exactly what Hunter wanted. That and the evidence he needed to bring the Syndicate down. So far, they had been careful not to leave anything that would lead back to them. All Hunter had was a gut full of suspicion and no real evidence to back it up. "You won't get it. Not from me. I won't have them burying me with a cloud over my grave."

"Like they did Abbott Connolly?"

His father mustered up enough energy to glare at him. When he spoke, the words came with effort, staggered and slow. "Bastard never knew when to leave well enough alone. Been a thorn in my side since the day he arrived in town."

"Well you took care of that, didn't you?"

His father's eyes burned. "I saved his worthless life."

"You kept him alive to save your own skin."

His father didn't refute the claim. "The man is dead. What does it matter now?"

"It matters to Meredith."

"Her." He spoke the word with derision, strength returning to his voice for one brief second before fading away again. "You think she'll want you, boy, when she finds it was you who convinced the council members to vote her down so you could run her outta town?"

Hunter didn't bother correcting him. He didn't have the time. "Not that it matters, since it doesn't appear you kept up your end of the bargain. The Syndicate still came gunning for her. You want to explain that?"

Hate sparked in Vernon's eyes. "I spoke to them. See what it got me? You remember that when I take my last breath. My blood is on your hands."

Hunter refused to feel guilty. "This is your doing, not mine. Who are the other members of the Syndicate?" His father said nothing and Hunter's frustration mounted. Time was running out. "They just tried to kill you. What loyalty can you possibly have to them?"

"You want to know who they are, find the evidence Connolly hid. I ain't doing your work for you."

His father coughed and bloody spittle dotted his lips and chin. It wouldn't be long now.

Hunter stood and stared down at his father. Abbott Connolly had spent the last seven years of his life in prison—his wife dead, his daughter on the other side of the country. Yet still, he was freer than Vernon had ever been, trapped in a prison of his own design, the bars fortified with bitterness and hate.

Hunter turned to leave, then stopped. Meredith stood in the doorway connecting the two rooms and from the expression on her face, she hadn't just arrived.

"Mere…" How much had she heard?

She held up a hand to stop him and when she spoke, her voice was low and hollow. "You made a deal with your father? When were you planning on telling me?"

He didn't answer right away. He didn't have one to give her. He hadn't figured it all out yet. All he wanted to do was get her somewhere safe, to take down the Syndicate. Everything else he'd figure out later.

But later came sooner than he expected and the moment for explanations passed. Meredith dropped her hand, turned and left the room as silently as she had entered it. The expression on her face took with her any hope he'd had of a future together.

Despair wrapped around Hunter like a heavy blanket. She no longer trusted him. There was no going back.

"Caleb went to take a walk around, see if he could find anything," Doc Whyte said. Meredith heard his words, watched as Hunter nodded in response, but it meant nothing. It was as if she were standing outside her body watching the events unfold. People moved and talked around her, made plans. She nodded from time to time but it was all a jumble of noise.

He was going to send her away. Again. Worse, he had been the one to convince the council to vote down her shop. Destroy her dreams.

How could she have been so foolish to believe he loved her? That he wanted to build a life with her? Oh, he would dole out the same excuse as last time. That he loved her, that he wanted her safe. But this wasn't seven years ago, and she had thought they were working together.

But they weren't. He was working with his father, pulling strings behind the scenes to keep her from succeeding. To keep her from staying.

It had all been a ruse.

Why he did it hardly mattered. In the end, the result was the same.

Meredith returned to the bench and sat down, her hands firmly clasped in her lap.

"I'll stick around here," Kincaid said to Hunter. "Just in case."

Hunter walked over and stopped in front of her. She couldn't look at him. If she did, she would fall apart. She stared at the button on his coat, at the bloodstain next to it. "I'll take you back to the office."

"I'll need to stop at the hotel first to gather a few things." Her voice sounded flat even to her own ears.

Bertram joined Hunter and crouched down, taking her hands in his. "Please reconsider and stay with me, Meredith."

It was a tempting offer. She could go with Bertram. Hide. Bury her head under blankets and wrap herself in sorrow, but then what? The Syndicate would still be out there. They would still be looking for her. Her father would still be thought of as guilty for crimes he didn't commit.

She stood, forcing Bertram to his feet, as well. She kissed his bearded cheek. "I'll be fine, Bertram. Please don't worry."

They left the warmth of Doc's office for the cold street, Hunter by her side. He had offered his arm but she ignored it, using her hands to hold the ends of her wool shawl together. The streets were deserted; everyone at the Town Hall had rushed back to the safety of their homes. The walk to the hotel was a short one, and Meredith wasted little time ducking behind the dressing curtain to change into her riding habit and exchange her shawl for her cape. It was better suited for movement than the fancy dress she donned to impress people who had already made up their minds. Thanks to Hunter. They said nothing to each other during the walk over, or while in the room. The oppressive silence hung heavy between them.

It wasn't until they were on their way to the jailhouse that Hunter finally spoke.

"You okay?"

"I suppose I should be thankful Mr. Kincaid's reflexes were not dulled by whiskey this evening."

"I should have stayed."

"Why? To see your handiwork in action? Well, you can rest assured you were successful. The vote went as you intended. They turned down my proposal. Although I must applaud your performance. Really, you and Vernon were born for the stage."

From the corner of her eye she saw his head

bow and the mouth she'd kissed so passion-
ately—had it only been the night before?—pull
into a tight line.

"It...it isn't what it seems. I had a good reason—"

"To lie to me? To steal the ledger sheet from
me? To make some deal with your father whom
we both know is a part of the Syndicate? And it
all worked out so well, didn't it?" She couldn't
help the angry edge to her voice. It was a struggle to contain it, to keep it from bubbling over.

"Mere—"

How she wished he would stop calling her
that! She cut him off again, not wanting to hear
his reasons. They paled against the outcome.
They reached the steps of the jailhouse and she
marched up them then whirled around, her cape
whipping about her legs. "It was the Syndicate
that shot at me, I assume?"

He nodded.

"When did you find out your father was involved?"

"Last night."

The air around them stilled. Last night. When
he'd made love to her. "And yet you said nothing?"

"I needed to be sure before I told you."

"When?" One hand gripped the railing. How

could this be happening again? She kept waiting to wake up from the nightmare, but the cold air biting into her skin told her this was no dream. It was real. It was happening. "When you told me you stole the ledger sheet from me?"

He looked at her, his gaze ravaged. Part of her, the foolish part that insisted on still loving him, on praying for an explanation that would make her forgive him one more time, wanted to reach out and touch his face, soothe away the desperation pulling the skin tight against his bones.

"Come inside. We'll talk." He walked up the stairs past her and pushed the door open for her.

A small scream escaped. Was that her? Then Hunter rushed past her and the nightmare took on a new dimension and hurtled her down a dark abyss.

Chapter Nineteen

Meredith's scream echoed off the walls of the dark office. The only light filtered in from the open door and cast a murky shadow over the prone body laid out on the floor.

"Dammit!"

Hunter raced inside and skidded to a stop on his knees next to Jenkins, grabbing the young man. Somewhere behind him Meredith lit a lamp and the weak light edged over the body of his deputy.

"Jenkins!" He turned him over. A deep gash cut into his forehead and left his blond hair crusted with blood. A small pool had soaked into the pine slats beneath him.

"Jenkins, wake up." He gave him a shake. A low moan seeped out and his eyes flickered before closing again. Relief swept through Hunter. He was alive.

"Yucton," Jenkins mumbled, his head falling to one side. An unmoving lump filled the prisoner's bed.

Hunter leaped to his feet and ran to the middle cell but Meredith had beaten him there. The door swung open on its hinges. A quiet creaking noise filled the room. He tried to stop her from pulling the blanket back, but she ignored him.

She staggered back. It wasn't Bill Yucton beneath the blanket.

Even in the pale light, he could see the sickly pallor of her ivory skin as she stared in horror at Wallace Platt's lifeless body, a surprised expression forever locked in his dead eyes.

He grabbed her hand and pulled her out of the cell and into his arms, but she fought against him, pushing him away. She didn't want his comfort. She didn't want him. He'd destroyed any trust he'd rebuilt in one fell swoop and this time, there would be no pardon, no second chance.

"Where's Bill?" Her voice cracked and her eyes shot daggers into his as if somehow he would know. "Where is he? What have they done with him?"

He held out a hand to calm her, knowing it was useless. "I don't know."

"We have to find him!"

"We will." That was a promise he intended to keep.

Whether Bill would be alive, however, was a different thing altogether. He didn't make any promise in that regard. He'd lied to her enough for one day.

Meredith shook off the paralysis wrought by seeing Mr. Platt's dead eyes staring into hers and rushed over to Rory Jenkins. The deputy had taken a nasty hit to the head but he was alive. She issued a swift prayer of thanks, then gently tapped the deputy's face.

"Rory? It's Meredith. Can you wake up?" He opened his eyes again.

"Head hurts."

"I know. We'll take care of you." She tried to keep the urgency and fear out of her voice with mixed results. "Can you tell us what happened?"

Rory closed his eyes and lifted a hand to his head to probe the injured area. Meredith stopped him. She didn't need him doing further damage or making the area bleed again. Based on the pool of blood on the floor, he'd lost enough.

"Don't know. Was sittin' in front of Bill's cell. He was tryin' to teach me how to play chess. Heard a shot and was gonna investigate, but he told me to stay put. I told him I could make my own decisions, then the door burst open. 'Fore I could draw, they got the drop on me. Bill okay?"

Hunter knelt down on the opposite side of Rory. "Did you see who it was?"

"They wore masks, but I swear one of 'em sounded just like Roddy Lewis."

Meredith glanced over at Hunter. Roddy Lewis worked on Vernon's ranch.

"Anything else?"

The deputy shook his head then winced, regretting the motion. "Is Bill okay?"

Meredith took the handkerchief from her reticule and pressed it against Rory's wound. "He's missing. But we'll find him, don't you worry. For now, though, we need to get you looked after." Fear clawed at her insides. What if it was already too late? What if Bill had met the same fate as Wallace Platt?

No. She couldn't think like that. If they had wanted Bill dead, it would be him in the middle cell with a bullet through his head instead of Mr. Platt. If they took him alive, they must need him. Maybe they believed he knew the whereabouts of the evidence Pa had hidden. It might buy them some time.

"C'mon, let's get you over to Doc's," Hunter said, interrupting the thoughts racing through her head. He bent and helped Rory to his feet.

The young deputy wobbled, his balance shot from the knock to the head. Hunter staggered under the bigger man's weight as he readjusted his stance to keep them both upright. His foot knocked against the turned-over table, scattering chess pieces across the floor. The chessboard, which had been teetering on its edge wobbled, then toppled over with a bang.

The sound echoed like a gunshot and made Meredith jump. She stared at the wooden board her father had made her and a funny tingle pulled at the hairs on the back of her neck. She stared it a moment, little pieces of memory trickling back.

Hollowed out the insides, Pa had said. *You just slide this section back. Meant to keep the pieces in there but they don't fit.* He'd chuckled as he tried to fit the hand-carved pieces past the narrow opening. He'd made them too big. He'd shrugged. *No matter. Now you have a secret place to put things. Your ma says every little girl needs a secret place.*

She'd been maybe ten years old then. She shook her head. It had been under her nose the entire time.

Meredith rose to her feet and walked over to the chessboard. She picked it up and hugged it to her. Blood rushed and pounded in her ears until she feared Hunter would hear and wonder why, but she had no plans on telling him. No doubt he would take it from her, then try to send her away like a child who had no business meddling in the affairs of men. Well this was her affair. It was her father and it was her right to prove his innocence.

And she'd be damned if she'd let anyone— Hunter included—stop her from doing that.

If Hunter noticed anything amiss, he gave no indication. He jostled Rory, then glanced her way. "C'mon. I need to set out to find Yucton and I can't leave you here unprotected."

Meredith didn't kick up a fuss. She had no desire to stay here sharing space with Mr. Platt's dead body.

The clouds had shifted and thinned as they stepped outside allowing a sliver of moonlight reflected off the snow and lit their way up Main Street to Doc Whyte's. Hunter kept up a dialogue with Rory in an effort to keep him conscious. As they stumbled inside the office, Kincaid jumped to his feet, gun drawn before all three of them made it through the door.

"What happened?" He reholstered his gun and rushed forward to help with Rory. They wrestled him onto the table Vernon had occupied earlier.

"Yucton's been taken," Hunter said. "How are your tracking skills?"

Mr. Kincaid took the time to look affronted by Hunter's question. "I'm a bounty hunter, what do you think?"

"Then saddle up. Because we've got to go hunt down Yucton and whoever took him."

"Think we both know who took him," Mr. Kincaid said, picking his jacket and hat from the peg near the door.

Meredith stared at the bounty hunter. "You know about the Syndicate?"

Mr. Kincaid returned her level gaze with one of his own as he shrugged into his coat, but didn't answer. He transferred his attention back to Hunter. "We best get going."

"Going where?" Doc Whyte came out of his back office. He nodded toward Hunter. "Your father is holding on." Despite the news, his tone didn't convey much hope. It was just a matter of time.

Hunter nodded and gave the doctor a brief rundown of what had transpired at the jail. "Can you take Meredith to Bertram's?"

Doc Whyte waved him off. "Done, done. Everything's taken care of here."

Hunter turned to her, his hands holding her shoulders. "I'm sorry. I have to go."

She remained silent.

"We'll talk when I get back." He leaned down

and, heedless of Doc Whyte standing behind them, pressed an urgent kiss on her lips. "I will explain everything, just stay out of sight until I get back. Promise?"

She didn't respond. Her mouth still burned from the kiss.

Then he was gone.

She turned to Doc Whyte. "I should stay here." She held a hand up when he made to protest. "I know what Hunter said, but he also told me to stay out of sight. Bertram's apartments are farther up the street. Plus, you've got your hands full here. You could use the help."

"I suppose…" Doc Whyte didn't sound convinced.

"What if something happened to Mr. Donovan or Rory while you were escorting me to Bertram?"

To his credit, Rory managed a well-timed groan, necessitating Doc's attention. "All right, all right. Truth is I could use some help."

"Perfect," Meredith forced a smile. "I'll sit with Mr. Donovan while you tend to Rory."

Doc Whyte, already engrossed in examining Hunter's deputy, nodded absently toward the adjoining room where Vernon was housed. "Fine, fine."

Meredith hurried into the other room. She sat

on the low stool by Vernon's bedside and flipped the chessboard over on her lap. The compartment her father had created was well hidden, seamless. The perfect hiding spot.

She pressed against it and slowly slid the back away from the edges a few inches then held the board up, giving it a hard shake. A piece of paper tumbled out and fell into her lap. She set the chessboard down and picked up the paper, unfolding it. Her hand shook as she held it up to the lamp next to the bed. It was a legend of sorts. A list of six surnames, each with a corresponding code. The same codes used on the missing ledger sheet.

She read them off. "Laidlow. Donovan. McLaren. Kirkpatrick. Reynolds M and Reynolds A."

McLaren. The old sheriff. Hunter would be devastated when he discovered his old mentor had been part of the conspiracy. Or did he already know? Donovan and Laidlow, neither surprised her. Of the final three names, Shamus Kirkpatrick was no longer a threat, having taken on more than he could chew in Rachel and Caleb six months previous, but the Reynolds were not familiar to her.

The Syndicate. Six men who had destroyed her family. Still, the list meant nothing without corresponding proof. And that proof had been stolen from her. Even with the ledger sheet, how did she prove it tied them to the injustice perpetrated against her father? All the ledger sheet showed was payments made to these men. Payments that could be for anything.

She needed more. She needed to find the evidence her father had. Surely this wasn't all of it. She flipped the paper over. Written in her father's hand at the top were the words: *Look into yourself.*

"Oh, Pa, this isn't the time for riddles," she muttered. Her brain was overtaxed as it was with everything that had happened tonight and the words he'd written made no sense to her at all. If she was to look into herself right now, likely all she would see was an ugly, writhing mass of anger and hurt.

Next to her, Vernon's labored breathing rattled, the sound taking on a liquid quality. She glanced at him, his cheeks had sunken somewhat, as if already the solidity of his body was giving over to what came next. It took her a moment to realize his eyes had opened and he was staring at her.

"What are you doing here?" His words were spoken between breaths, the effort leaving him visibly weakened.

"What I came back to Salvation Falls to do. I'm proving my father's innocence." She flipped the paper over and showed him the list. "Recognize this?"

The fever in Vernon's eyes flared briefly, then died. "Doesn't matter now."

But it did. It mattered to her. She'd lost everything because of the men on this list. "I want to know what my father knew, what evidence he had against the Syndicate. I already have a torn ledger page and the legend to decode its meaning, but there's more, isn't there?"

She read the confirmation through his pained expression. "Your pa took what was mine. Deserved what he got."

Anger blazed within her. Even now, on his deathbed, Vernon had the audacity to spout such lies against her father. "My father was a good man. He never stole a thing from you."

"Vivienne." The name was spoken with a reverent mix of love and hate. It disgusted her. His obsession with her mother had never waned, it colored everything he did and twisted him into a bitter, hateful man. He claimed her father had stolen her away, but she'd never been his to start with.

"My mother never belonged to you and she certainly never loved you."

"No." She couldn't tell if the one-word response was a denial to her claim, or an agreement. Meredith shook her head and for the first time in her life she saw Vernon Donovan for what he really was. Not a monster she needed to fear, but a sad, pathetic man who had convinced himself of a lie because he couldn't face the truth. A man who threw away everything of value in his bid to seek revenge on her father for doing nothing more than being the better man. He'd lost his wife, his son and now his life. And for what?

Vernon fell silent and his eyes closed. Meredith berated herself. This wasn't what she'd come here for. She needed information.

"Vernon?"

He opened his eyes again. The color in them had begun to fade as his life slowly ebbed away inch by inch.

"Who is Reynolds?"

"Dead."

"Both of them?"

"One."

It appeared the Syndicate did not come out of their treachery unscathed. She wondered who did them in, but that was neither here nor there at the moment. "Who is the other Reynolds?"

He looked at her. She could see defeat and re-sentment in his gaze. "Bancroft."

She sat up straight. "Anson Bancroft?"

Vernon nodded. Meredith couldn't believe it. She shook her head in disbelief, but it was a fleeting sensation. There had been something about him—a coldness—that had been unde-niable. Had Charlotte known? Is that why she had remained so aloof, not inviting friendship or conversation? Or was it the impetus for Mrs. Bancroft's nervous chatter? She shook her head again. She would deal with that information later. First she needed something to deal with. She needed evidence.

"What is it my father held over you that kept him alive?"

Vernon glared at her but gave up nothing.

She leaned forward and put her mouth close to Vernon's ear. He smelled of sweat, blood and death. "They're after your son now, do you re-alize that? If I don't stop them, if I can't get my hands on this evidence, in all likelihood he will follow you to the grave. I need to know what evidence my father had on the Syndicate. If you won't do it for me, or to clear your own con-science before you meet your Maker, then do it for the sake of your son. You owe him that much, at least."

Vernon shook, whether from anger or from death sinking its talons in a little deeper, she couldn't say. His lips and skin had turned ashen gray.

"The last ledger." Vernon took a shallow breath. It rattled around in his chest before he spoke again. "Had details from that night. Bank accounts. A legend. Plans. Would expose everyone. Your pa hid it. Can't find." His sentences grew shorter, each one requiring a new breath that came harder and harder.

Meredith had the legend. All she needed now was the ledger and plans to put it all together. "Did he give any indication where he hid it?"

Vernon gave a slight shake of his head. "Said it was…staring me right…in the…face but I'd… never…see it… Tried…"

Vernon's eyes closed. Staring him right in the face?

Look into yourself.

She turned her father's words over in her mind, reworked them, changed them around and then it dawned on her. She didn't bother trying to wake Vernon. She had what she needed. The man would meet his Maker, likely before sunrise. He could atone for his sins with Him.

He opened his eyes briefly and stared at her.

"My son…did this for you…damn Connolly women…death of us all…"

She shook her head. "Your son lied to me and tried to send me away."

"He tried…save you…at his own expense… not worth it…"

At his own expense? What was he talking about? She looked down at the man who had wreaked such havoc in her life. Should she say something—a prayer, forgiveness? No words came. In the end, Vernon Donovan had made his bed, and now he lay there dying in it. A profound sadness settled around her. Such a wasted life.

She turned and left the room. "How is he?" she asked, walking over to the table where Rory's large frame had been wrestled into a sitting position. He smiled when he saw her, though it was obvious the poor boy was in pain.

"Doc says I'm gonna be okay, but I gotta stay awake. Guess he wants me to be able to enjoy the doozy of a headache I got."

She returned Rory's smile and patted his shoulder. "I'm just thankful that's all you have to contend with."

"Yes, ma'am."

Meredith turned to Doc Whyte. "Mr. Donovan isn't doing so well. He was asking for you." She didn't much care for lying to the good doctor, but she needed to slip away and that would be easier done without a roomful of people.

She waited until Doc disappeared into the other room and closed the door behind him before she turned her attention back to the injured deputy. "Rory, I need to go back to the hotel for a minute. If Doc comes out, please tell him I'll be careful and not to worry."

Rory nodded then winced, putting a hand to his head. "You're not really going to the hotel are you?"

Meredith twisted her mouth to one side. She hated lying. It didn't come naturally to her.

"Doc said Mr. Beckett went looking for Bancroft. My guess is he likely left Jasper in Doc's stables out back. In case you need a horse or somethin'. Jus' don't tell him I mentioned it. I already got one lump on my head."

She didn't like hearing Caleb had gone to confront Mr. Bancroft, or Reynolds, or whatever his real name was. But she had learned enough about Rachel's husband to know he was capable of handling himself and going up against the worst. She had to believe he would be okay.

"Thank you, Rory."

He nodded. "Just be careful. Sheriff Donovan will have my hide if'n anything happens to you.

That is if Mr. Beckett don't get to me first 'cause I told you to take his horse."

"I will. You be sure and follow Doc's instructions." She left Doc's office and headed to the stables.

She knew exactly where her father had hidden the evidence.

"You want to tell me how it is you know so much about these men we're tracking," Hunter asked, surprised at how quickly Kincaid picked up the trail in the dark. The clouds had blown to the other side of the mountains by now, leaving ample moonlight to guide their way until they hit the wooded area. Kincaid had had the foresight to grab a lamp from Doc's office on his way out the door and every now and again he'd hold it up to confirm he was where he wanted to be. The bounty hunter seemed to have a sixth sense about how the men who took Bill would react.

He shrugged. Hunter had learned Kincaid was not big on sharing. "Idiots generally all act the same. Isn't that hard to figure them out."

The horses plodded along side by side. "Then how about you tell me why you agreed to help Bill Yucton."

"Told you. The man paid me to do a job."

"Uh-huh. And what was that job again?"

Hunter had an easier time dislodging a deeply embedded splinter than he did getting a straight answer from Kincaid.

"You aren't the only one who's got a beef with these men."

"And what's your beef with them?"

"Shh!" Kincaid held up a hand and shot him a sharp glare.

They reined in their horses and fell silent. He thought Kincaid was overreacting. They weren't far from town at this point. It didn't make sense the men who took Yucton would stop here. But he held his position and kept his mouth shut. If Kincaid had the right of it, then they weren't looking to get away. They expected to be followed.

The only sound Hunter heard was the occasional hoot of an owl in the far distance and the deep breathing of the animals they rode. Then it came. A swift crack of a twig to his right from somewhere inside the dense thatch of trees where the moonlight couldn't penetrate. Hunter drew his Colt and tried to see through the darkness, but there was nothing. He chanced a look toward Kincaid, but the bounty hunter was searching in the opposite direction.

A shot rang out and spooked the horses. His horse reared as Kincaid's shimmied, its hindquarters slamming into his horse and throwing him off balance. Hunter jumped off amidst the sound of Kincaid's answering shot. He hit the cold ground hard and rolled down the gradual slope leading toward the forest. That's when he saw it. The shadowy movement about twenty feet away.

Shots sounded simultaneously. It happened in seconds, maybe even less than that, but time had lost meaning at that point, stretching out until everything slowed to a crawl. Hunter recognized the sickening sound of a bullet hitting flesh and a coinciding grunt. His or the shooter's? Heat seared up his arm, the shock causing him to stumble and lose his footing.

His back hit the ground first, then his head. Pain exploded through his skull, then everything went black.

Chapter Twenty

Hunter's head and arm throbbed fiercely, taking turns until it reminded him of a pendulum clock. He managed to stem the blood from the wound in his arm, but there wasn't much to be done about his head. Near as he could tell the damage to his skull was minimal save for the egg-size lump where he'd hit the rock beneath him. At this rate, he and Jenkins would be sporting matching bandages. He wondered if his deputy's brains felt as scrambled as his did at the moment. He'd tried twice to stand and both times his head swam and knocked the legs out from beneath him. Finally, he dragged himself over to rest against the thick trunk of a white-bark pine.

The shooter lay about a hundred yards away. It was Roddy Lewis, one of his father's men. He hadn't moved, twitched or groaned since Hunter had come to. If he wasn't dead he was on his way there.

The quiet of the forest unnerved him. Kincaid was long gone—alive or dead, Hunter had no way of knowing, but it didn't appear he would be returning any time soon. His own horse grazed nearby, making a meal of the moss scrambling over a large rock, apparently unconcerned his rider sat on the leaf-strewn ground, the cold soaking through his clothes until he forgot what warmth felt like.

"Don't suppose you want to go for help?" The horse's ears flickered but he continued with his meal. "No…didn't think so."

"This your idea of a rescue posse?"

The words came from the other side of the path beaten through the middle of the forest. Hunter drew his gun, thankful the bullet had hit his left arm. He couldn't see through the darkness to find where the voice had come from, but he recognized it just the same. "Come out where I can see you," he yelled. He didn't want to take the chance Yucton was being used as bait to lure him out.

Yucton ambled out from behind a tree, a lantern swinging from his hand. He patted Hunter's disloyal mount on the hindquarters as he walked past. The man moved as if he was out for an evening stroll. Hunter wondered if his head injury wasn't more severe than he'd originally thought because there was no way on earth Yucton should be alive, let alone walking free.

He lowered his revolver when it was clear Yucton was alone. "How the hell—"

The outlaw crouched down next to him. "You took out one of 'em and Kincaid took off after the other two. Left me all by my lonesome. Just had to work myself free. Turns out not one of those three idiots could tie a decent knot."

Hunter shook his head and regretted the action instantly. "Kincaid hasn't come back."

"Doubt he will either."

"You think he's dead?"

"No." Yucton reached for Hunter's uninjured arm and helped him to his feet. "I think the man is chasing a ghost and he won't stop until he lays it to rest."

Hunter winced with each step he took toward his horse but bit by bit he regained his footing and felt a little less like tossing the contents of his stomach. Though he expected that situation would change drastically once he sat atop his horse.

"What's that mean?"

"Means those demons you kept accusing Kincaid of chasing are the same ones we're after now. If he caught up with the other two, I suspect he'll be on his way back to Colorado to try and put those demons to rest."

"Are you talking in riddles or has the lump on my head made me daft?"

Yucton chuckled and leaned on the saddle horn. "This Syndicate reaches a lot further than just your little town. And unfortunately, Kincaid found himself in their crosshairs. It didn't end well and the man wants his retribution. Our meeting up was no accident. He searched me out and not for the bounty."

"So it's safe to say we can cross him off the posse list for now, then."

"I wouldn't sit around bleeding like a stuck pig waiting for him to return." Yucton set the lantern on the ground and gave Hunter a leg up on his horse. The sudden movement forced him to grip the pommel and close his eyes as the landscape tilted.

Once the world righted itself, Hunter opened his eyes again. "You mean to tell me Kincaid knew the names of the men involved in the Syndicate this whole time?"

Yucton shook his head. "He knew one man. Reynolds. But didn't have a face to go with the name. He suspected Laidlow based on past dealings and through him he traced the Syndicate to Salvation Falls and to me. By then, Bertram had wired me to let me know Meredith was returning to town. Figured that would stir up a big mess, especially if they thought she knew where Abbott had hidden the evidence. I made a deal with Kincaid—he could bring me in and collect the bounty on the promise he'd stay long enough to ensure Meredith was safe."

"What did this Reynolds do to him?"

"He never gave specifics and I didn't ask. Case you hadn't noticed, Kincaid ain't much of a talker."

"I noticed."

"Hang tight. Got a horse just over that hill." He tossed Hunter a handkerchief. "Try and tie that wound off."

A minute later, Yucton returned mounted on a chestnut-colored mare. Hunter had wrapped the wound in his arm as best he could, securing the knot with his teeth and gun hand. It would have to suffice.

Hunter took the reins. "We need to get back to town." He'd left a mess in his wake, worse than the one seven years ago. He needed to find Meredith. What she must be thinking of him right now, guilty of trying to run her out of town twice and lying to her both times. There had been no time to explain to her it was just a temporary measure. Even less time than that to convince her he loved her more than his next breath.

She'd heard the words before, but it was his actions she'd remember.

"Town is exactly where we're heading," Yucton said, pulling Hunter out of his muddled thoughts. "The jailhouse to be exact."

Hunter shook his head, then wished he hadn't. "Why?" He didn't want to go back to the jailhouse, he wanted to find Meredith, to apologize, to try and make things right.

Yucton leaned on his saddle and grinned. "Abbott Connolly was a crafty bugger. He liked to build things. Now and again, he'd build a little hideaway in things. I hadn't thought anything of it until they came to get me. I put up a bit of a struggle, knocked over the chessboard. When it hit the ground, I noticed a piece at the back split. It was then I remembered. We get that chessboard and find out what he hid inside of it and I bet we get our evidence, or at least a clue as to where he hid it."

"There's only one problem with that idea."

"Which is?"

"Meredith took the chessboard with her." She had picked it up when they'd transported Jenkins to Doc's. He hadn't thought anything of it other than she had a sentimental attachment given her father had made it. But what if she had seen the compartment, as well? If Yucton was right, and the evidence was hidden inside, what would she do?

She'd use it to prove her father's innocence.

"We need to get back to town. Now!"

Meredith ignored the pinch of guilt about borrowing Caleb's horse. The escalated situation dictated urgency. The less time she spent out in the open, the better. She worried the Syndicate might be watching her every move, but several checks over her shoulder revealed she was alone. Still, she pushed her heels into Jasper to hurry him along. He was a fine piece of horseflesh, strong and sleek. He widened his stride with ease and the ground passed beneath her in a blur.

She leaned over the horse's neck and held on tight. It had been a long time since she'd ridden like this, but the feeling left her exhilarated despite the dangers.

Relief swept through her as the homestead came into sight. She pulled up on the reins and slid from the saddle, leading Jasper to the side of the house. She tethered him by the water barrel, breaking the thin layer of ice on top.

"Stay out of sight, handsome." She patted the horse's neck. "I won't be long."

She nudged the door of the cabin open, putting her shoulder into it where the top corner liked to stick against the frame when the weather turned cold. The interior was silent as a tomb and in a way she guessed that's what it was. An altar to her past, to a time before the world had come crashing down around them and taken it all away.

When she first returned, she had hoped to move back here once she established her business. Now she knew better. Hunter would get his wish after all. She couldn't stay here. She couldn't stay anywhere in Salvation Falls. Her heart would never survive seeing him every day, knowing she had hung her hopes on him once again only to be played the fool. She had wondered once how much pain a body could stand before it just gave up. Now she had her answer.

She walked into the cabin and fished in her pocket for the matches she'd filched from Doc Whyte's table. She struck one against the mantel above the fireplace. The flame burst from the end and she placed it against the wick of a candle that had sat there these past seven years. It was almost down to its nub, but it should suffice. She didn't need much time.

Said it was...staring me right in the face, but I'd never see it...

Vernon Donovan's words echoed in Meredith's mind coupled with the words written on the list containing names of the Syndicate's members. She put two and two together. Pa was right—Vernon would never have seen it, even if he had found her father's clue in the chessboard. But she knew her father better than most, understood the way his mind worked. She'd been deciphering his riddles since she was a girl and she'd deciphered this one.

Memories washed over her as she stepped away from the fireplace, taking the candle with her. Her footsteps echoed through the empty home. Her heart ached over the loss of her family, but deep inside she was thankful for what she'd had. Hunter hadn't been so lucky, with a father twisted with bitterness and a mother who had run off without a backward glance. He'd once told her when they were married he would make sure their home was filled with love and laughter. He didn't want their children to grow up in the cold and lifeless atmosphere he had.

Well, it hardly mattered now. None of them would get their wish on that account.

She turned to her left and walked down the short hallway into the back room that had been her parents' bedroom. Over the bureau, an oval mirror hung on the wall. It was the only one in the house. Pa had saved for a year to buy it for

Mama. A crack ran through the middle, something that hadn't been there when she'd left seven years ago.

She stared at it a moment. Had the Syndicate been here already? But of course they had. No doubt they would have turned the place upside down and inside out. That had been why the furniture had looked slightly out of place on her last visit. Someone would have cleaned up after them. Hunter?

She hurried over to the mirror and carefully lifted it off the wall. She rested it on the floor, facedown. The back was covered with a thin layer of wood nailed into the frame. Fishing in her pocket, she pulled out the sharp knifelike instrument she'd taken from Doc and used it to pry the backing off at one edge, lifting it far enough to see inside. She pulled the candle closer. The flickering light revealed a small rectangular object wrapped in cloth and wedged near the bottom.

Outside, Jasper nickered and snorted in the cold. Meredith stopped, her muscles rigid as she listened. Blood rushed and pounded in her ears.

Was that...?

The pace of her heart increased tenfold. She let the backing snap back into place and rushed to the window pulling back the dusty curtain to peer outside.

Two riders came down the sloping hill toward the house. They were fewer than a hundred yards away. Too close for her to make a run for it. She let the curtain fall back into place and rushed back to the mirror. It was too heavy to lift back over the tall bureau. She scanned the room quickly then shoved it under the bed. She pulled at the bed's sideboard and it fell open. A breath of relief escaped her as she found her father's rifle in its old hiding place. She grabbed it as a cold burst of air blew in and guttered the candle on the floor.

"You can set that down nice and easy, Miss Connolly, lest Tyrone here might be tempted to blow a hole in your back with his."

"Rider," Yucton said, nodding straight ahead.

Hunter squinted into the distance. The buildings of the town formed a dark shadow on the horizon. It had started to snow again and big flakes filled the air. The tracks they'd made earlier were nowhere in sight.

"Caleb." He recognized the ease with which his friend rode, the relaxed posture in the saddle as if he'd been born in it. "But that's not his horse." He had become accustomed to associating the two together as if they were one entity.

Hunter pressed his heels into his own horse and immediately regretted the faster trot. He was happy to finally draw up on the reins when they reached Caleb.

"What happened to your horse?"

"Meredith Connolly happened to my horse." Caleb arched an eyebrow. "What happened to your arm?"

"Meredith? Is she hurt?" He pointed to his wound as an afterthought. "Kincaid and I ran into some trouble."

"Meredith left Doc's on the premise of going back to the hotel."

"Did you find her?"

Caleb shook his head. "I was at the hotel looking for Bancroft. He's gone by the way. Cleared out."

"Where is she, then?" His stomach clenched, his worst fears realized. She *had* found something in the chessboard.

Caleb shook his head. "The snow had covered her trail by the time I returned. She was in with your father for a few minutes. When Doc went in to check on him she snuck out, taking my horse with her. Jenkins admitted the hotel story was just a ruse. I thought maybe she'd come after the two of you. Where's Kincaid?"

Yucton answered, "Kincaid lit out after the men who took me."

"Meredith didn't come after us," Hunter said. "She didn't know which trail we were taking either way. What did my father tell her?"

The old mare shifted under Caleb. Puffs of white streamed out of her nose with each heavy breath. Caleb sat silent in the saddle for a moment, his steady gaze unwavering. His father was gone. He knew before Caleb said the words. "I'm sorry, Hunter."

Hunter nodded, pushing back the mixed emotions that came with the news. He didn't have time to deal with them now. He could pick through them later. Right now he needed to find Meredith.

"There's more," Caleb said. "Laidlow came by Doc's office. Said he was there to see Vernon, old friends that they were. Doc wasn't sure what was said, but when he went back in to check on your father, he was gone."

"Helped along by the judge, no doubt," Yucton said. "If Donovan held on to the ledgers detailing the Syndicate's operations, he made himself a liability."

"He made himself a liability the minute he

signed up with them," Hunter said, his voice grim. "C'mon. We need to find Meredith."

Caleb's mare shook its mane, the snow clinging to it flying off. "Any idea where she might have gone?"

"Same place we're going would be my guess," Yucton said. "The old homestead."

Chapter Twenty-One

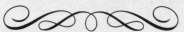

Judge Laidlow's voice cut through Meredith and the wild beating of her heart stuttered to a stop. For a fleeting second, she considered taking her chances, but she knew by the time she raised the rifle to her shoulder, she'd be dead. It wasn't worth the risk. She had to find another way out of this.

She set the rifle down. Would they shoot her in the back anyway? Her insides had turned to jelly. There was no reason in the world for them to let her out of here alive. If she offered them up the evidence as an exchange, they would kill her once they had their hands on it. If she didn't, they would kill her anyway. It was safer that way. With her gone, no one would care one whit about the Syndicate or bringing them down.

"That's my girl. Now step backward slowly

and let me see those hands of yours lifted nice and high."

She glanced over her shoulder. As promised, Laidlow's hired gun had his own rifle raised and ready. She supposed she should be flattered they considered her such a threat. She wished she possessed the ability to live up to it, but in truth, she had no idea what to do to protect herself or stop them from doing whatever it was they intended.

Is this where it ended? It seemed a strange kind of symmetry to leave this world in the same place you came into it. Sadness crept upon her. There was so much she had left to do. Goodbyes she wanted to make. Conversations left to be had. Funny, how you always think there's all the time in the world to take care of these things, then when the time comes you look back and see all the minutes you wasted not doing them.

She could have come home sooner. Left Aunt Erma and spent more time with Pa. She could have returned to Salvation Falls and made a life for herself, a life she wanted and not one foisted onto her by circumstance. Maybe she could have loved a little more. Shrugged off her anger a little sooner. Forgiven a little easier. Listened a little better. Hunter told her he could explain why he'd done what he had, that things weren't what they seemed. What had he meant? Now she would never know.

Maybe if she'd known the kiss Hunter gave her when he left Doc Whyte's to find Bill was to be her last, she would have accepted it with more grace. Pulled him a little closer, kissed him a little harder.

Maybe.

Now it was too late.

Having a gun pointed at your back and no way to escape could put things into stark perspective for you. Not that Hunter didn't have a lot to answer for, but suddenly, she realized she wanted to hear his explanation, weigh out his reasoning and balance it against the hurt it had caused. She wanted the chance to know if she could get over it, find a way to walk past the hurt and eventually leave it behind.

All the things you never think about in the moment when the hurt is happening and your only reaction is to pull away, lash out. Shut down.

She stopped walking backward. She swallowed her fear and turned around. If they were going to kill her, they could look her straight in the eye when they did it.

"What do you want?"

"Oh, I think that's obvious, don't you?" Laidlow walked over to the table and set his lamp on top of it, turning up the wick to spread a pool of light across the floor. She stood just outside its reach.

"What's obvious is that you've broken into my home and are now holding me hostage at gunpoint. I'd like to know how you're going to explain that one to the authorities should anything happen to me."

Laidlow laughed causing his jowls to vibrate. "The way I see it, no one will be the wiser. Tyrone will put a bullet through your head and a gun in your hand. We'll ride away and it will look as if you couldn't cope with the disappointment of your family name ruined and your business proposal rejected. Quite sad, really."

"You'll leave a trail. People will know I wasn't alone."

Laidlow gestured toward the window. "It's snowing, my dear. Our tracks will be well covered by the time anyone thinks to come looking for you." Her gaze flitted toward the window to her left. True to his word, the snow fell in fat flakes obscuring her view of anything beyond the hill that led down to the homestead. It was as if Fate conspired against her, giving Laidlow every opportunity to pull off what he needed.

"Hunter will—"

"I wouldn't hold out any hope your sheriff will come. I took care of that little issue."

Fear strangled her, making it difficult to get the words out. "What do you mean?"

The judge's mouth twisted into a sick grin. "I'm afraid dear Bill's abduction was just a distraction. My men have instructions to lie in wait. It pains me to inform you Sheriff Donovan and Bill Yucton will not be making the return trip to town."

Her body trembled. "Hunter will figure out what you've done. He won't fall for it."

"He will. And even if he doesn't, my men will find him and kill him, then ride on. It will look like what it was—an ambush that your dear sheriff did not survive. One way or the other, I will have my way." He took a step toward her, his shadow crawling over her. She shuddered as if he'd touched her. "As you may have noticed, I am not one for leaving loose ends."

"Is that why you tried to kill Vernon?" Meredith shifted her feet, taking a small step forward, allowing herself a brief glimpse out the window. Dark forms appeared on the horizon. Her heart leaped, but she quickly tamped it down and looked away. For all she knew, it could be more of Laidlow's men. There was no reason anyone would come looking for her here. No one knew of her plans or the information she had found.

She was alone in this. So close to proving her father's innocence and yet now, with a gun pointed at her heart, so far away.

The judge's expression darkened. "I did more than try, I succeeded. Vernon got sloppy. He never should have kept those ledgers. If he had dealt more efficiently with your father in the beginning, this mess would have been over and done with long ago. It's been left to me to clean up his mistakes."

Tyrone sneered and sniffed and Meredith would have bet her last dollar he was the one who had put the bullet through Vernon's chest.

"So you're the leader of the Syndicate, then?" She had to keep him talking. She needed to buy herself time, to at least try to find a way to escape.

She chanced another furtive glance out the window. The dark shadow grew closer but the snow kept it obscured.

"I wouldn't worry your pretty little head about the particulars of our group."

She ignored him. "Who is Reynolds?" Laidlow's nostrils flared. She'd obviously hit on a sore spot. The pompous judge was not the one calling the shots. "I see. Perhaps it isn't so much that *you* don't like loose ends but that your boss doesn't. Did he tell you to clean up your mess or you would end up like Vernon?" She remembered the cold look Anson Bancroft had given her at lunch that day. The man had ice in his veins.

"Reynolds is long gone. I am the one in charge now."

She chanced one last glance out the window. Her heart sank. The shadow on the ridge was gone. It had been nothing more than the play of light and a figment of her imagination. An imagination that wanted to live, to have another chance.

"Where is the evidence?" Laidlow took a step forward.

"I don't know." She hated how her voice shook.

"I think you do. And I think you'd best tell me. My patience is wearing very thin."

Meredith didn't doubt he would kill her. He would put a bullet straight through her and walk away without a moment's remorse. He would have done the same to her father had Pa not been smart enough to see it coming and cagey enough to do something about it.

"What makes you think I'll just hand it over?"

"What other choice do you have if you value your life?"

It was an empty threat. "You're going to kill me either way. I'm a loose end, remember?"

"Indeed you are. The question is, will I show mercy and kill you quickly, or will I let Tyrone here have his fun first?" Tyrone grinned and bile burned Meredith's throat. "Where is the evidence?"

She swallowed. Her time was up. No one was coming. "It's in here."

"Show me."

Pa's rifle lay on the floor near the bed. She edged toward it. If she was going down, she would go down shooting. Maybe if she could kill one or both of them before they did her in, the story of a despondent woman killing herself wouldn't be as believable. Maybe someone would look a little closer, find the evidence hidden in the mirror and Pa's name would be cleared.

She'd like to see that, though right now the chances were not looking good.

She took a step forward closer to the rifle. "How does Sheriff McLaren figure into this?"

"A means to an end, nothing more. The man wanted to retire. We offered to make that a more profitable prospect, provided he looked the other way while we did business. Every man has his price. Unfortunately, his conscience started to get the better of him after your father was arrested."

"For a crime he didn't commit."

Laidlow shrugged in response as if her father's innocence was irrelevant. As if lives hadn't been changed forever. Destroyed beyond repair. She hoped there was a special place in hell for him where he would be the one judged and sentenced for all the pain he'd caused in the name of greed.

"You're stalling." Laidlow waved a hand at the room. "Where is it?"

She pointed. "Under the bed."

"Get it."

Her mind worked quickly. "I can't. It's hidden in the far end of the bed, next to the wall. The bed is too low to fit under and too heavy for me to move on my own."

Laidlow motioned to Tyrone. "Help her."

Tyrone set his gun against the wall, well out of her reach and Laidlow bent and picked up her father's rifle. She bit back the desperation clawing at her insides. She had no weapon, no hopes of escape and within a matter of minutes they would have the evidence in their bloodstained hands. She needed more time. She needed—

Before she could finish the thought, the front door exploded inward. Tyrone turned and lunged for his rifle. Without thinking, Meredith kicked blindly, her boot connecting with bone and throwing him off balance. A shot rang out. Tyrone slumped against the wall and slid to the floor. Her gaze flew to the bedroom door. A thin plume of smoke curled up from the barrel of Hunter's gun. He was alive! Caleb Beckett pointed his Colt at Laidlow's head.

She would have sighed in relief if Laidlow didn't still have her father's rifle aimed directly at her.

"Move and she's dead," he growled.

Meredith didn't dare breathe.

"It won't do you any good," Hunter said. "You're a dead man before you even pull the trigger."

"And if you're wrong?"

"Then you're a dead man either way."

Laidlow lifted the rifle a little higher, settling it tightly against his shoulder. Her knees shook. "If he shoots—"

"He won't," Hunter said, his voice laced with steel. The lamplight wavered and for the first time she noticed the makeshift bandage around his arm. Laidlow hadn't been lying about the ambush.

"Will you lookee here?" Meredith jumped as Bill Yucton waltzed into the room with a casual saunter as if nothing unusual was going on. He had no gun she could see and his hands were buried in the back pockets of his pants. He smiled at

Laidlow. "Doesn't appear to be your lucky day, does it, Judge?"

"You'll never prove a thing. It'll be your word against mine. Who do you think they'll believe? An outlaw, a gunman? The daughter of a cattle rustler?"

"I found the evidence," Meredith pointed out.

If Laidlow's gaze had been daggers she would have expired on the spot.

Hunter looked at her for the first time and she caught a glint of fear and relief etched into his face. He was alive. He was standing here before her when she'd feared she would never see him again and he was alive. All the maybes, would haves, should haves rushed back to her and in the back of her mind a question formed: Could she? Could she forgive? Could she at least try?

She wasn't sure and right now it didn't matter. The only thing that mattered was that he was alive. The rest they could figure out later.

"It's under the bed," she continued. "Vernon said Pa had enough evidence on the Syndicate to see them all hang."

Laidlow jerked the rifle harder against his shoulder and pulled the trigger. Two shots rang out, but Meredith didn't see either of them. Bill's saunter had brought him closer to her and the second Laidlow's finger pulled the trigger, Bill turned so all she could see was his back.

A scream caught in her throat as she waited for Bill to fall to the floor. It didn't happen. He turned around and smiled at her. Smiled!

"Your pa never loaded that damn rifle of his. He was too afraid you'd get your hands on it once you figured out where he kept it hidden."

When Bill stepped away, Hunter and Caleb were hauling Laidlow to his feet, a bullet hole in each leg.

"He's not dead," she whispered.

Hunter turned to her and his expression softened. "Thought it might be better to let the law deal with him." He nodded toward the bed. "Bring the evidence. I'm sure a jury will love to see the truth for a change."

Breath rushed in and out of her lungs. Bill nudged Hunter out of the way and he and Caleb struggled with the barely conscious judge, pushing and pulling him through the bedroom door to the horses waiting outside.

Hunter walked over to where she was rooted to the spot, unable to move. "Are you okay?" She nodded. Yes. No. Maybe. "You think when all this is said and done we might get a chance to talk?"

Meredith nodded again. "I think I'd like that."

Chapter Twenty-Two

Meredith swept the dust on the floor of the back room into a tidy little pile, humming as she went. The fire in the woodstove created a cozy warmth that spread into the shop area out front. It would be a few weeks yet before she opened for business, but for now she was enjoying the preparation. Trunks containing bolts of cloth were stacked along a far wall waiting to be unpacked and put on display, her books of patterns resting on top. She'd also ordered accessories, though it would be another month or so before they arrived.

It had been almost two weeks since the incident at the homestead. Laidlow sat in the jail cell once occupied by Bill and awaited his own trial, scheduled to start early next week. Meredith was set to testify, but most of the evidence against him would come from her father.

She had visited Pa's grave, let him know his permanent marker was on the way, though below his name she had decided against the epitaph of an innocent man. By now, everyone in town knew he was exactly that. Instead, she requested below his name the phrase: *Look into yourself.*

She had realized in the days following, her father's cryptic riddle had also been wonderful advice and she had taken it. She examined her feelings, let go of the anger and resentment she had carried for so long, and learned to forgive. It hadn't been easy, and at times it hadn't been pretty, but she'd forced herself to do it. She'd put herself in Hunter's shoes and asked what would she have done to save him? The answer came swift and easy. She would have done anything. How could she blame him for doing the same?

She had been on the precipice of death, gazed down its gaping jaws and been snatched to safety by Hunter, Caleb and Bill. It gave her a different perspective on things. And her father's letter helped.

Inside the package hidden behind the mirror, Pa had left something else. A letter to his daughter, filled with fatherly advice. He reminded her of the love he shared with her mother, but he also reminded her of the past they both needed to overcome. He had not come to her mother a gentleman of honor, he claimed, but a man with a past far less respectable than she deserved. But their love allowed her to forgive his past mistakes and forge a new future. The words hit home and she wondered if her father hadn't foreseen the problems the promise he'd extracted from Hunter would cause down the road.

Her father always did have a habit of thinking a few steps ahead of everyone else.

The thought made her smile.

"Nice place you got here."

She spun around, broom in her hand. "Hunter."

He leaned against the door frame separating the front and back of the shop. One arm was tied up in a sling while it healed from the bullet wound. She hadn't seen much of him. He'd spent two days on strict bed rest insisted upon by Doc Whyte and after that…well, after that he'd simply made himself scarce, though she had noticed a bunch of fresh lavender and herbs on her mother's grave.

"Getting settled, I see." He glanced around the room. Her worktables were in place, thanks to Bill, and the sign rested on top of one of them waiting to be hung over the door.

Connolly Designs & Dresses.

"I'm trying. The council reversed their decision." The ruling had come down within a week of the events at the homestead. A special meeting had been called to deal with it. She was certain both Hunter and Bertram had had a hand in it, and she would be forever grateful. Preparing the shop for opening had given her something to do. A bit of a respite from all the thoughts and emotions she'd dealt with in the aftermath.

She and Hunter hadn't spoken about the ordeal. She had seen him during the sparsely attended service for Vernon and gave her condolences but the exchange was stilted and awkward. He'd told her he wanted to talk, but so far, he had kept his distance. She didn't press, giving him the space he needed to grieve and heal.

"Has there been any word on Mr. Kincaid?"

Hunter shook his head. "Not yet. I'll keep you posted if you like."

"Please." She worried about the bounty hunter. He had saved her life, pulling her out of harm's way at the Town Hall. She didn't want to see him come to any harm, self-inflicted or otherwise. "Thank you for the flowers at Mama's grave."

"You're welcome."

Meredith's fingers tapped against the broom handle as she struggled to find something else to say. The weather had been nice, despite an early snowfall. Rachel had complained Caleb was becoming a nervous nursemaid the more her belly grew. Bertram was talking about retirement again, which would never come to fruition. Bill seemed happy in his newly installed position of foreman at the Diamond D Ranch, leaving Hunter free to continue on as sheriff.

But those topics were just fillers, words put in the way of the things that really needed to be said, so she held her tongue, and her breath, and she waited.

Hunter didn't disappoint.

"I owe you an apology."

She remained silent and waited.

"I shouldn't have kept you in the dark like I did," he said, walking into the room. His footsteps echoed against the walls and beat against her heart. He stopped a few feet from her and she gripped the broom handle tighter to keep from reaching out and drawing him in closer.

"Why did you?"

He hesitated and stared down at the floor between them. The fingers of his injured arm flexed. When he looked up, reflected in his dark eyes was everything they had been through, everything they'd lost and gained and lost again. He looked as battered as her heart felt and she suddenly understood she wasn't the only casualty in all of this.

"When your room was broken into, it scared

the hell out of me." He shook his head at the admission. "Right to the bones. The idea that you could have been in there, not gotten away. And when you showed me the ledger sheet, I recognized the writing and that scared me even more. My own father had a hand in it. My own father, Mere!"

She took a step forward and touched his uninjured arm, offering what comfort she could. "I'm sorry, Hunter."

He nodded and took a breath. "I wanted to be sure, before I said anything. I kept hoping I was wrong. When I found the rest of the ledgers and confronted him, I realized who he really was. *What* he really was. He offered me a deal—if I got you out of Salvation Falls and promised to quit my job and take over the ranch, he'd ensure no harm came to you."

Meredith's eyes widened. That was the agreement Vernon had referred to. The news staggered her. She couldn't imagine Hunter working with his father, knowing what he did. It was a little like selling your soul to the devil. Only he hadn't done it for riches, or for power. He'd done it for her. To keep her safe.

Shades of her father who had sacrificed himself to save her. Because he had loved her. And she smiled again, through the pain in her heart.

One dark eyebrow arched upward. "You're smiling?"

"Why did you agree to such a thing?"

He threw up his good arm. "I did it to save you. You were so bullheaded stubborn about proving your father's innocence that you refused to stop for even a minute to realize the danger you were in. When my father threatened you—"

"Vernon threatened me?"

"Of course he threatened you! That's what he does when he wants someone to comply. He threatens and he bullies and he—" Hunter stopped and suddenly quieted. "Well, I guess he doesn't do any of that anymore."

"No," she agreed, seeing the conflicted emotions cross Hunter's face. She stepped closer and slipped her hand into his for comfort. The contact of skin on skin sent a wash of warmth spreading through her and her body sighed in relief.

"Anyway." He squeezed her hand as if acknowledging he felt the same thing. "I couldn't risk anything happening to you."

"So you convinced the council to vote down my proposal."

He smirked. "No. I lied to Vernon. I needed him to believe it, to buy us some time. I figured I could get you out of town where you were safe. Maybe send Bill with you to make sure."

"Bill? He was in on it?" Hunter gave her a sheepish look and shrugged. "So what was your plan after you sent me packing?"

"I would pressure my father into admitting to the crimes or uncover enough evidence to force him to reveal who the other members of the Syndicate were and bring them down."

"Then what?"

He grinned. "Then I would ride up on my white horse like some ridiculous knight in shining armor, tell you it was safe to return and ask for your hand in marriage—at which point you would be so grateful you would fall into my arms and profess your undying love."

She pulled her lips in to hide her smile. "I see. That's quite the plan."

"Not really. I messed it up from the get-go."

"How'd you do that?" She moved a little closer until she could feel the heat from his body mingled with the cold air still clinging to his sheepskin coat. He smelled of the outdoors and she breathed him in.

"I treated you like a damsel in distress. Truth is, you were anything but. If it wasn't for you, we wouldn't have found the evidence your father had hidden." He let go of her hand and placed his under her chin, tilting her face up to his. "I shouldn't have excluded you. I was an idiot."

"You were."

"I promise you, I won't do it again." His voice dropped to a whisper and his thumb caressed the edge of her bottom lip. Need pulsated deep inside of her. "I messed this up. I messed *us* up, and I know I have no right to ask your forgiveness, but…"

"But?"

He smiled. A real smile this time so it reached all the way up to his eyes and crinkled their edges. "But I'm going to anyway. I love you Meredith Connolly. I've loved you from the first time you agreed to dance with me at the Autumn Festival and I've loved you every day since. God knows I don't deserve you after everything I've done, but if you'll have me, I'll spend every day for the rest of our lives making up for my mistakes."

Her heart soared, straight out of her chest and past the clouds and all the way up to heaven where she was quite certain Pa and Mama could see it. Love roared in her ears. Yes, roared. Because it wasn't a quiet kind of thing. Not theirs anyway. It was loud and passionate and messy and riddled with missteps and mistakes. But in the end, it had made them what they were.

Just like it had Mama and Pa.

"I forgive you," she whispered, pressing the words into his lips.

Hunter wrapped his good arm around her and pulled her close, kissing her with a fierce passion that swept her away, and it was good. Good and solid and everything her heart had ever desired.

"I love you, Mere. Will you marry me?"

She hugged him tight and put her mouth near his ear so he would be sure and hear her. "I love you, too. And yes. Yes, yes, yes, yes, yes."

He swung her round and the shop walls blurred around her and echoed with her laughter. It had been a long and bumpy road home.

But she was glad she made the trip.

* * * * *

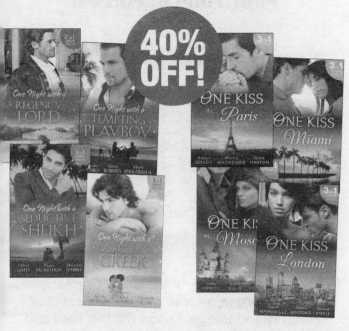

MILLS & BOON®

HISTORICAL

AWAKEN THE ROMANCE OF THE PAST

A sneak peek at next month's titles...

In stores from 6th March 2015:

- **The Soldier's Dark Secret** – Marguerite Kaye
- **Reunited with the Major** – Anne Herries
- **The Rake to Rescue Her** – Julia Justiss
- **Lord Gawain's Forbidden Mistress** – Carol Townend
- **A Debt Paid in Marriage** – Georgie Lee
- **Morrow Creek Runaway** – Lisa Plumley
